Snapshots

Cath Cole

First published in 2023

Copyright © Cath Cole

The moral right of this author has been asserted.

All characters and events in this publication, other than those clearly in the public domain, are fictitious and any resemblance to real persons, living or dead, is purely coincidental.

All rights reserved.

No part of this publication may be reproduced, stored in a retrieval system, or transmitted, in any form or by any means, without the prior permission in writing of the publisher, nor be otherwise circulated in any form of binding or cover other than that in which it is published and without a similar condition including this condition being imposed on the subsequent purchaser.

Editing, design, typesetting and publishing by UK Book Publishing

www.ukbookpublishing.com

ISBN: 978-1-916572-48-5

Snapshots

About the Author

Cath Cole had a working-class childhood in Bolton. She trained as a nurse and health visitor and subsequently as a further education lecturer and nurse tutor. She enjoyed a successful career in further education, which culminated in her becoming a principal of a further education college. After working with college staff to rescue a college judged to be failing, she was awarded the OBE.

The impact of State Registered Nurse training has underpinned her professional success. She was awarded a Master of Arts (Creative Writing) from Edge Hill University in 2013. Her first novel *Home from Home* was published in 2015 and has reached #1 in the Amazon Medical Fiction charts in the UK and Australia. *Everyday Lies* was published in 2021.

Cath travels, reads and spends time with family and friends. She is married and has three grandchildren.

Also by Cath Cole

Home from Home

Everyday Lies

For Kearsley Girls

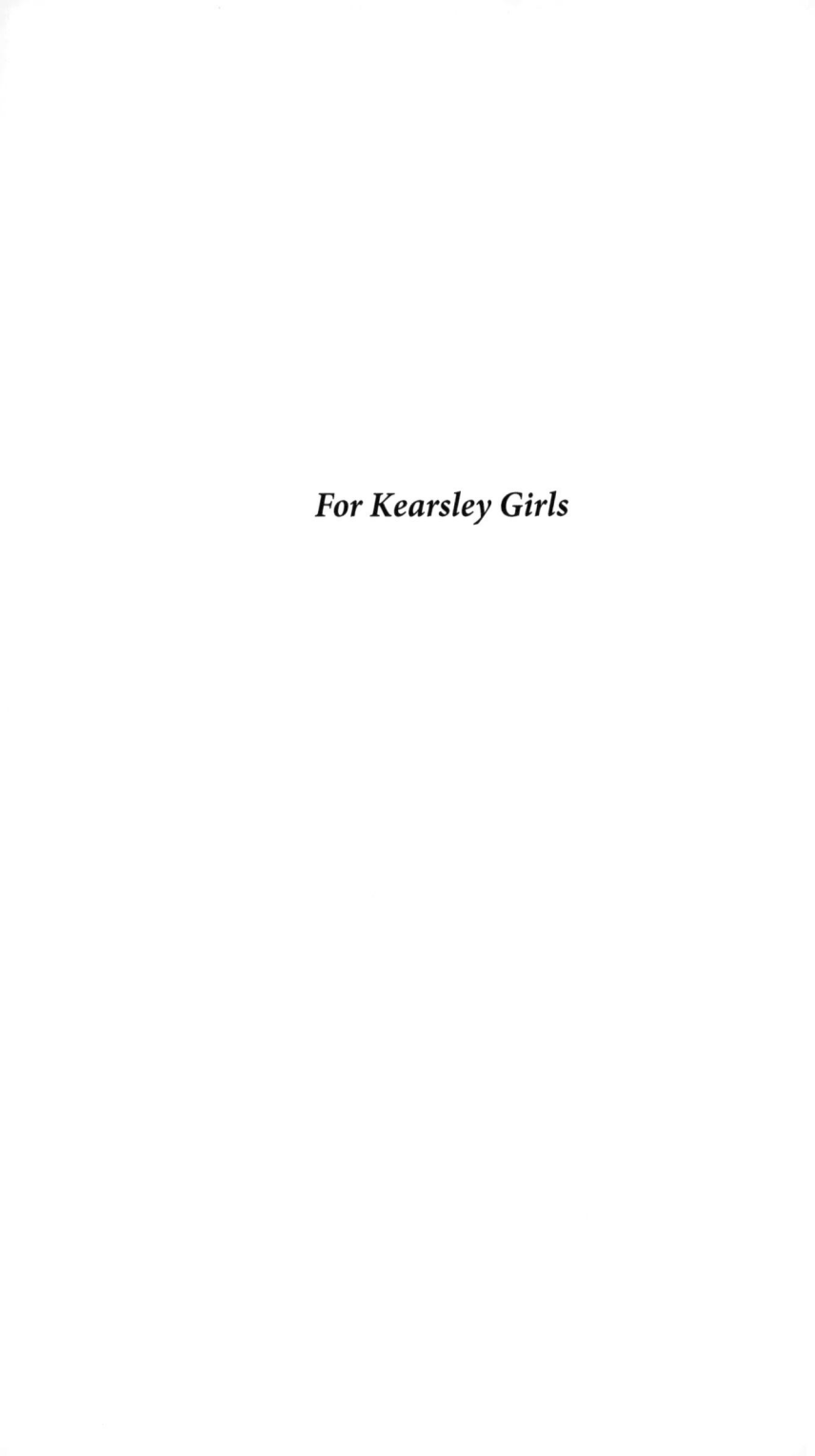

Snapshots

"There is no complete life. There are only fragments."
James Salter *Light Years*

Cath Cole

Chapter One

Izzy's Journal

May 2016

This is my journal. It is somewhere for me to write every day. My teacher, Mrs Berry, says a journal is good for sorting out the way you think about yourself and how you feel about your life and what's going on around you. She said it is good to make lists and write things down. I mostly feel odd. I looked odd up and found synonyms for it. Synonyms are words that have the same meaning. The synonym thingy on the computer said that odd is an adjective. I know what an adjective is we did it for SATS ages ago. Synonyms for odd are —

   strange,
   peculiar,
   weird,
   queer,
   funny,
   bizarre,
   eccentric,
   unusual,
   abnormal

CHAPTER ONE

quirky,
special,
unique.

There are a lot more on the list.

I feel odd because –

I have a funny name. Izzie is good. People think it means Isabel or Isabella. For other girls it does but for me it means Isalene.
My daddy is really old. He looks like a grandad.
I have a sister who is older than my mum.
I have started my periods.
I need to wear a bra.
I am fat.
My grandma has a boyfriend.

Mrs Berry says a journal could include

Things To do
Thoughts
Notes
Poems and other sayings
Goals — things I want to do
Books I like
Writing about family and friends
Drawings and Pictures. I am no good at art.
Stuff to be happy about
Sad things.

I'm not sure where to start so I'll start at the bottom of Mrs Berry's list and work up.

- Sad things I think I am more fed up than sad. I am sad about big things on the telly like wars and cruelty to animals and people starving and bombs in Paris and people being shot in America. I can tell when I'm meant to be sad by the way the person reading the news tells us the story and the way they hold their face and shuffle their papers or close their computer. I am fed up with the EU and the referendum thing. I don't really understand it but my dad says it is VERY, EXTREMELY IMPORTANT and that it is a ONCE IN A LIFETIME OPPORTUNITY. He must be very eccentric. I am not bothered about being old it looks very, very, very boring. I think it is best to die before you are thirty. My once in a lifetime opportunity would be to make my mum understand that I am not a stupid little kid who is going to do something really silly, daft and bonkers. I can only have access to technology, on my mum's iPad, for an hour a day. I am not allowed a smartphone.

- Stuff to be happy about. My friends. I think it would be good to say my family make me happy. They don't make me laugh or skip about or anything happy like that but they are nice and kind, most of the time, and my grandma gives the best hugs in the world. I think she likes hugging her boyfriend. On her Facebook page it says she is in a relationship. Ugh, Ugh, Ugh. It is truly, absolutely disgusting, at her age.

CHAPTER ONE

- Drawings and Picture. I don't understand what I'm supposed to do here and anyway I'm useless at art.

- Writing about family and friends.

My best friends are Olivia and Becca. Olivia has two older brothers she says they are smelly and horrible. They fart a lot and mess about on Facebook. They take pictures of their willies and post them to their friends. One of the reasons I'm not allowed a smartphone is that I might see dick pics. I see them all the time when I am at Olivia's house. Olivia is clever and pretty and boys like her. She gets loads and loads of likes and retweets. Her mum lets her experiment with make-up. Becca is clever as well and ace at drawing and painting. Her mum is my mum's best friend. Her sister Molly used to be nice and friendly but she's mostly sulky and moody now. She shouts and cries and sits in her room squeezing her spots and putting cream and other stuff on them. We sometimes go on holiday with Becca, Molly and their mum and dad.

My mum is called Paula. She is little, like my grandma. I am nearly as tall as both of them. She is a physiotherapist who works at the STATE OF THE ART CAPTALIST MEDICAL EMPOREEUM OF NIPS TUCKS AND FALSE HOPES. Well that's what my dad calls it. When he says it I hear it in capital letters. She really works at Euxton Hospital helping people get better after operations or injuryies. She worries about me, well what I really mean is she is a nuisance, a nice nuisance, because she worries and worries and worries. She reads books about the problems girls might have growing up. She went to our doctor's last week and sneakily tore two stories out of magazines about what it feels like to be a teenage girl in the 21st Century. She "pops" into my bathroom, to check on the toothpaste or the towels, or to see if I need any **Always,** when I'm in the bath. She pretends to be looking in the bathroom cupboard but I can see her giving me the once over to see if I'm cutting myself or losing weight or if I've pierced anything or whatever else she thinks I'm up to. Does she not trust me or what? She won't let me lock the bathroom door — in case I faint. I've never fainted in my whole life.

My dad is called Douglas. He is the best dad in the world even though he looks like Father Christmas with white hair and a white beard. He is very old, nearly as old as grandma's boyfriend. He met my mum when she was at university. He is a professor of ~~phiseeology~~ physiology. He swears a lot when he gets mad and throws stuff at the wall in his very untidy, messy, disgusting tip of a room. He doesn't work at the university anymore not since he told the Deen where to stick his (rude f word) job. He writes books and papers and gives talks. He goes to Canada and somewhere in South America a lot. He is a visitors professor. He has another daughter, my sister Amy, who is older than my mum. She lives in a house with other people like her.

My grandma is little and cuddly and I love her lots and lots and lots. She looks after me while my mum is at work. I go to her house in a morning and from school, sometimes I sleep over. She is called Jean and is sixty-eight. She reads a lot and goes to a writers' group. She has written a book about nurses. Ron, her boyfriend, goes to the writers' as well. She likes nice clothes and gets her nails done. She lets me experiment with a bit of make-up. We measure ourselves against each other every day. It won't be long now before I'm as tall as she is. She says she will soon be able to borrow my shoes. She has loads of shoes. I wear them sometimes, although they are beginning to pinch a bit.

Grandma Mary is ninety-two. Everybody says she is remarkable. She lives on her own with some help from carers and Grandma because she wants to stay at in her bungalow and not go in a home. She calls them death palaces. She likes nice clothes and high heel shoes although since she had her fall and had to go in hospital she has to wear "bloody coal barges". She goes to a dancing club although she can't keep up with the music anymore. When I go to see her she tells me to push the settee back and we have a little dance. She hums the tune and tells me the steps at the same time. Grandma thinks Grandma Mary sleeps on the settee instead of going upstairs to bed. Grandma Mary says it's "none of her bloody business". She does sleep downstairs, it's our secret. It's because the toilet is downstairs and the bedroom is upstairs in her little dormer and she's not having a "bloody commode". She says bloody a lot especially when she's cross.

Books I like

> The Fault in Our Stars by John Green
> Little Women by Louisa May Alcott
> Goals — Things I want to do are -

Be like everybody else. Perhaps when I start at Parklands there will be more girls who are what Grandma Mary calls well developed then they will have started their periods and need a bra. It would be good if they were fat as well. At least I'm going to Parklands High School and not Bolton School. My mum wanted me to go to Bolton because she went and they have small classes and are strict about uniform and get girls into important universities. Oxford and Cambridge that's it. I couldn't remember their names, Durham and St Andrews, they are two more. When we were falling out with Mum on the Bolton School side and me and Dad on the Parklands side she said them over and over again. On the day of the entrance exam I refused to get dressed. Mum cried and promised me anything I wanted if I would go and sit the exam. Dad said she was wasting her time. He stuck up for me and said if I was as bright as we thought then I was old enough to have a say in my own future. So me and Dad won. Dad had a quiet word and said that he respected my decision but it was made and there was no going back and that I had to live with the ~~consse~~ consequences. Grandma said he meant put up and shut up and that anyway it suited his politics. I don't know what that means.

Poems and other sayings. I don't understand poetry. Ron is a poet but what he writes doesn't rhyme. Well he doesn't really write some of the stuff he shows me. He cuts words out of newspapers and magazines and rips bits off bus and train tickets and food packets then shuffles them up and copies words off them. How is that poetry? He sometimes writes stuff that I can understand — well some of. It is mostly about what he did when he was younger. It is rude. Grandma says it is called confessional poetry. It doesn't rhyme either.

Notes. I'm not sure about this either but perhaps it means ideas. Whatever. Or perhaps it's to remind myself of stuff. In that case I need to ask Mum to get me a present for Mrs Berry. I will miss her she is old but understands children. She suggested us writing a journal because we are facing a difficult time with growing up into ~~adoless~~ teenagers. She says it's one of the most difficult times in your life because of raging hormones. I'd rather be a girl than a boy at least I don't splodge in my bed every night.

Thoughts. I think I'm lucky. My mum and dad live together. They fall out but then get all yucky again. A lot of children in my class have step-parents and loads of brothers and sisters that are not real brothers and sisters. I have two grandmas who I love loads and loads. I think mum should stop worrying so much. Her next big worry after me, is Ron and Grandma's money.

Things to do. I need to get ready for bed. If I'm quick, I can be in and out of the bath before my mum finishes her glass of wine. I don't like showers.

Ps. I will write again when I've time. I don't think it will be tomorrow I go to guides on a Monday and Tuesday I have my piano lesson. I will write something again later, when I have time. Does that mean you aren't a journal if I don't write every day? I will ask Mrs Berry.

Paula *June 2016*

Monday morning – again. Paula breathed, in one breath, out one breath, held her breath and prepared to face the reality of yet another weekend hangover. She had Izzy to get off to school and Douglas was, as usual, absent; on his way to London on the early train. With a groan that verged on a whimper Paula swung her legs out of bed and hoisted her body to a sitting position. She lingered for a second, her hands braced against the security of the mattress, then, with a push, propelled herself into the en-suite.

With her eyes half closed she unhooked the Roman blind; the dull grey light from the bathroom window offended the slits between her eyelids. She turned and stumbled into the shower where the pin pricks of hot water lashed her into wakefulness. Tilting her head backwards Paula let the water sting her face to punish her self-loathing at the realisation that she had stepped into the shower in her nightie. The iridescent dark satin clung like an oil slick emphasising the rounded contours of her body. She fought the sodden nightie grunting and fuming as she dragged it over her head before kicking it into the corner of the shower cubicle. Towelled dry and wrapped in her dressing gown, she headed for the kitchen.

'Are you all right, Mum?'

'Fine, just fine, a bit of a migraine, don't worry, Sweetie.' Paula flicked on the kettle. 'Eat your cereal.'

'Do you think Daddy liked his mug?'

'He was over the moon, love. It mattered, to him, that you had thought of it yourself and used your own money.'

'Why did Amy send him a scarf for Father's Day, when it's the start of summer?'

CHAPTER ONE

'Amy? Perhaps because the people she lives with chose it for her...come on, love, get your bag sorted while I pull some clothes on or we'll be late.'

As she turned from the school gate Paula let out a giant phew that vibrated her lips. She'd missed Sue who'd been and gone, having dropped Becca off at breakfast club.

Paula had periods of regret and recrimination related to her drinking. She could go for days, well two, perhaps three, then she treated herself to a small glass of Pinot Grigio rose, or failing that Chardonnay or Sauvignon Blanc, or whatever was to hand, then another and then another. *Why do I do it? To be sociable? Don't kid yourself, you drink more when you're on your own. Because I like the feeling, free floating, carefree. Yes, free of care, that's it. Christ, I am losing it talking to myself, even if it is all in my head. I will get myself sorted, stop worrying, stop needing the oblivion that booze ever so gently bestows.* Paula shrugged. *Very profound and poetic, Paula. You're beginning to sound like that shyster, Ron.*

The ping of her mobile dragged Paula back to a dull Monday morning in June. She stopped in the middle of the pavement and rootled in her bag. A text.

Is there any chance you can you come in today? Jackie on holiday. Karen phoned in sick.

Paula hesitated, then keyed in a reply as she walked.

Be with you in half an hour.

My one day off, still it sorts out what I'm going to do for the day. As she waited to cross the road she scrolled to her mother's mobile number.

'Hello, Paula love...Bye, see you on Thursday...I was just saying goodbye to Ron.'

'He's stayed the weekend – again?'

'There's no need to be like that.'

'Like what?'

'Shall we start again? Good morning, Paula. How are you this morning?'

'I'm fine, Mum, fine. Why wouldn't I be? Will you be able to pick Izzy up from school? Work have just called…'

'No problem. She can have her tea with me.'

'Thanks, and Mum, will you be able to bring her round to ours so she can get changed? It's Guides tonight.'

'See you later, and Paula… stop upsetting yourself about Ron. I know what I'm doing.'

Paula leaped back onto the pavement as a passing car sped past. *Thinking about that bloody man, nearly got me killed. She won't be happy until he's fleeced her, then we'll see if she knows what she's doing. My poor dad. I don't know what he'd have to say about her gadding about with a Jeremy Corbyn look alike.*

*

Paula craned her neck looking for a parking space at the front of the Palladian mansion that housed a state-of-the-art private hospital. There was nothing for it: she'd have to park at the rear of the building and trudge back. Giving the front car park a last hopeful glance, she spotted John Smithfield's car tucked in one of the consultants' spaces. She gulped as her heart raced. She breathed deeply. She glanced in her rear-view mirror. A flick of her mascara and a coat of lipstick wouldn't go amiss. Parking at the back wasn't a bad idea after all. A quick nip into the ladies' changing rooms and she'd soon brighten herself up.

The patients in the reception area were being entertained by a tall, distinguished looking man stating, with casual arrogance, that he was not used to being kept waiting especially when he was paying, in more ways than one, for the privilege of seeing a physiotherapist.

'Time is money. Time is money,' he said to the assembled patients.

'Can I help?' Paula stopped at the desk and inclined her head toward the receptionist.

'Mrs Quayle, thank you for coming in.' The receptionist raised her eyebrows and flicked an upward glance at the man. 'Mr Benton has been waiting a full five minutes…I tried to explain.'

She handed Paula a set of medical notes.

Mr Benton glanced at his wristwatch. 'Eight and a half minutes to be precise.'

'Please, follow me,' said Paula.

'Are you the person in charge of this shambles?' Mr Benton said as he paced along the corridor beside Paula. *Douglas would love this. He'd put this pompous pillock in his place in no time.* 'No, Mr Benton. I'm here on my day off.' *Careful, Paula you're rising to the bait. Smile, relax and think of seeing John Smithfield's car.*

Paula asked her patient to remove his socks and shoes and settle himself on the couch while she looked through his notes. Absorbed in manipulating Mr Benton's right foot, she startled as the door to the therapy room opened.

'John! Mr Smithfield…' she said.

'Good morning, Brian. I see you are very literally in the best pair of physiotherapy hands we have.' Mr Smithfield turned to Paula. 'Isn't that right, Mrs Quayle?'

Paula unequivocally knew certain facts about herself. She drank too much, too often and Monday morning was the time to summon up her resolve to buy a range of slightly sparkling flavoured waters, tonic water and *Coke zero* and to move the elderflower pressé from the back of the larder shelves. She was, more or less, happily married to Douglas, but liked, nay needed, perhaps even craved, the fizz, risk taking and inherent "will I see him, will I not" buzz of a flirtation. In her more rational, sensible, married woman with a child, moments she acknowledged to herself that her various romantic attachments were no more than a distraction and a fantasy. Over the twenty-two years of her married life, she'd been besotted by a variety of different men including Izzy's headteacher; she had even given serious consideration to the validity of his left of centre views. When Douglas found her reading the leader in his copy of *The Guardian,* he'd regarded her as though she were an artefact in some fascinating exhibition and suggested one or both of them should lie in a darkened room until the aberration drifted away. Not long afterwards the headteacher left the school, and when she thought of him now Paula had difficulty remembering his name.

Then there was the landscape gardener she and Douglas had asked to remodel the back garden. Paula admitted to herself that he resembled a cheerful garden gnome. He was at least as tall as her, five feet one in his stocking feet, and those eyes, oh those eyes. Paula told herself he was no ordinary garden gnome, sorry, landscape gardener; he regularly exhibited at RHS Tatton Park and had been known to visit the Chelsea Flower Show. His girlfriend gave birth to twins, he finished the back garden and transplanted himself to a big job in Garstang and was never seen again.

Then there was the dangerous one, the one too close to home – Mike from the PTA. Paula and Mike been appointed by the main association, of which they were both longstanding members, to look, with another parent, at the suitability of the current school uniform. No easy brief given the demands of a school that espoused the word pluralism.

Every kind of -ism was to be considered and the needs of every child really and truly mattered. The other parent regularly left the meeting the minute it ended, leaving Mike and Paula waiting together for the caretaker to return to the school and lock up. One of Paula's bucket list wants was a nippy sports car, and it happened that Mike was general manager of a prestigious car showroom with a fund of amusing stories about customers. An imposing performance car was inevitably parked outside the school; a perk of the trade.

Douglas scoffed at Paula's yearning for a "with it" car. He said it reflected her materialistic right-wing leanings. He was adamant that his battered old Volvo did what he wanted it to do and that Paula only needed "a little runabout" to get her to the hospital or into Chorley for shopping. Mike pretended devastation when he heard Paula's tale of unrequited car ownership. There was one motoring trip around the town, after a meeting, then another into the local countryside, then a quick visit to a country pub one night when Douglas was away and her mum was babysitting. Then the kiss, tongues and wandering hands right outside her front door. Then up against the wall in year five's classroom. They heard the front door of the school bang shut. The bubble burst for Paula; she missed the following meeting, claiming a cold. In a rush of dread, panic and shame, she offered to increase her hours at work, resigned from the PTA due to work pressure, slunk in and out of school to avoid Mike's wife and vowed never again. She loved Douglas, there was no doubt about that. She had loved him from the moment she first saw him. He had taught her what love was, sustained her as she stood up to her parents, well, her mother. She would never leave him. Her mother rehearsed the age difference and the circumstances of their "hole in the corner" wedding at every opportunity. Paula knew without doubt that Douglas was her future; even when she fancied other men, she knew there would always be Douglas. Until, that is, Mr John Smithfield came along.

Jean *July 2016*

Ten o'clock on a Monday morning and Jean still isn't dressed. She couldn't give a jot if the whole of the WI committee marches up the drive and finds her unwashed and still in her dressing gown. She's happy, exhilarated and sore; between her legs throbs like billy-o.

She finishes the dregs of her second mug of tea, tightens the belt of her dressing gown and with a sigh heads for the bathroom. With joy and a sense of abandonment she squeezes *Molton Brown's Pink Pepperpod* body wash into the flowing water. She inhales deeply, sighs and smiles to herself.

'Ooh, aah, mmm.' Jean slides down the bath and lets the fragrant water flow over and around her body.

'Bloody idyllic,' she says to the bathroom walls. As the bubbles eddy and swirl, Jean's nipples and the mound of her abdomen emerge and disappear. She slipped into a reverie as the mountains and valleys of foam slip and slide against the sides of the bath. The chafing between her legs prompts vague thoughts of adding natural yoghurt to her shopping list. She is roused by the cooling of the water and inspired by a sudden decision: she is off to Marks and Spencer for new bras and knickers.

CHAPTER ONE

★

Ensconced in the bra fitting cubicle, Jean tries for a nonchalant attitude. The one women use when they go for a cervical smear or a mammogram. Flipping her legs open for the cervical smear crosses Jean's mind. Throwing the knees apart with apparent carelessness looks wanton with everything on show for a second or two too long, especially with a male doctor. Knees together too long and requiring a polite "would you open your legs for me" smacks of frigidity. For Jean, bra fitting is the second cousin once removed to the mammogram. Pretending you have nothing better to do than have a stranger scrutinise your breasts in the middle of a week-day morning while you force a world-weary smile is an indignity that can only be appreciated and understood by other women. Still, here she is in the cubicle. Eager to get started, she's stripped to the waist and waiting for the fitter to return with a selection of bras.

Should I have kept my bra on? I might pull my tee shirt back on. She is saved from further analysis when the cubicle door opens, and the bra fitter throws back the curtain that divides the large cubicle in two. There is no way Jean can avoid the sight of her naked torso in the full length mirror that now confronts her.

Dear God, she leans forward to peer in the mirror. *No, it can't be.*

The fitter fixes her eyes on a space over Jean's right shoulder as Jean pushes her arms through the straps of the proffered bra.

They must be taught not to gawp at their clients. She won't have noticed.

'If you turn round, I'll fasten the bra and adjust the straps.'

Jean chances a surreptitious glance at her left breast, just above the line of the cup. 'It's warm in here.' She fans her face with her hands and looks down again. *A bloody love bite. What must she think?*

'Turn round and slide a hand in the opposite cup to lift your breast,' the fitter says. She stands back to watch Jean carry out the task. 'Perfect,' the fitter says as she runs a finger around the rim of each cup, straightening the lace trim as she goes. Then she steps back again, head on one side to admire her work. 'Did you want to try on the other ones I brought for you?'

'Yes, I want three sets.' *It's too late now, she doesn't look as though she's seen it. Perhaps she's left her specs at home.*

'Are you having a fresh start?' The fitter smiles as she unhooks the next bra from its hanger.

'You could say that,' Jean says. 'I'm…it doesn't matter… I'm treating myself.'

'Well done, you,' says the fitter, indicating that Jean should turn round again to have the straps adjusted on bra number two. 'There's nothing like a new set of underwear to make you feel good about yourself. I usually change my eye make-up if I want a bit of a change.'

Fortified by a cup of tea and a toasted teacake in Mark's café, Jean heads into the next door *Boots*. She looks at the women staffing the various cosmetic stands and decides to approach a counter where the assistant looks as though she was still at school when The Beatles first made albums.

'Could you advise me on updating my make-up?'

'I certainly can, love.'

CHAPTER ONE

An hour and six minutes later Jean feels as though she has a new best friend. She knows the women's gynae history: three babies, two miscarriages, everything taken away and the need to use *Tena Lady* on a long journey. *I really do need to stop telling people I was a nurse.* She has parted with the best part of £156 and is frightened of smiling in case the layer of foundation cracks.

'I've never been in love before…la, la, but now it's you… la la.' Jean heads to the car park.

Hair on Wednesday, this boring bob is going. Something short and spikey like Julie Walters or Helen Mirren. Once she's in the car, Jean reaches for her mobile phone.

'Mum…Hello, it's me. How are you?'

'Fine. You're late. I thought you weren't coming… I've eaten my sandwiches.'

Jean slumps in the car seat, the weight of her commitments and responsibilities takes its usual vice like grip across her shoulders. She glances at her watch.

Bloody hell. 'I'm sorry, Mum. I lost track of time.'

'It's alright for some – I haven't spoken to a soul since you phoned last night.'

'The carer? Who made the sandwiches?'

'Yes well – she's been. It were that chirpy one, the one with the withered arm.'

'Put the kettle on, Mum, I'll be with you in ten minutes, and Mum, what about coming home with me? I'm meeting Izzy from school. You could have your tea with us.'

'She's the light of my life that kiddie…She got me one of them Mark's meals out of the freezer, her with the withered arm. I'm surprised they take cripples on in them jobs.'

'You can have it tomorrow, Bye.'

'If it hasn't gone off by then.'

As she pulls up outside her mother's dormer bungalow, Jean takes a deep breath to steady herself. Her mother is loved, liked and revered by one and all. Marvellous, love, treasure, remarkable, are all words that Jean is used to hearing to describe her mother. Despite her deteriorating health, she is the star of the dance club, the doyenne of the youth club, the sweetheart of her neighbours. Yet, she is Jean's mother and with that comes responsibility for a fiercely independent woman who believes her admirers and holds Jean responsible for anything and everything that might be amiss in her life. She treats Jean as her personal assistant, secretary, lady's maid and chauffeur. Terry, Jean's dead brother, is mourned by their mother. She beseeches Jean to tell her "why was the best kiddie that was ever born taken before his time?".

'Yoo hoo, it's me,' Jean says as she steps into the hall.

'Hello, Me, I thought you'd forgotten about your poor old mum.'

Jean sighs and pauses for a second before walking into the front room. *You miserable cow, she's old, half-blind and house bound;* she pushes her shoulders back and pastes a smile on her face as she steps into the front room.

'Well you're here now,' her mother says. 'Sit yourself down.' She pushes herself out of her chair. 'No ifs or buts. I'll put the kettle on.'

Jean shudders as she contemplates the mug of tea. Being partially sighted had added to the decline of her mother's always dubious housekeeping. The walls of the downstairs of the bungalow are yellowed from years of accumulated cigarette smoke. The surfaces in the kitchen and sitting room are sticky where drinks have been spilt. The push-along trolley and its contents of address book, photographs, junk mail and Liquorice Allsorts are tacky and bound together by gunge. Any attempt, by Jean, to set to with hot water and bleach, are met with derision. Jean needs to be desperate to use the bathroom.

'Let's get off, then we can have a cup of tea at my house before we go and get Izzy.'

'Well, if that's what you want; help yourself to a liquorice allsort while I get me coat.'

Jean casts a surreptitious glance around the sitting room.

Mary *July 2016*

After she had seen Jean off, Mary turned from the hall window and lowered herself onto the second step of the stairs. She fished up her cardigan sleeve for a hanky. Careful to avoid the corner containing the glob of yellow sputum she'd coughed up, when Jean was fetching her coat, she wiped away the threatening tears and shoved the sodden hanky back up her sleeve. *How the bloody hell have I come to this – a doddery old woman?*

Slowly, very slowly, she made her way into the front room, her stick and the wall used for support as she navigated her way around the bag of shopping, and the parcel of paperbacks Jean had donated to the youth club. *Youth club! That Douglas is a cheeky bugger but t'name's stuck. Even him from the Town Hall calls it that now.* Mary's chest heaved in syncopation to the unpredictable lubb, dub of her heart as she edged her way around the arm of the settee. When her bum made contact with the seat she dropped back into the settee's soft, welcoming arms.

She wriggled around until she'd made a nest of the scatter cushions. With a root down the side of the settee she found the remote and switched on the telly.

You silly bugger, you should have gone to the lav while you were up. Posh folk were talking about Europe and Brexit. Mary closed her eyes and dozed.

Roused by the phone, she contemplated letting it ring: *Leave it; it's probably only Madge ringing for a mither. No, more like our Jean. Better answer it or she'll have Jim round to check on me.*

'Hi, Ma, it's me, I'm back home. Did you put your shopping away?'

'Yes, course I did; as soon as I got in.'

'Did you enjoy your afternoon?'

'It were alright, best part were seeing our Izzy, she's a bonny child. Let's 'ope she doesn't turn out like our Paula.' Mary sighed. 'She were a bad un when she were our Izzy's age. Good night and God bless.'

'Bye, Mum, I'll pick you up about eleven on Wednesday, for the hairdresser's.'

Mary made it to the lavatory, her knickers only slightly damp. Then bracing herself for the task ahead she set about transferring the afternoon's shopping to the kitchen. Using the hook on her stick she dragged the plastic bag to the bottom of the stairs and then, steadying herself against the newel post, hoisted the bag onto the bottom step. A small tin of beans toppled out and rolled under the hall table.

Bugger it.

With stops to catch her breath, Mary, with grim determination, grappled with the job of shifting the packets and tins onto the two-tier trolley. The social worker had provided the trolley. Mary had agreed to have an assessment

CHAPTER ONE

by Social Services following a stay in hospital. She told anyone who would listen, that it was all a lot of fuss and bother after a bit of a fall and an asthmatic attack and resented everybody else's insistence that it was something serious to do with her heart and bunged up airways. She now had a chair in the bath, the trolley and carers who came to check on Mondays and Thursdays. The carers' jobs included helping her in the shower and doing a bit of washing, ironing and cleaning for her.

"Just do the washing and ironing and help me in't bath. There's nowt much to do with only me living here," Mary instructed the women every time they called to see her.

On Sunday mornings, she had set herself a special job. She huffs and puffs up the stairs to lie on the bed and roll about a bit. Then she sets-to and pummels the pillows and throws the covers about before a return huff and puff downstairs. She's jiggered the rest of the day but it's worth it.

I'll not have em telling our Jean, and them from the Town Hall, that I don't sleep upstairs. They'll carry me out in a bloody box before I go into one of them death palaces. There's no way they can make me, while I can manage. And I can bloody manage on my own, well, with a bit of help from Jim fetching my paper and checking up on me. Our Jean must think I'm gormless. I know she's asked him to spy on me; still, he's a real gent; he'd do anything for anybody. Our Jean's a good kid; she's not like our Terry though. He were a bit of a rogue but lovely with it; very loving. She does her best taking me shopping, and calling in when she's passing, even though she doesn't stay long. I've told her "you've got your own life to live, what with your writing and being on them committees and that". And she's got that man. Ron, they call him. In idle moments Mary finds it useful to mentally review, practise

23

and amend her life story in case she's called upon to account for herself.

During the long evening, the phone rang twice.

'Hello.'

'Mary, is that you? I thought you weren't in.'

'It – takes – me – bloody – ages -to – get – to – the - phone. I have to get yon trolley in gear.' Mary gasped for breath.

'I thought your Jean had fixed summat up next to your settee.'

'It's buggered up. Did you want me for something or other?'

'Let me think…There were something I wanted to tell you… It's come to me now. Our Gemma's getting a divorce.' Madge dropped her voice. 'He can't manage it.'

'Speak up. Did you say ravage it?'

'Manage it. In bed. Doing it – that.' Madge dropped her voice again. 'Sex.'

'Really?' Mary took a deep breath and pondered a second or two. 'They've been wed five years, last March. I remember it were that time me and our Jean went to Scotland on that coach trip.'

'I had that blue two-piece, it's still like new,' said Madge.

'Well, our Paula's husband might be getting on, but he can obviously do what's necessary; our Izzy's a lovely child. I must say though, I didn't care for it much myself.'

'I'll ring again.'

'Good night then,' Mary said to the ring tone.

Rifling through her trolley Mary shuffled the contents to find her notepad and pen and wrote Divorce. She contemplated the seriousness of Madge's information and decided a phone call was in order.

CHAPTER ONE

'Jean, I've summat to tell you.'

'Are you all right, Mum?'

'Course I'm all right, I only saw you a couple of hours ago. It's that Gemma, that grandchild of Madge's. Her as were always full of herself. You'll never guess. Are you there, Jean?'

'Yes, Mum. Is Gemma al'…'

'She's not had it consecrated. Now what do you think to that?'

'Consecrated?'

'You know – bed and that – IT.'

'Consummated.'

'That's what I said.' Mary put the phone down.

Mary trundled her trolley back to the lounge. She flicked between the channels and settled on a quiz programme. When she woke from her doze the luminescent evening light had dimmed and the news was rambling on about Brexit – again. She wouldn't be voting. *Does no bugger remember the war?* She shook her head and pushed herself up. *A trip to the lav and time for bed.* Dragging the trolley towards her, she hoisted herself off the settee. *You clumsy bugger.* A half empty glass of dandelion and burdock she'd fetched on her return journey from the telephone went over the top of the tray and onto the carpet. *I'll mop it up in't morning.* In the bathroom, Mary had a swill, eased out her teeth, rinsed them under the cold-water tap, reinserted them and smacked her lips. Dressed in her nighty, dressing gown and her knickers – in case she was "taken badly" during the night – she hobbled back to the settee and rearranged the cushions. She pulled the blanket out of its hiding place, curled up on the settee and settled down for the night.

Chapter Two

Izzy's Journal

Hello Journal, September 2016

I am sorry I've not written but I've been away nearly all summer and I forgot to take you with me. I've been with Grandma and Ron to Scotland. They were on a writing retreat. They didn't do much writing, well not unless they did it when I was in bed. Most of the time they went on walks and said how lovely the wet, misty, mostly very boring scenery was. Ron took a lot of photos. He likes photography he says it gives him an inspiration for his poetry. That seems silly to me when most of the stuff doesn't make sense and you can't tell what the poems are about. He sometimes uses very rude words when he's writing about Grandma — words beginning with c and f that I'm not supposed to know about. I hope he never shows my mum any of his poems. She'd go ape-shit. That's two more words I'm not supposed to know but Olivia's brothers say them all the time. Ape-shit is my favourite saying now. I say it all the time to myself if I'm really fed up and sometimes when I'm not. I'm not as fed up as I was last time I wrote to you. I think I was bothered about leaving primary school and starting at Parklands as well as my mum always bothering about the POTENTIAL DANGERS FACING YOUNG GIRLS. She hasn't been as bad since she started working full-time. She's happy and smiley and very kissy with me and Dad. I have a lot to write to you. Where shall I start? Well, first of all. No it can wait, perhaps I should keep to the headings Mrs Berry gave me. No, I have to tell you before I do the lists because it is so exciting and very daring — I have dip ~~died,~~ dyed my hair and my mum doesn't know — yet. It's been two days and she hasn't noticed. I twist my hair in a bun for school and make sure its tucked down behind my shoulders and that I am lying slid down in the bath when she bobs in to check on me. Me and Becca did it on Sunday afternoon. We found a website called "Ombre Hair: How To Dip Dye At Home Without Looking Shit". I really, really love swear words and swearing. It makes me feel strong and in charge and its fun. Anyway, we put our money together and went to Boots to buy the stuff. It took a long time to go through the instructions, but we did it. Becca's looks better than mine because she's got darker hair but you can tell with mine. I'm really pleased, my friends at school think it looks awesome. The other thing I've done this summer is find out a bit more about sex, well me and Becca have. I'd be in big, ape-shit type trouble if I used my technology time on my mum's iPad to look up naughty words. It all started when I read one of Ron's poems. I thought I understood it for once, it was obviously about him kissing somebody all over, yuk, yuk double yuk and ape-shit if it was about Grandma. He was once married to another lady, so it could be her — I hope so. Anyway, he went on about tasting cum. Well it didn't make sense to me. Had he spelt cream wrong and why would the lady have cream on her body or did he mean cone like in ice cream? But that didn't make sense either. Well its double disgusting with knobs on because Becca's IPad said it means

1. to orgasm
2. whiteish fluid from aforementioned orgasm
3. how internet sluts say "come"

Next me and Becca looked up orgasm. Well!!!! Ape-shit. I don't think I want to grow up and have to do all the sex and touching stuff. (I should tell my mum to save her a lot of worry and me a lot of pretending to listen time.) Orgasm means "the climax of sexual excitement, characterised by intensely pleasurable feeling centred in the genitals and (in men) experienced as an accompaniment to ejaculation". That urban dictionary on the internet is awesome. We knew about boys splodging in bed, Mrs Berry told us when she was getting us ready for leaving primary school but who would have thought they splodged for ever, all the rest of their lives and with a lady there? Thousands and thousands of yuks and ape-shits. Then it got worse. And honestly it made me feel a bit sick because the next explanation said. "a male or female orgasm resulting in sometimes unexpected amounts of love juice spurting vociferously."

So that means Ron has licked ladies stuff that comes from out of their vagina. Me and Olivia told our friends at school and they laughed, one nearly fainted. One girl has a sister who's a lot older than us — she's at university. Well she's not gone back yet so she asked her about it and she said it was true. I've been watching my Mum and Dad for signs that they do it. I can't look at Grandma and Ron without screwing up my face just in case it is Grandma and not his once wife. Grandma asked me if I'd got tooth-ache last week. What do you think about that?

Me, Mum and Dad had two weeks in a cottage in the Lake District. We couldn't go on holiday with Becca and Molly and their Mum and Dad because my Dad is getting ready for something or other to do with advising Mr Hunt who's in charge of the NHS. I can always remember his name because it rhymes with the rude c word. That's what my dad calls him rude C word then unt. He has promised us a Caribbean cruise after Christmas to make up for being wet and windy in Windermere. I've just done alliteration — hurray. I'll do the list now.

Drawings and Pictures. I still don't have any.

Writing about my family and friends.

Mum and Dad. - They are both very busy with work. Our cleaning lady comes twice a week. We are SLAVES TO THE BLACK ECONOMY because if anybody asks Rita is a friend of the family who likes cleaning more than my mum does. In exchange for the cleaning Rita gets her envelope (with money in it) and my mum's old clothes and shoes. Although Rita says she can't walk in high heels. We have a man who comes to do the garden. He has his name on the side of his van and sends us a bill so we don't expect anybody to ask about him. I'm as tall as my mum and grandma now, but Grandma says I shouldn't put too much store by it because she and my mum didn't grow after they were 12.

Grandma Mary told me my mum was a "little bugger" when she was younger and that she led my grandma and grandad a pretty dance. It helps knowing that because I'm not as bothered about her, my mum I mean. I'm trying to think what I mean — I mean she might be protecting me because she got up to stuff when she was a girl and she doesn't want me to do that stuff. I don't know what the stuff would be though because in the olden days they didn't have iPads and Facebook. I'd like to know though.

Sometimes when I think about her being a "little bugger" I think she is a ~~hyppocrit~~ hypocrite and then I think apeshit she's blighting my youth. But she loves me very much so I'll keep on swearing to myself and doing stuff like my hair. I might pierece my belly button next except I am not old enough to go to a shop.

I need to talk to Becca and Olivia and Georgia and Leah our new friends at school.

Grandma and Grandma Mary. I've said about the holiday with Grandma and Ron. Grandma is busy with a new book. She's pleased with the old one — it has good reviews on Amazon. I haven't read her first book yet but I will one day. She says not to rush because it has a bit of sex in it. I told her that sex doesn't bother me because I have seen sex stuff in films and on television and reading about it can't be as bad as seeing it.

Grandma Mary is lovely although her house is a bit sticky. She still goes dancing although she doesn't dance but she talks to everybody and gives out liquorice allsorts. She goes to Grandma's every week for Sunday lunch. Ron runs her home afterwards. She says he's an intalectual layabout but a gent all the same.

Books I'm Reading. I'm reading Harry Potter. I didn't think I would like them but there was a set in the cottage in Windemere.

One rainy day I started reading and I can't stop.

Poems and other sayings. I'll leave them and think about this for Next time I write.

Notes, thoughts and things to do. I'm tired now so will do more on this next time. Goodnight — I wish you could see my hair it is truly awesome.

Paula *November 2016*

As she reached into the cupboard to retrieve two glasses, Paula relished the idea of a glass of wine. She could almost taste the crisp, dry, vaguely fruity Pinot Grigio rosé. She licked her lips in anticipation; it was a wine-free night but who in their right mind would have a steak without a glass of wine? She was doing it for Sue.

'Wine on a Wednesday?' said Izzy, wandering toward the fridge. 'You've got work tomorrow.'

'Thanks for that, Miss Bossy Boots.' Paula set the glasses on the table. 'Pass me that bottle.' She nodded toward the open fridge. 'The pink one; and the steaks.'

'I'm only saying.' Izzy passed the bottle and reached back into the fridge for the parcel of meat. 'Why is Aunty Sue coming round on her own, and how come Becca can stay in without a sitter?'

'She doesn't need a sitter.' Paula unwrapped the meat and placed it on a plate. 'She's with Molly.'

'And what's with the steak? I thought you'd given up red meat.'

'Izzy, what's got into you? Pour me a drink, put the bottle back in the fridge, get your milk, drink it and then head upstairs…after you've given me a kiss.'

Izzy pushed the fridge door shut so that the bottles and jars lodged in the shelves of the door tinkled and jingled out a syncopated rhythm as they clattered and rattled against each other.

'Was that really necessary?' said Paula.

'I did what I was told.' Izzy swallowed the dregs of her milk and moved toward the dishwasher. 'Didn't I?'

'Izzy, for the last time – bed.' As Paula nodded toward the kitchen door the front doorbell rang. 'There's Sue now.'

'I'll answer the door,' said Izzy.

'You scoot to bed, young lady. Sleep tight.'

Izzy lingered at the bottom of the stairs.

'Night, Aunty Sue.'

'Goodnight, Izzy love. God bless.'

Sue followed Paula into the kitchen, shrugging off her coat and tossing it onto the settee that took up the corner of the spacious open plan kitchen.

CHAPTER TWO

'Drink?' said Paula opening the fridge and holding up the bottle of wine.

Sue nodded and settled herself onto one of the high stools at the island unit.

'You look knackered,' said Paula, moving toward the island hob that faced Sue. 'Do you want to talk now, or shall we wait until we've eaten?'

Sue shrugged. 'Now's as good a time as any,' and twisted her wedding ring.

Paula sipped her wine and scrutinised Sue. 'How bad is it?'

'I'm not sure. He's had the odd dalliance before, looking – not sex or anything. I might be wrong.'

'Are you sure he doesn't just fancy her a bit.'

'Could be, but it's about me as well. I feel dowdy, run down – the girls – the house – college – bloody hormones. When does the menopause kick in? I'm sick and tired of being me, and somewhere deep inside I'm half expecting him to be cheesed off with me.' Sue folded her arms, hung her head and muttered into her chest, 'Look at me. I'm drab and dowdy. Why wouldn't he look somewhere else?'

'Sue–' Paula threw water onto the griddle pan then waited until it squealed and sizzled before setting the steaks down in the hot pan– 'let's face it, we've had the conversation about fancying other men, and the husbands looking but not touching, loads of times. What I don't understand is all this guff about you.'

'Basically, I'm pissed off with everybody and everything.' Sue rootled in her bag and pulled out a packet of tissues.

Paula left the steaks to their own devices to move round the central island to hug Sue.

'Come on, drink up and let's plan on sorting you out. Bloody hell, the steaks.' Paula scuttled back round the island to flip the meat over. 'You could take a leaf out of my mum's book and revamp yourself completely. Although why she bothers for that slug, I don't know. Anyway, you've already started with Slimming World…can you eat chocolate brownies for dessert?'

'She looks amazing, and let's face it, she deserves happiness.' Sue dabbed at her eyes. 'After all this time.'

'Sixty-eight and behaving like a teenager, she encourages Izzy with make-up and cleansing routines.'

'I wish somebody would encourage me?'

'That's my job.' Paula flipped the steaks onto the waiting plates. 'Let's eat and plan at the same time.'

Two bottles of wine and a large brandy later, and with a plan of attack sorted, Sue pulled on her coat for the walk home.

'Look at yourself, not Bob. He won't risk upsetting the girls for a fling, and think of the personal shopper, I'll ring her tomorrow. And get that application form for the vice-principal's job and make an appointment at the hairdresser's.'

'Yes, Miss.' Sue kissed Paula on the cheek. 'Thanks for listening.'

★

Paula undressed, cleansed off her makeup, and peered at her chin in the magnifying mirror. The sudden and unexpected appearance of a single, dark chin hair, a few weeks ago had, after the initial shock, galvanised her into frequent scrutiny and when necessary a terror attack with tweezers. In bed, she tossed and turned.

I'm vigilant. Trying to understand what it's like for young girls today. What would I have been like with a mobile phone and the internet? Up to no good, that's for sure; but it was different for me. Dad was always at work, mostly it was me and Mum. I must have been about twelve when I had my first good snog. Douglas is away a lot and I've been distracted what with work and John. And she's started answering back and looking at me as though I'm a lab specimen. Then Mum and Him, and Grandma – I must go and see her. And Sue…Who the hell's ringing at this time?

'Hello.'

'This is the Admissions Unit at The Princess Royal Hospital. Could I speak to Professor Quayle please?'

'Admissions Unit? I'm sorry, my husband isn't here.' Paula swung her legs out of bed.

'Are you Mrs Quayle?'

'Yes, is something…?'

'I'm afraid I have some bad news, Mrs Quayle. Is anyone with you?'

'Yes. No, I mean. What is it?'

'It's about Amy, your daughter.'

'She's my stepdaughter.'

'Your husband is listed as her next of kin.'

'He is, but he's away. Look, what is it?' Paula's voice ratcheted up. 'What's happened to Amy? Do you need consent for something?'

'Mrs Quayle, your stepdaughter died half an hour ago, I have tried Professor Quayle's mobile phone number several times without success and…'

'Died? How? I'm sorry, I didn't mean to snap – before.'

'She collapsed, her heart. I'm sorry, I'm afraid I can't give more details over the phone. Will you be able to contact your husband?'

'Leave it with me, Douglas, my husband, will be in touch. Thank you.'

'Shit, piss and bloody hell,' mumbled Paula as she speed-dialled Douglas's mobile. *Where in the name of God is he? In a bar ranting on about Donald Trump.* She tried again and again. *IPad! Find the number of the hotel and ring them, you numpty.*

'Lo.'

'Douglas, what the hell…'

'Paula? What time is it?'

'Douglas, are you awake? Have you been drinking?'

'Yes – not much. Why? What is it, love?'

Paula took a deep breath and paused. 'Douglas, are you properly awake?'

'Izzy, has something happened to Izzy?'

Paula felt tears prickle her eyes. She gulped.

'No, love not Izzy. It's Amy.'

'Amy!'

'Oh Douglas. She, she. The poor girl died about an hour ago. They rang, from the Princess Royal.'

'Died. Dear God, Why? How? When?'

'Her heart they said. They wouldn't give me more details.'

'Right. I'll ring, then get back to you.'

'Fine. Douglas, I'm so sorry.'

'Paula, I love you – and Izzy, thank God it wasn't Izzy. Speak soon.'

'I love you. We both do.'

CHAPTER TWO

★

Paula was desolate. Sue was dead and Bob didn't care, he refused to organise a funeral. Paula was pleading with him to let the personal shopper choose a shroud…

'Mum, Mum!' Paula heard Izzy's voice; she felt cold.

'What?' She shivered and screwed up her eyes at the sudden light.

'Mum, the alarm's gone off. Mum.'

'Yes, yes, what time is it?' Paula swallowed, her mouth was dry, her head felt fuzzy. She reached to pull the duvet over herself.

'Mum, are you drunk?' Izzy reached to once more pull the duvet away from Paula.

'No. No.' Paula rubbed her eyes and pushed herself upright. 'I've not had much sleep.'

'Was it Aunty Sue? Is she leaving Uncle Bob?'

'Sue? No, why would you think that; were you listening? Anyway, that doesn't matter, it wasn't, isn't Sue.'

'Come on, Mum. We'll be late.' Izzy walked toward the bedroom door. 'Get up.'

'No, Izzy, wait, it's important.' Paula hesitated. 'It's Amy. She died late last night.' Paula reached toward the bottom of the bed for her dressing gown and patted the bed. 'Sit down, love. Please.'

'Dead! How can she be dead?' Izzy waved her hands in dismissal. 'She's my sister. I only spoke to her at the weekend. You must have dreamt it.' Izzy stood, frozen to the spot. 'Have you told Dad?'

'Yes, of course. He's going to the hospital on his way home, to sort things out.' Pushing her feet into her slippers Paula made move-along motions with her hands. 'Get going, love. Izzy? What's wrong?'

Izzy was like a statue leaning against the side of the tall boy.

'Why?' she whispered. 'Why did she die?'

'Her heart; part of her disability. Izzy, please. We're already late. Come on.' Paula reached out to stroke Izzy's face. 'It's sad, but with her condition we knew it was bound to happen sooner or later. You knew that. We talked about it; about the need for you to not get over involved.'

Paula stepped back as Izzy flicked her head to one side to avoid her touch. As she gasped at the sting of Izzy's rejection, her hand flew to her mouth at the sight of her daughter's hair.

'What!' She reached out again. 'What have you done to your hair?'

'What the bloody hell do you think I've done?'

'Izzy, what's happening? What's got into you?'

'You, that's what's got into me. I hate you, and so does,' she sobbed, 'did Amy. You never wanted her as part of this family. Not like me or Dad.' Izzy sank to the ground to fold in on herself and sob.

'Izzy, please we need to…'

'Getlostleavemealone,' the crouched little girl mumbled between sobs and loud sniffs.

'Please, love, get up or I'm going to have to leave you here.' Paula bent toward Izzy.

'Leave me then.' Izzy raised her head. 'See if I care.'

'Please, Izzy.' Paula's head felt ready to burst. 'It is sad but… I'm going for a shower and when I get back, we can talk.'

'How can you carry on as though nothing's happened?' Izzy dragged her pyjama sleeve under her nose and turned her blotched face toward her mother. 'All you care about is your patients. My sister, my dad's other daughter, is dead. You're a selfish bitch.' She sat up. 'I'm going to get ready, at least my friends care about me. And by the way, I've had my belly button pierced.'

Paula plonked down on the edge of the bed, her hands were shaking; she felt a surge of nausea, she belched as the contents of her stomach fought for freedom. With her hands, over her mouth she stumbled and tripped over the thrown back duvet as she attempted to stagger toward the en-suite.

As the first lot of vomit hit the shag pile of the bedroom carpet, she felt her consciousness stutter and tremble.

Breathe you, stupid bugger. Breathe.

As she fought the battle for her consciousness, her jumbled thoughts held her to ransom.

What the hell. I feel like shit and let's face it, Paula, you made a balls up with Izzy.

She vomited again and again until she was retching up mucous. Any attempt to move threatened her delicate level of consciousness.

'Izzy, please. I'm sorry,' she croaked. She heard the shower in Izzy's bathroom, then the smash of her bedroom door, the sound of footsteps stamping downstairs and the front door slammed shut. 'Izzy, I'm truly sorry about Amy.' She rolled on her side and sobbed.

Jean *December 2016*

Not another, Jean read the note in the Christmas card again. A friend from long ago, from another lifetime, when Paula was a sweet biddable child, and Geoff a young sergeant.

They'd been neighbours supporting each other while their husbands built their careers. Now she was dead, since June the card said; cancer, bravely fought. Jean pondered the phrase.

What does it mean, "bravely fought"? Cancer is crap, so which way you look at it. You either give in or put up and shut up. Would I fight bravely if it came to it? The sound of a car beeping roused her from the gloom crawling around her. She waved and smiled as she dropped the card onto the accumulated pile nestled on the windowsill.

'Are you okay? You looked absorbed, sad, when I pulled into the drive.'

'Yes, fine, it's–' Jean fiddled over her shoulder, feeling for the seat belt– 'just that's the third card I've had announcing a death.'

'Nobody close?'

'We were once. In the early days, when we were young.'

'What do you mean, "when we were young"? Old is always going to be two years older than us, no matter what age we are.'

Jean chuckled and shook her head.

'Di, you remember her, she was a primary school teacher – red hair.'

'Vaguely, she lived next door to you in the police houses, didn't she make a big thing of Nursing having been her second choice, if she hadn't got into teacher training college?'

'That's her, she was a good neighbour and a good friend despite being full of herself. We lost touch, well other than Christmas cards.'

Jean and Gwen synchronised a silence for a second or so, to allow Gwen to negotiate the roundabout that had notoriety as a danger spot. Locals obeyed the rule to drift to the right if they had no intention of driving into Chorley town centre. There was no road sign to indicate this requirement and hapless strangers had been known to cause road traffic accidents. Danger over, the two old friends were free to talk. After a simultaneous intake of breath, an in-depth analysis of life and its meaning could begin.

'How's Bill, still enjoying retirement?'

'Same as ever; if he says retirement is "twenty-four seven" once more I'll throttle him.'

'He always was easy going.'

'Easy going! I've a job to get him to do anything. I sometimes wonder what I saw in him, although I don't know what I'd do without the old git.' Gwen groaned and banged the steering wheel. 'Sorry, me and my big mouth.'

'Gwen? Don't be daft. I often wonder how Geoff and me would have been, growing old together.'

'Then you wouldn't have had another chance–' a smile skittered across Gwen's face– 'with Ron. Oops I think we've missed the turning. I should have used the sat nav.'

After reversing into a wide drive and a narrow miss with an ornate gate post, Gwen pulled out into the stream of traffic despite the threat of oncoming vehicles.

'I can't be doing with shilly-shallying about. I sometimes wish I could have another go, with a man and me a grown up. I mean, we were kids. I've only ever done it with Bill. Look, we're here…Cunnilingus…it sounds like an exotic airline.'

Jean, relieved to have arrived in one piece, hoisted herself out of Gwen's SLK. Death and sex, what more could two sixty-eight-year-old women talk about on their way to a Christmas lunch with old nursing friends? The remnants of the earlier gloom scuttled at the edge of Jean's thoughts as they left the car and made their way toward the posh café.

Three of the group had arrived and were relaxed and sipping drinks on the squelchy Chesterfields in the bar area. Jean had booked for eight people and felt responsible for liaising with the café staff to let them know the status of the numbers. After a quick wave and a blown kiss, Jean dumped her coat and handbag and made her way to the reception desk.

'Wow, who's the glamour puss, that looks a bit like Jean?' one of the group said loud enough for Jean to hear.

Jean gave a half-hearted wave to the assembled group. She was about to turn toward the receptionist when, through the window, she spied the remainder of the September 66 squad piling out of a car. *Four of them? Four, surely not?*

'Has everybody arrived?' said the receptionist, following Jean's line of vision.

'Yes, but I'm confused. Can you give me a minute?' Jean meandered over to the front door while trying to make sense of the appearance of a plump, rumpled looking woman who looked vaguely familiar.

'Jean,' Val, Jean's oldest and closest friend, said as she forced a smile. 'You remember Maggie, she took her finals with us?'

'Yes, we worked together once, in theatre.'

'We bumped into each other in *Marks* late yesterday.' Val stepped back to allow Maggie and the other two women to precede her into the bar area. 'Sorry,' whispered Val. 'She invited herself. I tried to ring you, then left a message on your mobile.'

'I was round at Paula's, my mobile was probably out of juice. Don't worry, I'll sort it or Maggie can sit on your knee.'

Jean sighed and headed back to reception; the uneasy mood that had nibbled at her all morning reasserted itself to gnaw at the base of her skull. She rubbed the back of her neck as she waited for the receptionist to finish her phone call. *There's an eight-week waiting list to get into this place. Trust Maggie Smithfield to show up without warning.*

The receptionist finished her call and turned to Jean.

'I'm sorry,' said Jean, 'we seem to have an extra person.'

'Extra person! I'll need to speak to the manager.'

Jean felt her heart rate increase as a flash of red crossed her vision.

'Is everything alright?' Val said as she appeared at Jean's side.

'Mrs Fletcher. How are you?' The receptionist flashed a smile at Val. 'Are you with this lady?'

'Yes, she's my friend.' Val gave Jean a rueful look. 'Well, she used to be.'

'I'll fetch an extra chair and place setting and call you when your table is relayed,' said the receptionist.

'What the hell's up with you? You look as though you're at a wake, not a Christmas bash?' Val said.

'Nothing – everything. Mood swings. Family: a dreadful row, Gwen's driving. How do you know the receptionist?'

'I delivered her, it's a long story.' Val linked Jean as they headed back to the group. 'Come on, let's get you a drink. You miserable old bugger.'

★

Jean was home and had no sooner kicked off her shoes and slung her coat over the banister rail when the phone rang.

'It's me. Jean, I'm really, really sorry about Maggie Smithfield. Are you pissed off with me?'

'No. It's not you or Maggie Smithfield. It's the family; nothing new but every now and then the ongoing story of *A Family at War* with Paula and Izzy as well as my mum gets to me. Oh, and I think my thyroid's on the blink; constant mood swings being tired and fed up.'

'So long as you weren't pissed off with me.'

'Pissed off doesn't begin to cover it. Forget the family, let's get down to Maggie. I didn't catch half of what she was going on about with Ann on one side of me ranting on about her daughter-in-law, who does appear to win hands down in the in-law-from-hell stakes. Then Di deciding she'd had enough of being dumped on by her family and threatening to move without leaving a forwarding address.' Jean sighed and pictured a lovely cup of tea. 'It did cross my mind I might join her.'

'What about Ron, and me for that matter?' said Val.

'Okay, you and Ron can come, and Izzy,' Jean said as she walked to the kitchen.

'Are you having a wee?'

'No, running the tap to fill the kettle.'

'Sounds to me like you'd be better with a glass of wine. Well, at my end of the table Maggie was telling us about her son and his wedding.' Val slurped. 'He's done well for himself.'

'Is that wine?'

'Yes.'

'Hang on I'll get a glass and then we can settle down.' Glass in hand, Jean picked up the phone. 'Go on, about Maggie.'

'Her son, how old will he be?'

'Forty-six, forty-seven.'

'He's a consultant, orthopaedics and he's engaged to a consultant ophthalmologist.'

'Wasn't his father supposed to be that quiet, little Egyptian houseman?'

'I never knew that,' said Val, sounding doubtful.

'Is he local? Paula and Douglas might know him.'

'Both him and his future–' Val paused for effect– 'husband, work in Chorley and Preston.'

'Wife?'

'Husband.'

'Well, each to their own. What can I say, with Paula eloping and all the stuff that went with it?' Jean paused and sighed. 'Stuff that's still going on.'

'Do you want to talk about it. Whatever's going on with Paula? Your voice is shaky and you keep mentioning a row.'

'Sometime. Not now. Let's not spoil the day.'

★

Jean reached for the bedside light switch. Wine and rich food had her abdomen gurgling and spluttering like the plumbing in an Edwardian semi. Her thoughts, bloated abdomen and the urge to fart and belch told her that sleep was not on the agenda. She surrendered to the inevitable wakefulness, dragged on her dressing gown and headed to the kitchen for a mug of peppermint tea. Back in bed and sipping the tea in the quiet glow of the bedside light, Jean told herself to relax. A full ten seconds passed then she belched, and her thoughts cascaded, crashed and clattered into her almost, very nearly, relaxed state.

What the hell's wrong with me? It must be my thyroid, I'm tired all the time, no energy and weepy. I'll ring the GP tomorrow. I can't move in with Ron, I'd lose Geoff's pension. I can't face the thought of moving. And anyway, Paula would go bananas. What business is it of hers what I do?

She's making a real mess of things with Izzy. The poor kid wants to grow up. Perhaps she could live with me – don't be ridiculous. Perhaps she's starting with the change, she's short tempered at the least thing. What was all that about when I asked her if she knew Maggie's son? She rings to ask if Izzy can have a sleepover and we end up having a set-to about Maggie Smithfield and her son. I'm going to try sleep and ringing the GP in the morning to see about a blood test.

*

'Jean, love, it's me, Jim. Have I woken you?'

'Er no. Yes, what time is it?'

'Quarter to nine. I've just been with your mam's paper and I've found her at the bottom of the stairs. I've called an ambulance.'

Mary *February 2017*

Mary looked around the ward from her vantage point at the top end of the ten-bedded room. It was her favourite time of the day; the beds were made, the ward tidied and there was plenty going on for her to watch and listen to. Mary had persuaded the nurses to position her chair with its back to the wall so that she could keep her eyes on the various comings and goings that made the day in the ward

CHAPTER TWO

interesting. She was well aware that the women in the green overalls were care assistants really, not proper nurses like Jean had been, but they smiled when she called them "nurse". It was a pity that they didn't speak up so she would know for sure what was going on at each bed. Bed making, medicine rounds, patients pottering around their bed space, new admissions, tantalising, half heard, conversations, Mary watched and listened. It was almost as good as watching *Holby*. Her favourite was the doctors' rounds, especially when they didn't bother drawing the curtains round the individual beds.

'Cup of tea, Mary?' said the nurse, pausing at the foot of Mary's bed.

'Please.' Mary shifted her position to look beyond the nurse. A wheelchair carrying a youngish woman had been positioned by the bed on the left of the ward door. 'No sugar. I've got diabetes, you know.' Mary held out her hand for the cup of tea while watching the transfer of the patient into bed. 'She looks done in. Poor bugger.'

'Mary.' The nurse glanced toward the door. 'Don't worry about her. What about you, any chance of going home?'

'Home! I shouldn't think so. Not for a good while yet.' Mary shook her head and tutted. 'Not with all that's wrong with me. Is the hairdresser coming this afternoon?' She sipped her tea.

'I'll have to ask Sister, it's something she arranges.'

'She's good at her job, is that one.' Mary wrinkled her nose as she held out her cup and saucer to the nurse. 'This tea's stewed.'

The nurse moved on while Mary harrumphed as the curtains were pulled around the bed of the new patient. She thought back to the day she was admitted. She'd been against the admission even though she had to admit she felt buggered with spending the best part of the night at the bottom of the stairs. Every now and again she had a pang of guilt that she'd not told the truth about what had happened. *No bugger thought to ask me, they just thought I'd fallen downstairs and let's face it we all know what thought did. Well Jim and them ambulance men sure as heck followed a muck cart and thought it were a wedding. If truth be known I'm not really sure what happened. All I know is, I didn't fall downstairs. Still, it's turned out grand; there's always summat going on, the food's tasty and I gets plenty visitors. It's a pity I'm missing Emmerdale and Coronation Street but I'm managing to keep up with t'Express telly page.*

As she shifted her position to reach for the *Daily Express*, and her glasses that lay on her bed, Mary felt the need to use the lavatory. *I've never bint same since they took that caffither out. I'm sure I don't make water like I used to.*

'Nurse, nurse will you help me to the lav…toilet, love?'

In her shuffle to the lavatory and back, Mary concentrated on showing her mastery of the walking frame. "Both hands on the chair arms, push forward and stand up. DO NOT use the frame to pull up. Move one arm at a time from chair to frame. Move frame forward. Step into frame with bad leg then good leg." Mary could hear the physiotherapist's mantra as she shuffled along. The physiotherapy girl, who'd instructed Mary, knew Paula; they'd done some training together.

Mary hadn't been able to resist asking the girl if she'd wanted to be a doctor like Paula. She was happy to pass on the family history of Paula and Douglas's elopement and Paula's subsequent switch to physiotherapy at another university "so as Douglas wouldn't get into bother and be struck off". She looked forward to the girl's visits and always had a titbit of family information to keep the conversation going.

'Here, nurse, look at this.' Mary held out the *Express* as a nurse paused at the foot of her bed to jot something on the charts. 'The Queen, God bless her, she's been on the throne for sixty-five years. She's had her ups and downs, like the rest of us.'

'She'll be your age?' The nurse cocked her head to one side.

'I'm a bit older than her. I wouldn't have wanted her life, alus on show, and 'im, Phil the Greek, being no better than he should be. And then that girl, Diana, dying–' Mary shook her head and pursed her lips– 'leaving them kiddies.'

'See you later, Mary.' The nurse strode off down the ward leaving Mary to her newspaper.

Brexit, and that Trump man, there's nowt in the news, well other than the bit about The Queen. Mary smiled to herself. *When I were little we called a fart a trump… President Fart.*

'Something's making you smile,' the Sister said as she ran her hands over the duvet on Mary's bed.

'It's him that new President, he's not fit. Whatever is the world coming to. I asks myself over and over, does nobody remember the war?'

'Anyway, Mary. I think we need a little chat at visiting. Me, you and your Jean.'

'Chat! What about?' Mary sensed danger. 'Is summat up with them blood tests?'

'No, everything is fine…within normal limits. It's just that we need to talk about next steps.'

'Next steps?' Mary took a surreptitious glance at the walking frame. 'Next steps?'

'Discharge; what might be best for you.'

'Well, that's easy. Going home is what'll be best for me.'

'Like I said, let's have a talk when Jean arrives. She's coming in at two o clock.'

Two o clock. There is summat up, our Jean comes at six. There's no way I'm going to one of them death palaces. They'll carry me out feet first before they put me in one of them homes. I have a home and that's where I'm going, come hell or bloody high water.

The morning dragged on. Mary's eyes fixated on the clock over the ward door. *That clock must be slow or has it stopped?*

'Nurse, love, what time is it?'

'Ten minutes further on than last time you asked,' said the nurse, checking the catheter bag of the patient in the next bed to Mary. 'Is something bothering you, Mary? You seem mithered.'

'No. Yes. Can they make me go in one of them homes, you know the Sister and that stuck up doctor and our Jean?'

'They usually have a plan before you're discharged to make sure you're ready–' the nurse hooked the catheter bag back in position– 'for what they think is best for you.'

'Don't I get a say?'

'Have you spoken to your daughter about going home?'

'No and I'm not going to. I managed before and I'll manage again.' Her voice quivered. 'I'll tell you this, our Terry, God bless him, would never have put me in a home.' Mary rested her head back and closed her eyes.

I'll do as I bloody well please.

'Mary, please don't cry,' said the nurse.

CHAPTER TWO

Mary opened her eyes to see the nurse crouching at her side. 'I want to stay here until I'm fit. Pass me a tissue, love.'

'Perhaps you're jumping to conclusions. Do you want me to have a word with Sister?'

'No! They're all in it together. I'll wait and see what our Jean has to say for herself.'

★

The large finger of the clock clicked to twelve; two o clock at last. Mary craned her neck: no sign of Jean. *Perhaps I've dreamt it?* Ten past two, twenty past two. *Must have done. You're a daft bugger getting in a state.*

'Mum, Mum.'

'Jean?' Mary pushed her glasses up from her cheeks and rubbed her eyes. 'What are you doing here?'

'Didn't Sister mention I was coming in? I'll just get a chair.'

Mary felt her heart flutter, her mouth was dry, her hands were sweaty, and her head felt clammy. *I'll not be bossed about. I know my own mind.* She belched: *Brussels sprouts.*

'Sorry, Mum, did you say something?'

Mary shook her head as Jean settled in the chair, leant forward and took her mother's hand.

'Are you okay, you feel warm?' She raised her hand to feel Mary's forehead.

'I'm fine, stop mithering,' Mary said, flinching away.

'Mum? What's the matter?'

'You can't make me. I've not signed anything, not like Doris at the Youth Club. I've not given you one of them–' Mary whisked away the tears trotting down her face– 'enduringly powerful things.'

'Mum, you're getting yourself in a state over nothing.'

'Nothing! You could have had the common decency to talk to me about it first.'

'Mum, what are you going on about?'

'Have you not come to take me to a home?' Mary sniffed then wiped her hand under her nose. 'Pass me a hanky.'

'I've come to begin to talk to you about what you want to do next. What your options are?'

'Options?'

'You need to get a bit better before you are ready to be discharged, but the team here, and me, well we need to look at your short term and long-term care needs.'

'Short term, long term, what does all that mean when it's at home?'

'Well, perhaps you could move to somewhere to convalesce, until you put some weight on and get steady on your feet.'

'They've stopped my liquorice allsorts and my dandelion and burdock, and biscuits and jelly babies. That's why I've lost weight.'

'Because, they've found out you're diabetic and anaemic.'

'Anyway, why can't I stay here?'

'Because you're on an acute ward and they need the beds.' Jean picked up Mary's newspaper. 'You read your paper every day, you can see what state the NHS is in.'

'I've paid my dues all my life, and so did your dad and our Terry.'

'That's why you can have a period of convalescence. You could wear your own clothes and have a television in your room.'

'Where is this place then?'

CHAPTER TWO

'We would need to wait for a bed to become available. But, somewhere here in Chorley.'

'You mean a bloody home.'

'A home, with convalescent beds.'

'Then what?'

'We would need to see how you progressed.'

'Then I could go home. Couldn't I?'

'It would depend, you could perhaps think about living with me. We need to wait and see.'

Mary paused. 'Move in with you? What would he say, that Ron?'

'It was his idea.'

'I always said he were a belter. Convalescence, you say. Would that mean my own telly and proper clothes?'

Chapter Three

Izzy's Journal

Hello again. I'm upstairs hiding from my mum. I've finished my homework, but she doesn't know that. The reason I don't want to see her is in the last few weeks she's changed for the better but at the same time for the worse. Fuck wit. That's my new swear word. It would really make her mad if she knew — but ape shit what does it matter? To be honest, she's trying too hard to be nice. Her face must really ache with smiling and being chirpy all the time. Mr Coupe my English teacher says nice is a lazy word. To pass the time on and not be lazy I've looked up nice on the internet. That's a surprise "the internet". Fuck wit, it is awesome I got a mini iPad for Christmas!!!!!!!! Anyway, there are 45 synonyms for nice. My favourites are

    Fine and dandy
    Ducky
    Swell
    Nifty and
    Copacetic. I've never heard this word before. I like it, it sounds as though a doctor would say it. It means "in excellent order".

CHAPTER THREE

The other words on the list are a bit boring. I must say that everything is not copacetic with my mum, Grandma or Grandma Mary. That's why we're going to Tenerife next week and taking Grandma with us. Fuck wit, Mum's coming.

Here I am in bed. We've had our GIRLS CHAT. We have one every night now since the big, shocking, massive, row.

Good things about the row.

> I've got an iPad
> My ears are pierced. I'm not going to bother with my belly button. I wish I hadn't wound Mum up; telling her I had. It made me feel good at the time but I'm sad about it now.
> Dad is trying really, really, hard to be at home
> Ron has been for a meal.
> Like I said before we're going to Tenerife but not the Caribbean. We can't go there until next year.
> Mum doesn't pull her face or look fed up if me and Dad talk about Amy and she is only drinking wine with meals at weekend. Which day does the weekend start?

Bad things about the row.

> GIRLS CHATS every fuck wit night.
> Awesomely bad, secret news about my mum.

I understand, a bit about why Mum was mean about Amy. Amy was jealous when my dad took Mum to meet her after they had eloped. She tried to hit and scratch Mum and spat at her.

The people that looked after Amy said it was best if Mum stayed away because Amy fretted and was violent, when she saw Mum. And for ages afterwards she threw food and messed with her poo. Poor Dad. He only had Amy because he did sex with her mum once when he was still at school. Grandma says he faced up to his responsibilities. I think that means he sent money to her mum until she died, Amy's mum I mean. Then he had to put Amy into a home with her mum's money. Amy's money is mine now, but I'm not allowed to touch it. How mean is that? And I've got two of her favourite Charlie bears. She had loads but they've gone to the children's hospice. I'll miss going to visit her she was lovely and cuddly and I loved her with all my heart.

What else, Grandma — she's better now she's on the Vitamin D, not as tired and fed up. She's always kind to me and Ron and Aunty Val. She was fuck witted with my mum. That's how I got my ears pierced and the iPad because during the BIG ROW, after I ran to Grandma's, when my mum told me Amy had died Grandma told my mum she was sick and tired of her arping on about me and growing up. She told my mum she had a short memory if she'd forgotten what a bloody awful dance she'd led her and Grandad. If I'm half as promisquas as my mum I'll be a soddin angel — that's what my grandma shouted at my mum. Grandma got very upset, she was crying and gulping she said my mum was spoiling my childhood and wearing her out with worry. Then fuck wit she said something awesome that is BEST KEPT BETWEEN US which means I've not to tell my friends about not one but two abortions and then eloping and creating a scandal at the medical school.

CHAPTER THREE

I couldn't quite hear everything because of all the crying. And anyway, I couldn't breathe and my eyes went blurry and sick came in my mouth. But I swallowed it.

My mum screamed dead loud at my grandma to get out of the house and never comeback then she said grandma would never see me again. That's when I jumped downstairs and ran in the kitchen and said I wanted to live with grandma and then I told my mum to bugger off. Then my dad walked in. So now we're all pretending we're getting on which we mostly are but it's hard work. Grandma Mary is in a home, she thinks it is for the time being but we all know, except her, that she won't be going back to her bungalow.

Adults tell a lot of lies to each other. I didn't intend to write all that about the row but I'm glad I did. I think about my mum and her being promisquous a lot. I could have had brothers and sisters, except they wouldn't be my dad's children. She got rid of them. We've done about abortion and contraception I know what happens to the unborn baby, the foetus. It gets sucked out. Why didn't she get contraception? I wonder who she did sex with and how old she was and where she did it and what it feels like to have a boy's willie in your vagina? I'm practising the words to ask her during our GIRLS CHATS but it's difficult because it's mostly, well really all about mum and her very, extremely boring concerns about school and my friends and boys urges and being careful around boys!!!! She should talk!!!!!!!!

Well we've been to Tenerife. It was good except when we were going to land a gust of wind made the aeroplane wobble and the pilot had to abort the landing. It was fuck wit frightening and exciting at the same time. Everybody clapped when we finally landed. Me and Grandma shared the room next door to Mum and Dad. Me and Dad went on a Segway tour and we all went to the top, well nearly to the top of Mount Teide some of the paths were closed because of ice. It was awesome, cold and crisp and truly lovely. Ron would have written a poem. Grandma didn't want to leave Grandma Mary because of her only just being in the home but we all ganged up on her, in a nice way, and persuaded her. Ron and Aunty Val sorted out visiting Grandma Mary. We went to see her yesterday she is very settled and smiley happy and though she won't say she likes it you can tell she does. She says it's like the youth club with bedrooms. She joins in all the activities so that she can see "what's what". She says the handy-man has his finger in the pie and must be related to the owners.

She has her bedroom door open all the time and sees him prowling about where he has no cause to be. She is getting about on her frame and likes watching television in bed. She didn't mention the smell of wee and something else that pongs.

This is mixed up again and not like Mrs Berry said a journal should be. I'll try harder next time.

My mum will be coming for the CHAT soon and I can guess what it will be about. — Zoella. My dad showed me an article in yesterday's Guardian. YOUR MUM'S READ THIS he said with a wink. We didn't talk about it last night because Mum and Dad were out. Anyway, this Zoella is really called Zoe and has made lots of money giving advice to girls my age. She seems sensible to me but she is old — 26. She says good things like "Every time you post something online you have a choice. You can either make it something that adds to the happiness levels in the world — or make it something that takes away." Zoella's obsessed with staying safe. Who does that remind you off? Mum's on her way.

Next time I write I am going to go back to Mrs Berry's way.

Promise.

Paula   *March 2017*

The light from the mobile phone, on the bedside table, cast a blue tinge around Douglas's side of the bed, highlighting his bulk. Paula snuggled closer to him, her arm tight around his waist. Her knees tucked up against his. Her hand cupping his balls. He groaned, half asleep; his penis stirred.

'Whatsup,' he said, rolling onto his back.

'Do you still love me?'

'What?' He snuffled. 'Course I do.' He made to roll back onto his side.

'Why?'

'I just do, you're my wife – Izzy's mum.' Douglas yawned. 'Are you having a bad period again?' He swung his legs out of bed, sat up and scrubbed his face with his hands. 'I'll fetch you some paracetamol.'

'I don't need paracetamol. I need to be…I don't know how I need to be. I'm a dead loss; everything I do or feel or say, it's wrong.'

'Come here.' Douglas settled back into bed and squirmed to lie facing Paula. He stroked her face. 'What's brought this on?'

'I'm no better now than when I was a mixed-up kid.'

Douglas kissed her eyes then her lips. Paula's lukewarm response of a tug and pull on his balls and a pump or two of his penis were a catalyst for the familiar pattern and well rehearsed moves of their coupling. Before Paula had finished wiping herself with a tissue Douglas had turned on his side and was puffing and snorting like the Flying Scotsman. Paula gave up on sleep and headed for the kitchen. Rationalising the glug of whisky she added to her mug of tea as "for medicinal purposes", she trudged back upstairs. With care, she turned the door handle of Izzy's bedroom and moved toward the sleeping figure.

I so don't want you to be like me, little girl. I want you to be a child, forever, for as long as possible. But that's not fair. Is it? It's not what you want. How do I help you? How do I help myself? I love you so much. Paula was so taken up with her musings that bending to kiss Izzy she forgot the mug in her hand.

'Shit!' she yelped as the scalding liquid hit her bare foot.

Izzy stirred and murmured as Paula tried to examine her foot in the light from the landing.

You stupid bloody fool, you can't even kiss Izzy goodnight without scalding yourself. You are well and truly fucked up. And besides that, you're a drunkard. Ashamed and dejected,

CHAPTER THREE

Paula took the two steps into Izzy's shower room. In her haste and determination to rid herself of the adulterated tea, she flung the tea and the mug into the sink. The midnight quiet of the house was shattered, along with the mug. Paula stumbled back into the darkness of Izzy's room to find her befuddled husband blocking the light from the hall and her sleepy daughter rubbing her eyes and pushing herself up her bed.

'What the fuck? Paula, what's going on?' said Douglas, moving toward a puzzled Izzy.

'Douglas, Izzy.' Paula shuffled toward the bed. 'I love you both so much but all I do is mess up.' Paula plonked herself on the end of the bed. She hung her head and sniffed back tears. 'I'm a selfish bitch who doesn't deserve either of you.' Escalating breaths caused her shoulders to shudder. Her eyes closed and her hands shook. 'It should have been me that died, not Amy, at least she was happy with her lot in life. Well apart from when she was spitting at me and trying to claw my eyes out; I probably deserved it. That set-to with my mum has finally made me realise what a bitch I've been for years and years and years.'

'Hush, love, you're frightening Izzy, and me,' Douglas said as he pulled Paula against his chest. 'Izzy, sweetheart, go downstairs and make us all a cup of tea. Give us a shout when it's ready.' Douglas kissed Paula's head and then gently pushed her away so that he could see her face. 'Into the bathroom, wash your face, put your dressing gown on and then come downstairs; we're going to sort you out, once and for all.'

★

With her dressing gown belted tight, her hair dishevelled and with shoulders hunched, Paula joined her husband and daughter to sit on the edge of the settee in the family room.

'Come on, love, sit back and relax because we're staying here until we're all in a more settled state.'

'Should I go to bed, Dad?' Izzy wriggled to the end of the settee.

'No, love. Pass your mum her tea. You need to know what's going on. We all do. Paula?'

Paula looked mournfully at Douglas and Izzy. 'I hate myself. That's what's going on. I hate and despise myself, I have done for a long time, since I was a kid. I hate how I am with you both. How I am with my mum. How I've been with Ron and Amy. I'm bored at work, and more than anything I'm frightened of Izzy growing up in this horrible world. I'm a fucking mess, Douglas, and like I said–' Paula paused at the sound of Izzy crying. 'Izzy, I love you so much.' She turned and held out her arms.'

As Izzy lurched into her mother's embrace, she skittled all three mugs sitting on the floor.

'See, I can't do anything right,' Paula said as Douglas grabbed a tea towel to set about, mopping up the tea seeping under the settee.

'I did that, Mum, not you, and anyway I think the milk was off,' said Izzy.

'You did us all a favour, Izzy, saved us from food poisoning, botulism and God knows what else. Come on, Paula love, let's try and understand what's happening, then we can work out what to do.' Douglas turned from washing out the tea towel at the sink. 'Start at the beginning, wherever you think that is.'

CHAPTER THREE

'See, you think I'm useless, "the beginning, wherever I think that is",' Paula parodied Douglas's voice.

'Paula, you are, as usual deciding what I think.' Douglas crossed the room to kneel in front of his wife; he paused. 'My love, you need to take things at face value without deciding that everything and everybody is against you.' He sighed. 'Just start where you want but please, please, please, let us in, let us help you. Now hutch up you two, so that I can put an arm round you both.'

Snuggled against Douglas, Paula focused on a small puddle of tea that had settled between two of the floor tiles.

'I've thought and thought since the row. I was happy as a child. I spent a lot of time with my mum and grandma and Uncle Terry, when he was at home. My dad was mostly at work. I had friends, was in the Guides and then I don't know. I started at Bolton School, I got on well, at first anyway, I did my homework, got good marks and then something in me changed. I started doing stupid things, taking risks. It was nothing to do with the school or my friends. When Mum got exasperated with me, she'd ground me and say I'd got my Uncle Terry's "bloody selfish genes".'

'Why?' said Izzy.

'He was a law unto himself, a tearaway, albeit funny and kind, but he didn't conform. My grandma idolised him, and, according to Mum, let him get away with murder. He left school as soon as he could and got a job, as a labourer. He swapped jobs whenever he fancied, tipped his wage up every week and went his own sweet way, coming in when he wanted, disappearing for weeks on end. Your grandma will give you chapter and verse. What I'm saying is he did as he pleased and san fairy ann, to everybody else.'

'I don't understand how that makes you like him,' said Douglas.

'He was never contented, never happy to be still.'

'And is that how you feel, felt as a young girl?'

'Yes, it was as if – as if I could take risks and getting caught, found out, proved how useless I was.'

'Like what, Mum?' Izzy leant forward.

'Well you were there, involved in the row. So, you heard Grandma get upset about…' Paula chewed her lips and looked into the middle distance… 'the abortions and daft tricks like pinching stuff from British Home Stores, the police called and my dad a chief inspector, smoking at school, threatened with expulsion. It confirmed to me that I was a tramp, no good, a waste of space. Then, well, you know the rest. I ended up at university doing something I had no real interest in. And here we are.' Paula sat upright and ran her hands over her face and through her hair. 'Then it turns out I'm useless at what comes naturally for most women; getting pregnant, when I wanted to, took years. I'm an excuse for a wife, and mother. I hate myself.'

She turned to look at Izzy and Douglas. 'Why can't I be happy?'

'Dear God, Paula, why haven't you talked about all this before?'

Paula held her hands wide in supplication. 'I think, it's because, well I've never admitted it, even to myself. The row started because Mum could see what a balls-up I was making with Izzy, and Ron, and the Amy situation. I'm empty, Douglas, so very sad and empty and oh so bloody tired.'

'Paula, love.' Douglas rubbed his chin on Paula's shoulder. 'If you're so bloody useless how come you manage to run a home, have a career and more important, from my point of view, be a caring, supportive wife and mother?' He clapped his hand. 'Izzy love, why don't you have a shower, change your pyjamas, have a dose of Calpol…'

'Calpol, Dad? How old do you think I am?'

'Whatever; but scoot. Go on, love, it'll give you something to do, something to settle you. I'll finish clearing up down here. I've spotted another couple of rivers of tea. Tomorrow we start afresh.'

★

The light seeping through the curtains tickled at the edges of Paula's consciousness. *What time is it? Half-ten?* She flung back the duvet to feel the room shift as her blood pressure adjusted to the sudden movement of her standing up. The house was quiet, Izzy's bedroom was empty, the bed unmade.

'Douglas,' said Paula, shuffling downstairs.

'Coming.' He emerged from his study.

'Work? Izzy? It's half-ten.'

Douglas checked his watch and nodded. 'I rang the hospital and told them you'd had a rough night, I implied it was gut rot and told them you'd be back on Monday. Izzy was up in time for school, so, well I thought it was best if she had a normal day–' he shrugged– 'after last night.'

'I'm sorry…' Paula headed for the kitchen.

'Stop that. I mean it, things change from today. Now. This minute. That milk is off by the way.'

'I'm sorry.' Paula gave up her journey toward the kettle and plonked herself down on the settee. 'I feel like death warmed up.'

'Yes, well it's a good thing I rang the surgery and made you an appointment for this afternoon.'

'The surgery? Why? Is that not pathologizing the way I am?'

'It's a starting point.' Douglas rummaged in the kitchen cupboard. 'Do you want black coffee or fruit tea?' As he waited for the kettle to boil, Douglas regarded his wife.

'Why are you looking at me like that?' Paula said.

'I have a question and I want you to answer straight away without thinking about it.'

Paula hesitated. 'Go on.' She took a deep breath.

'Answer straight away, no hesitation.'

'Okay.'

'If you could do any job, what would it be?'

'Personal shopper. Where did that come from?' Paula said.

'Personal shopper!?'

'See, you're thinking blatant consumerism, trite, what a waste of space…'

'Paula, here we go. Will you listen to yourself, yet again, deciding what I'm thinking. Making up your mind that I'm judging you, that I disapprove. I don't even know what a bloody personal shopper is.' He pouted, scowled and then smiled. 'Let's start again. Good morning, Paula. This is where you say good morning, Douglas.'

'Good morning, Douglas.'

Jean *March 2017*

The glass fronts and shelves of the two display cabinets sparkled. Jean felt noble as she stood in the kitchen and

CHAPTER THREE

considered the cheese dishes, her mother's coffee set and her grandma's tea service that she'd washed, dried and returned to be incarcerated in their usual places. *I could get rid of the cheese dishes. I've lost interest in kitchen antiques.* She knitted her arms across her chest. The ending of the Diana Krall CD that had kept her company during the spring clean diverted Jean's thoughts from the redundancy of the cheese dishes to a change of music; Brian Wilson letting rip on *Gershwin Reimagined*. She smiled, *go to it, Jean.* She was so engrossed in swabbing down the worktops, having sprayed the kitchen cleaner with dramatic flourish, while she bopped and sang, that she didn't hear the opening and closing of the front and vestibule doors. Emerging from an enthusiastic heel spin and in the middle of a *be-bop-de-do* chorus she was startled to find Paula standing in the kitchen doorway, holding a pot of orchids.

'Paula! What time is it,' said Jean glancing at the oven clock, 'why aren't you at work?'

She took the plant that Paula held out to her. 'What's this for?'

'I've had the day off sick and the plant is…it's, I don't know what it is, something and nothing to say…'

'Sick?' Jean filled the kettle.

'Mum, I'm in a mess.'

Jean held out her arms at the sight of Paula's tears.

'Mum? I don't know who I am.'

Jean guided Paula into the sitting room, sat next to her on the settee and with prodding and probing established the events of the previous night.

'Mum, I need to ask, to know when I started being a bitch, doing all that stupid stuff.' She followed Jean into the kitchen. 'Have I ever been happy, contented?'

Dear God, where do I go with this? Jean paused. 'There's no doubt, you were a beautiful child, full of joy, and then out of the blue…' A troubled look flitted across Jean's face. 'Over the years I've tormented myself; was it your dad and the long hours, or me working, albeit part-time so I could be at home for you – if you needed me.' Jean stiffed away tears. 'Which, let's face it, you made it abundantly clear that I was the last person you needed. Anyway, all that's all behind us now.' Jean's voice dropped. 'I've asked myself time after time was I too soft, particularly after your dad died?' She sighed. 'Tea or coffee?' Jean said, pointing the way toward the kitchen and then levering herself off the settee.

'Tea. What about Uncle Terry? You always said I was like him.'

'It's how I've explained it to myself. A family quirk, a trait maybe.' *Best not mention my selfish gene theory.*

'Was he ever happy?'

'After Dad died, he was more settled, more responsible, particularly with Mum, although he still had his moments, still disappeared for days on end. It was as though the shock of Dad's death triggered something better, more thoughtful, in him. Although he still came and went as he pleased. He thought the world of you.'

'I've done the same. Haven't I? Made everybody's life a misery?'

'I think that's going a bit far, love. Like I said, you've certainly had me worn to a frazzle over the years, especially when you were a teenager. And then it seemed to start again with you being beside yourself about Izzy.' Jean took a backward step to give Paula an intense look. 'But I've had my say and I don't want us ever to fall out like that again.'

CHAPTER THREE

'It's what I needed.' Paula sipped the tea, and turned to walk back to the sitting room. 'The row has woken me up to everything: Amy, my selfishness, my obsession with Izzy and growing up, Douglas, work, everything.'

'What did the doctor say?'

'He thinks I look anaemic, blood tests on Monday, and he mentioned me being deficient in Vitamin D.'

'It's doing me good, I thought it was my thyroid. What did you mean about work, I thought you were happy with Maggie's son.' *Oops careful, touchy subject.*

'I never really wanted medicine.' Paula gave her mother a sheepish look. 'And I'm bored stiff with physiotherapy.'

'Dear God, Paula, why didn't you say something years ago?'

'Because of the fuck up – sorry, Mum, language – I made at medical school and then eloping.'

'Shit, Paula. I never thought you were suited to medicine or physio for that matter.'

'Why didn't you say anything?' Paula looked aghast.

'Listen to what you're asking?' Jean's voice ratcheted up. 'If I'd have tried to interfere, what do you think would have happened?'

'See, I've been nothing but trouble. How bad is it when a mother can't talk to her own daughter?'

'You may well ask,' Jean muttered. 'Sorry, love. I don't want to go there again.'

'Where? You mean me and Izzy, don't you?' Paula stared at her mother.

Jean held her hands up as though to surrender. 'Like I said, I've had my say.'

'Mum! You don't get it, do you? YOU WERE RIGHT.' Paula's shoulders sagged and she shook her head, rivulets of tears coursed down her face. 'I have to change, to find some sort of, oh, I don't know – peace, equilibrium, happiness. Whatever that is.'

Jean reached out to Paula. 'I love you, you daft, unreasonable, sad girl, come here.'

'Mum, thank you, for sticking by me despite me being a waste of space. Don't cry, please, don't cry.'

Eyes dried, feeling drained and exhausted, the two women contemplated each other, searching for the right thing to say, the right move to make. Jean reached for Paula's hand.

'Let's make a pact, to be honest with each other and to take a deep breath and think–' Jean glanced at her watch– 'before we answer each other.'

'I agree.'

'I'm sorry, love, but I need to go and see your grandma, she'll wonder where I am.'

'Dear God, Mum.' Paula stood up straight and regarded her mother. 'You don't have it easy, do you, running round after all of us. I never realised?'

'I'm okay, love, I have Izzy and Ron and Val, and I love you and Douglas no matter what. Now come on, get yourself off home.' Jean stopped and paused as she contemplated her next move. 'No, don't. Put the kettle on. I'm going to ring the home.'

'Why? What about Grandma?'

'She's safe, and looked after, and now, at this minute, you are the most important person in the world to me.' Jean speed-dialled the home. 'We need more time. Hello it's Jean, Mary's daughter.' Jean nodded and smiled at the phone. 'Thank you, I'll expect a call in a minute or so.'

CHAPTER THREE

Now's your chance; tell her. 'Paula, I need... that'll be Grandma ringing back. Hello, Mum. Mum?'

'Is that you, Jean? They've given me this bloody thing to ring you on. Is summat up?'

'I can't come to visit until later. Paula isn't very well.'

'Well if you can't come before tea, don't come after, I'll be watching *Emmerdale* and you talk too much when it's on. And anyway, Madge and her daughter have just gone. How do I switch this thing off?'

'Mum? Well goodbye to you, Mum,' Jean said to the dead phone.

This is it, Jean steadied her breathing, aware that her heart was thudding. 'Paula, love... hello, Chorley, 67845.' Jean shrugged her shoulders and mouthed 'sorry' as she answered the ringing phone.

'What's up with our Paula?'

'Hello, Mum. She's a bit run down.'

'What with?'

'Work, running a home, different things.'

'They don't know what work is, these days. A shift in t'mill – that ud learn em what hard work is.'

Jean slotted the phone onto its stand. She paused, staring out of the window. *Where am I in all this? Mum, Paula, I need to be able to think, to decide.* 'Paula.' Jean continued to stare out of the window – her neighbour was raking dead twigs on his lawn. 'Ron has asked me to marry him.' She turned to look at her daughter. Paula choked and spluttered on her mouthful of tea. 'I'm going to tell him yes.' *That's it then, decision made.* Jean laughed as the room tipped, and a vague nausea threatened. She steadied herself against the window sill.

'I don't know what to say.' Paula enveloped her mother in her arms. 'I love you, Mum.'

The hackneyed phrase that Jean had, for so long, wanted to hear from her daughter shattered her. Held tight in her daughter's embrace she wept tears of frustration and joy at the overwhelming realisation that the daughter she felt she had lost thirty years ago, had somehow and from somewhere stumbled toward home.

Paula released Jean. 'Why didn't you say something before?'

'Because, I had you and Izzy and Grandma to think about. Let's face it, love, until we had the set-to you couldn't have given a toss about Ron.'

'Jesus, Mum. I'm a fucking liability. How've you coped all these years?'

'Izzy, Val, writing, keeping busy, reading, seeing friends, feeling pissed off. Wanting to be touched, to be held. And work, I loved nursing.'

'What can I do to make things right–' Paula reached for Jean's hands– 'better between us?'

'Get yourself sorted, health wise.' Jean squeezed Paula's hands. 'Think about work and try and be happy.'

'Happy? Huh, how do I do that?' Tears threatened again.

Jean sighed and looked skyward, her gaze fixing a corner of the ceiling: *cobwebs.* 'I'm not usually one for suggesting counselling, I usually worry something to death and talk to Val, but it might help.'

'I'm thinking about being a personal shopper,' Paula said.

'Personal shopper!'

'See, you're thinking what a waste of an education.' Paula stopped. 'Sorry, I'm doing it again, deciding what you think. Douglas says I decide what other people think about me, when it's me all the time using their supposed opinion to put myself down. How do I stop myself?'

'Self-esteem, feeling good about yourself. I don't know, love but I do know we need something stronger than tea.'

'Not for me, Mum. I drink too much. Now there's an admission. Why don't you and Ron come round over the weekend? I'll make a meal and then I'll have a drink as part of the engagement celebration.'

'That would be lovely, but I think I'd better ring Ron and let him have my answer before we make plans to celebrate our engagement.' Her hand covered her mouth. 'God only knows what your grandma's going to say.'

Mary *March 2017*

At the sound of the tea trolley Mary eased herself up the bed to glance at her alarm clock. The special mattress gave a slight wobble to accommodate her movements. She reached for the small plastic pot on her bed-side table, extracted her teeth from their bath and gave them a quick shake before pushing them home against her gums. As she smacked her lips together and wiggled her mouth to ensure a good fit, her bedroom door opened. It was a matter of pride that very few people saw her without her teeth. Well, other than Izzy who, from being a baby had chortled with laughter at the gurning faces her great grandma pulled, to amuse her when no one else was about.

'Good morning, Mary. Cup of tea?' Roza reached for the bed control on the bedside table. 'Let's wind you up.'

Mary patted her hair and straightened the top of her nighty as the position of the bed altered.

'Mornin', Roza love. I could murder a cuppa, that finny haddock last night weren't half salty.'

'Is it your daughter's party today?' Roza said as she drew back the curtains. 'It's a lovely day for it.'

'It is, but I've told em I have to be back here for four o clock. I'm not missing Edith's hundredth birthday tea. If they can't fetch me back, I'd rather not go in't first place.'

'But it's your daughter's engagement party.'

'Yes, but she's hardly a kid.' Mary slurped her tea while Roza gathered Mary's toilet bag and towels. 'Why a woman of nigh on sixty-nine wants to be getting wed for I do not understand.'

'Perhaps, for companionship, and friendship and who knows, perhaps love.'

'Well she's got me and her pal Val, she's been like another daughter to me.' Mary cocked her head on one side, a puzzled frown rippled across her face. 'She's surely not. Love? No, she can't be? Not at her age.'

'Are you thinking about sex and love and being cuddled?' said Roza, holding up a pair of knickers.

Mary tutted, *I'd done with all that by t'time I were forty-two, what with t'change and him passing on.* 'Not that pair, love. Elastic's a bit loose.'

★

Mary anticipated the warmth and gentle soothing of the scented water as Roza operated the hoist to lower her into the bath. She trembled with pleasure.

CHAPTER THREE

'Ooh that's bloody idyllic,' she said under her breath as she closed her eyes to savour the moment. 'Watch me hair, love. I only had it done on Friday.'

As the day gathered pace sounds of voices, the bump and thud of the lift and the ringing of the telephone were the background sounds of the Fairhaven Residential and Nursing Home.

Mary sniffed – bacon. Her mouth watered at the thought of a bacon butty. She had a lot to think about. Her fear and almighty dread of being put away in a "death palace" had been a waste of energy. The truth, that she was avoiding facing, was that she felt safe and happy being a resident in Fairhaven and, God forbid, she dreaded going home. *How the bloody hell am I going to sort out stopping here?*

'Come on, Mary, you will be dissolving if you sit in here much longer.' Roza manipulated the hoist until Mary was clear of the water then laid a bath towel over Mary's wet body.

'You like your work, then?' Mary smiled and patted Roza's hand.

'In my own country, I was a law student, but this is not possible here because I need to work. My husband he is student here.'

'You're a good kid, that's all I can say, Roza.' Mary clacked her teeth. 'There's summat as I need to ask you. What with you doing law and that.' She bit her bottom lip. 'How would I go on about stopping in here?'

★

Dressed in her best frock, Mary sat in the hall of Fairhaven with her shoulders back and a regal look on her face. She stroked the fabric on the skirt and sleeves as though she were soothing a precious pet. The thought of the £145.89 that Jean had paid for the frock discombobulated Mary. She couldn't relax when she wore the thing. *I don't know how the Queen manages dressed up like she's going to a wedding all t'time. Still, she'll have somebody as sponges her stuff down after each wearin.* Mary was conscious of a small gravy stain that had landed on her knee during Christmas dinner. Intent on massaging the gravy stain, with the spit she'd surreptitiously landed on the right index finger, she missed the front door opening and closing.

'Mary, you look gorgeous, as always.' Douglas bent to kiss her on the cheek.

Mary wiped her hands down her lap and made to pull herself out of the hard-backed hall chair.

'Let me help.' Before she could protest Douglas hoisted Mary to her feet and set her walker in front of her. 'Car's at the front.'

'Mary, let me help you and your visitor.' Roza bustled up and held the door open.

'Thanks very much, Roza. This is my grandson-in-law. He's an himportant man, you know; a professor and a doctor and in charge of that man who's ruining the NHS. Bloody ridicklus, if you ask me.' Mary nattered on as Roza eased her into the passenger seat of the car. Belted up, Mary eased herself back in her seat. The dress was rucked up under her bum.

Bloody thing 'll look like a rag bag by the time we get there.

'Are you alright, Mary?' Douglas glanced at her.

'Right as rain. What do you think about all this t'do?'

CHAPTER THREE

'T'do? Do you mean Jean and Ron being engaged, or Paula…?'

'Paula! What's up with our Paula. Is she tired, again?'

'Tired? No, she's been…she's jacking in physiotherapy and going to work as a personal shopper.'

'Personal shopper, what's that when it's at home? Sounds like a waste of all that posh schoolin' if you ask me.'

'Mary, if she says anything to you – well, let's just say it would be a great help to me if you would nod and smile.'

'Is summat up?' Mary scrutinised Douglas's profile. 'It's all our Jean's fault; spare the rod and spoil the child, that's what I allus say.'

'Here we are.' The car swung onto the drive. 'Look, the happy couple are waiting at the door for you.'

★

Mary hated eating from her knee. Her short legs meant her feet didn't reach the floor and trying to eat from a lopsided plate was more than she could cope with. A smear of piccalilli adorned one of the swirly flowers on the dress skirt while a piece of pork pie sat under her chair. A quick, serendipitous backward kick had hurtled the pie into hiding. Mary gave up on the food and settled back to watch the goings on.

'Here, Izzy love.' Mary raised her voice to catch Izzy's attention.

'Would you like a cup of tea?' Izzy took the plate. 'You haven't eaten very much.'

'I've had my dinner, before I come out, and there'll be a party tea when I get back. I hope your dad knows I've to be back for four o clock?' With a mug of tea in her hand

Mary monitored the gathering. *She looks happy, I'll say that for her. He can't keep his hands off her. Dear God, all that shoving and poking and mess. Ugh. I alus kept my nighty on. Other than our Terry's little un I've never seen a man's part, feelin it were enough.* Mary shivered, grimaced and slurped tea. *It's as well he passed when he did. Fifty odd years I've been on my own. I can hardly remember what he looked like.*

'It depends on Mum's level of mobility and the adaptations required…' Jean was talking to Paula's friend Sue.

'What's that they're saying? Bloody hell, they're talking about me living with em. I'm going to have to tell 'em I'm staying put, at Fairhaven.

'Hello. How are you?' Sue settled herself on the chair next to Mary. 'You look miles away.'

'I was listening to our Jean and him – Ron. What were they saying to you about me?'

'It's exciting, isn't it, a wedding and you moving in with them.'

'I dare say it is for them. Is that your Bob over there leaning against that cupboard?' Mary scrutinised the figure across the room. 'He looks buggered if you ask me. Now, where's Douglas, it's time I were gerrin back.' *Where I belong.*

Chapter Four

Izzy's Journal

April 2017

Here I am again and this time I really am going to stick to Mrs Berry's way of writing a journal. I've looked at my other journal writings and some of them make me sound fed up and miserable. Perhaps I was but now I feel different, better, more settled, less odd. Which is the opposite of how my mum was when she was a girl. I've learned a lot from all the upset and have decided that I'm going to like myself and my life because thinking she is bad and acting bad and mean as well as not liking her life has made my mum's life horrible. It's sad that she's got old and was lost and fuck wit miserable before she found out what she wanted. So, I'm going to start at the end of Mrs Berry's list and work backwards like I did the first time I wrote this journal.

Sad things. I'm not sad but I am bothered about my dad. He is going to explode before we have the election in June. It was the election in France yesterday. He worries about Trump and that French lady and Jeremy Corbyn being PRINCIPLED BUT FUCKING USELESS. He says he

CHAPTER FOUR

can't wait for the canvassers to come to the door. I will be hiding in my room when they call or better still out at Grandma's or one of my friends. He is truly embarrassing when he gets going.

Stuff to be happy about. Cleaning with the whole family. We've had an awesome time cleaning or as Grandma says "mucking out" Grandma Mary's house over the Easter holiday. It was mostly me, Grandma and Ron with Mum and Dad when they weren't working. First of all, went through all the drawers and cupboards. The kitchen was awesomely horrendous with thick grease in the cooker, the fridge had jam and sauce bottles stuck to the shelves like glue and packets of stuff with mould growing on them. Yuck, yuck and double yuck. Grandma was fuck-witted, she swore lots and lots. Ron made her go upstairs with me and start on the wardrobes while he set about in the kitchen. The smell of bleach made my eyes water. Mum and Dad were in charge of taking car-loads of stuff to the tip. We had a skip for the furniture. But best of all I don't know why, but we laughed a lot and we had fish and chips sitting on the floor in the front room. The carpet was a bit sticky but we were so mucky it didn't matter. There were liquorice allsorts everywhere down the sides of the settee, under the settee and stuck to the carpet. Some of the meat in the freezer was so old Ron said it was probably left over from the Last Supper. Poor Grandma Mary. I love her a lot but she wasn't good at housework. Grandma and Ron are having the estate agents round today so that we can sell the bungalow to pay for Grandma to be at Fairhaven.

Drawings and Pictures. I still don't have any. We're doing the colour wheel in art. Mine is a bit messy with the colours running into each other. Becca's is awesome with all the colours inside the bits of the circle.

Family and friends. Becca has a boyfriend, not the kiss sort like on the kids American TV shows. I think that comes when you are fifteen or perhaps fourteen if you really have a big crush. He's really a friend who's a boy. They hold hands and he's kissed her cheek. No mouths or funny touching. I like boys but wouldn't take my clothes off. Look what happened to Mum. Olivia is always crushing on somebody or other. Her brother's friends tease her a lot and you can tell she likes it. I can feel my face going hot, the heat grows from somewhere under my bra, when they tease me, it makes me feel daft and stupid and like a kid. I ape-shit dread them being at Olivia's when I go there.

Like I said, my mum is busy reinventing herself. That's what she calls it her trying to be different — "reinventing myself". She's resigned at the hospital and starts at the store soon. She has to work in the store until a vacancy for being a personal shopper happens. She looks better than she did, in her face I mean. She went with Grandma to the personal shopper to buy clothes and ask about the job. Then Grandma took her to have her make-up done. I'm going to have a lesson during the May half-term. Grandma is awesome persuading Mum. We are still having our chats but they are more about me and our family and trying to help Grandma get Grandma Mary sorted out then we can plan the wedding and decide where Grandma

CHAPTER FOUR

and Ron are going to live. Mum still cries when she talks about Grandma. It makes me sad when I think about them both. I don't want me and Mum to be like that so I suppose I am reinventing myself as well — well when I think of it we all are. Mum, Grandma, Dad, and even Grandma Mary who is enjoying being bossy at Fairhaven. Ron is being himself.

Dad is fizzing, it's as well we're all busy with being a family because otherwise he would have nothing to do but bother about Brexit, that cross looking Mrs Surgeon, who wants her own way and the election. He's been bouncing stuff around his room. He has the news running on his computer all the time. He's talked to me about Amy and her ~~conse~~ conception. Growing up feels like hard work and fuck wit scary but Dad says making mistakes teaches you more than everything being hunky dory all the time. I think it's good to write like this and the swearing, that helps as well.

Grandma is happier now she's engaged and Grandma Mary is settled. Her ring is lovely it is aqua marine in a square with diamonds round it.

Grandma Mary is very, very happy. She keeps watch on the odd job man who she says is a "shifty bugger". She's got them to set up a residents group like they had at the youth club — the old people didn't live at the youth club though.

I should say something about Ron. He's good and kind and Mum likes him now. Or she is making a good job of pretending.

Books I like. We are reading the Boy in the Striped Pyjamas at School. I knew a bit about the second world war but not how bad it was. It is sad and frightening.

Goals. I want to be happy with my family and friends. I understand about making mistakes. I wish I felt better around boys, - not clumsy and daft and sweaty and worst of all fat and wobbly.

Poems and other sayings. I'll think about this for next time. Grandma Mary has lots of sayings. I'll collect some for next time I write.

Notes. I need to get Grandma a birthday card and present she's 69 on Friday. Ron is taking her to see a singer. Franky Valley. Then they are going to a smart do on Saturday with Aunty Val and some of her nursing friends and their husbands. Grandma got a new posh dress when she went to the personal shopper with Mum. She has a special underskirt to hold her droopy bits up and in.

Thoughts. I think I have said them all.

Things to do. This is like goals — I think.

Back to school tomorrow. See you soon.

CHAPTER FOUR

Paula   *May 2017*

Life, for Paula, was changing. Her GP had set her on the road to being mindful. She was trying to be aware of being in a particular moment, in touch with the sights and sounds and sensations around her. The GP had suggested that she concentrate her attention on reading about mindfulness rather than being immersed in the dangers facing young girls. The young doctor had inspired her by listening carefully, and then describing her own path to believing in the benefits of mindfulness. Paula's interrogation of the internet led to a short introductory course. She attended the course, felt drawn to the principles outlined by the course leader, and was now signed on the next available eight-week course starting in September. It was hard going keeping thoughts of self-loathing and fear of relapse into her previous pathetic state from taking over and drowning her. The recriminations about what she had put her mum, Izzy, and Douglas through triggered a terrible guilt that hovered around her, its ghost-like malevolent presence threatening to push her back into despair and negativity.

I notice that I'm letting myself feel like shit again because I had too much to drink, yet again, last night.

'Mum, Dad says I've got to ask if you need any help,' Izzy crossed her parents' bedroom to stand at the window with her mum. 'What are you looking at?'

'Nothing, really, just thinking. Across the road have got a new car.'

'I thought you were sorting out your clothes for tomorrow.'

'I am, we are – you and me. Come on, let's get started. You go and fetch us a large glass of Vimto each and then we'll set-to and transform me from a miserable, boring, uniform-wearing physio to a happy, trendy looking, personal shopper.'

'I can't wait till you get to wear the store's clothes. Will I be able to borrow them?'

'You're only a young girl.' Paula paused, aware of the familiar, overbearing, protective mother thoughts creeping and crawling into her mind. *Bugger off, thoughts.* She kissed Izzy's cheek. 'Of course, love, if they fit and suit you and don't make you look too old. But, I need to get through the probationary period before I get the clothes allowance.'

'Are you practising your mindful thingy? It's good.'

'Scoot, and get us a drink, before I turn into your horrible, grumpy old mum again.'

'I'm practising being happy as well, then we can,' Izzy cocked her head on one side, 'all be awesome together.'

Dear God, help me be awesome for this child and my mum and Douglas. Please, I will do anything to be different.

*

Paula and Izzy piled the contents of Paula's wardrobe on the bed. Their aim was to achieve three distinct piles – keep, Rita, and charity shop.

'Can I try this on?' Izzy held up a multicoloured loose fitting top with a drawstring neck. 'It'll look good with my new jeans.'

'If you want to.' Paula watched Izzy pull her t shirt over her head. 'You're going to have a lovely figure, once you fill out in all the right places.'

'You mean I'm fat.' Izzy scowled.

CHAPTER FOUR

'You are not. You've not finished changing shape, that's all.' *Good job I stopped myself saying puppy fat.*

'What do you think?' Izzy studied herself in the cheval mirror. She smiled at her reflection. Mother and daughter ignored the ringing telephone.

'Perfect.' Paula paused, head on one side, a finger on her lips. 'Who's your dad ranting at now?'

'Paula, Izzy, come down, now,' Douglas shouted from the bottom of the stairs. 'We need to get round to Sue and Bob's. He's collapsed; unconscious. Sue's called an ambulance. I'll run ahead; you lock up and follow on.'

The front door opened and closed. Paula and Izzy looked at each other stunned.

'What does it mean, Mum – collapsed?' said Izzy, bewilderment playing across her face.

'Get some shoes on, love.' *What on earth? He's looked odd, distracted for weeks, since well before that night Sue came round.* 'Come on, love, we'd better get a move on, it sounds serious.'

Mother and daughter jog-walked past their neighbours' spacious houses and manicured gardens. As they turned the corner, they caught a glimpse of Sue as she climbed into the back of an ambulance. The doors slammed shut and, in a blur of blue flashing lights, the ambulance left Douglas on the pavement with his arms round Becca and Molly's shoulders.

'Douglas?'

'Thank God you're here. I'm going back for the car and following them to the hospital. Sue wants you to phone her mum and dad, and Bob's mum.' Douglas kissed the tops of Becca and Mollie's heads. 'Aunty Paula and Izzy will stay with you. Be brave. Take Izzy inside and put the kettle on.

Go on, I just need a word with Paula.'

'Bloody hell, what's happened?' said Paula as the three girls dawdled up the drive.

'Vascular accident – difficult to tell. I'll ring as soon as there's any news. Bye, love.'

★

Mollie and a softly weeping Becca were cuddled in one corner of the settee in the garden room with Izzy looking lost and forlorn propped in the other corner.

Keep calm, get a grip and make the phone calls. 'Mollie, love, do you know your grandma and grandad's phone numbers?' *I'll ring Lynn and Tom first, practise before I ring Bob's mum.* '…and Mollie, can you try and tell me what happened? They're bound to ask.'

Mollie gulped, sighed and looking somewhere over Paula's shoulder and said, 'Mum took a coffee out to Dad in the shed and screamed. I ran outside, and she yelled at me to ring for an ambulance. Is he dead, Aunty Paula?' Mollie hugged Becca close.

Fucking hell 'He's obviously not well, love, but we need to wait and see. Now what about those phone numbers?'

'They're on speed dial. Grandma and Grandad are 3 and Grandma Moira is 4.'

'Izzy, love, why don't you load the dishwasher, let's tidy up for Aunty Sue; give us something to do…eh?'

Paula took a deep breath as she punched 3 on the phone, *Lynn, bad news. No, the girls are fine. It's Bob, he's been taken to hospital.* Paula felt queasy; aware of the bump and thud of her heart as she willed to phone to be answered. *Here goes:*

'Lynn, it's Paula.'

CHAPTER FOUR

'Paula? – Hello, this is a surprise.'

'Lynn–' Paula licked her lip, her tongue felt as though it was stuck to the roof of her mouth. *Dear God, help me.*

'Sue! Paula, what's wrong? Has something happened to Sue?'

Paula swallowed; the pulse in her temple throbbed. 'No, Lynn, not Sue. It's Bob. Sue's with him,' she gabbled, 'and Douglas has gone as well – to the hospital.'

'Hospital! Where are the girls?'

'Here, at Sue's with me and Izzy.'

'What happened?'

'He collapsed, in the shed.'

'Collapsed?'

Paula hesitated. 'Douglas is worried that it might be a stroke.'

'A stroke! Bloody hell. Does Moira know?'

'No. I thought I'd tell you first. I don't know Moira all that well.' *Coward.*

'Don't ring her. I'll go round; she's on her own, best if she hears it face to face.' Lynn muttered to herself. 'Then I'll take her to the hospital and come to the girls. Tom's playing golf. Are you alright?'

'Sort of.' Paula's shoulders sagged. 'Take your time,' she said. Her fleeting feeling of relief at Lynn's assuming full command melting away as she turned from the phone and saw Mollie and Becca's expectant faces. She forced herself to stand tall, breathe deeply and announce with forced alacrity, 'Grandma Lynn is going to see Grandma Moira and take her to the hospital and then she'll come here to be with you. Your grandad's playing golf.'

Time dragged as Paula cajoled Mollie and Becca into making their beds and sorting out their uniforms for the following day. The sisters shuffled around the house with slumped shoulders and weary faces. They protested that their homework was up to date. Exasperated, frustrated and worried, Paula gave in to the moving wallpaper that was American teenage television. The lonely dregs of a bottle of white wine in the door of the fridge exerted its magnetic pull. *No, no, no.* The ringing of the house phone provided a welcome distraction.

'Hello.'

'Paula, it's me.'

Paula sighed with relief. 'Douglas, thank God. How is he?'

'Bad; the worst. Sue's agreed that ventilation can be withdrawn after the girls have said goodbye. Paula, love, are you ready for this? – Sue asks that you tell the girls what's going to happen; the ventilator and all that. And then bring them.'

'Jesus! Don't worry, I'll do my best. How's Sue, and his mum?'

'Sue's hyper and his mum's distraught; poor soul. I'd best get back to them.'

Paula was clutching the handset of the phone and contemplating the kitchen wall, breathing deeply when she became aware of Mollie leaning against the door jamb. She replaced the phone on its cradle and opened her arms to the wistful girl.

'Is he going to die?'

'I need to talk to you and Becca and then we'll go to the hospital. Come on.' Paula shook her head, downhearted and overwhelmed with the responsibility that Sue had thrust on her.

CHAPTER FOUR

Becca was curled up on the settee. 'Bless her, she's asleep, poor little soul.' Paula stroked the little girl's cheek. 'Becca, hon, wake up.' Becca struggled to consciousness, rubbed her eyes as she roused and fidgeted into a sitting position.

Mollie plonked herself between Becca and Izzy on the settee. 'Aunty Paula, tell me the truth. I'm old enough to know?'

'No, yes – well – we're going to walk to ours to get my car and then we're going to the hospital.'

'Is Daddy better now?' Becca's face brightened. She looked hopefully at Sue.

Shit, piss, fuck and bloody hell. 'No, no, he's not. You need to be brave, both of you. Your mum has asked that we go to the hospital so that you can see your dad…'

'I'll get his sudoku book and pencil.' Becca leapt off the settee.

'Don't bother, stay where you are.' The look that Mollie gave Paula pierced her heart with the certainty that she sensed the truth. 'He's dead, Aunty Paula. Isn't he?'

Paula sank on her knees in front of the girls to pull Becca toward her. She extended her arm to encircle Mollie who shrank from her touch. Izzy watched wide eyed.

'No. Well, we need to get you to your mum and then…'

'Then what?' demanded Mollie. 'Tell me the truth,' her voice quivered and then softened, 'please.'

'Your daddy's brain is very damaged.' *Bleeding hell, I can't do this.* Paula stroked Becca's head nestled against her chest. She stuttered with the effort of holding back tears. 'I'm so very sorry, girls.' Paula released Becca from her embrace and hoisted herself onto the settee extending her arms to pull the sisters into her embrace. *Christ Almighty, how do I do this?* A deep sniff and swallow were inadequate to dam the stream of tears that coursed down her face to drip from her chin onto the heads of the sisters who trembled and sobbed in her arms.

Over the top of the girls' heads Paula looked at Izzy alone, dejected and tearful, curled at the far end of the settee. 'I love you,' she mouthed. Izzy nodded.

Mollie shifted. 'I'm going to be sick.' She lurched toward the sink to retch.

Becca raised her head to look around, mystified and confused.

'Izzy, sit, shuffle next to Becca while I see to Mollie.'

A pale faced Mollie turned from the sink and belched. 'What does "very damaged" mean, Aunty Paula?' She swallowed, her hand over her mouth. 'Are you trying to tell us he's a cabbage?'

'You need to sit down, Mollie; if you're not going to be sick.'

'Just tell us, please.'

'Come and sit with Becca. Please, Mollie.' Paula held out her hand. 'Your mum needs you with her at the hospital.' *Mollie, please don't make this any harder than it bloody well is.*

'Why?' Mollie held her position at the sink.

Paula saw red. 'Because you need to say goodbye before the ventilator's switched off.' *Nice one, Paula.* 'Please, Mollie, take Becca upstairs and have a wash and brush your hair.'

'Why? Let's just go,' said Mollie. 'It's not as though he's going to notice. Is it? Get your shoes on, Becca. Come on.'

Well that went well. A resigned, sad, dejected and utterly drained Paula followed by the three girls headed for the front door, and a tortuous journey. She longed for the reassurance and security of Douglas's presence. And a

CHAPTER FOUR

drink; she could murder a drink.

★

Paula and Izzy pulled up outside their house. Paula turned off the ignition and hesitated.

'Are you alright, Mum?' Izzy said.

'I feel as though we've been to hell and back.'

'Put through the bloody wringer, that's what Grandma Mary says.'

'Well I agree with her, the fucking, bloody wringer.' Paula glanced at Izzy. 'Sorry, love, language and that.'

'It's fine. I swear to myself – sometimes.'

Paula turned sideways to regard her daughter who was holding her hands over her mouth. 'Well, I never.'

'Only sometimes.'

'I'm not having a go, sweetheart.' Paula stroked Izzy's arm. 'It's just that I do it, swear to myself, always have done, since I was your age. Good for you, swear away, love, if it helps. Only to yourself though.' Paula's shoulders slumped. 'Dear God, we've all those clothes to sort out.'

'I'll put them back, if you need a drink.'

Paula gasped; shame suffused her body. She shrank down in her seat, her head bowed, her eyes downcast. *This child can see into my rotten soul, she knows me inside out, you're nothing but a stupid, fucking bitch, Paula Quayle.*

'Are you swearing to yourself now?'

'Yes,' Paula whispered. 'I am, but I'll tell you what, we'll do those clothes together. Dad can manage to get egg and chips on the table while we get them sorted. I've finished drowning my sorrows.'

Jean *May 2017*

With her mother settled in Fairhaven and the dormer bungalow, at long last, on the market, Jean felt lighter, less ground down. For the first time in years, probably since she was a student nurse, her life was her own. Well, more or less. Her heart ached watching Paula struggle to reimagine herself. Jean, too, was aware of her need to adapt, particularly to the daughter who was trying desperately to be a responsible woman instead of the forty-two-year-old spoiled brat whose first reaction at being in the least bit frustrated had been to stamp her feet, sulk, and open a bottle of wine. She wasn't sure about the focus on mindfulness, dismissing it as likely to be another of Paula's transient obsessions, but she was willing to nod and smile and hope for the best. A peaceful, uncomplicated life, a concept that Jean had rarely considered, was a new country she was set to explore.

Sixty-nine! How many years are left? Does it bloody matter? Am I doing the right thing? A wedding, a new home, living with a man after all these years. Get a grip, get in the shower and get a move on, you miserable, ungrateful cow. You're due at the opticians in less than an hour.

Jean approached the opticians with her mind made up, she was having her cataracts removed. She'd postponed the inevitable at last year's opticians check, even though driving in the dark, to face the oncoming glare of headlights, was scary. Her overwhelming family responsibilities and ever-present tiredness had been all she could cope with. Now that the Vitamin D had worked its magic and with her new-found freedom, and with the support and encouragement of Ron, she was ready, yet scared stiff, of undergoing the procedure.

CHAPTER FOUR

Her experience of ophthalmic nursing had persuaded her that cataract removal was one of the operations she was never ever having, that and a sub mucous resection of the nose and haemorrhoid excision. As far as she knew there was nothing amiss with her nose, and her haemorrhoids, while needing the odd application of *Preparation H,* were manageable. So, with her courage well and truly screwed up tight, she was ready to ask the optometrist to refer her to meet the ophthalmic surgeon and his laser. Jean found herself humming *Onward Christian Soldiers* as she walked across the car park and pushed open the door to Boots Opticians.

*

As she signed the visitors register in the hall at Fairhaven, Jean heard laugher coming from the sunroom.

'That'll be your mam,' said the handyman, leaning out of the cubbyhole of the Sister's office, 'she's a right one, that's for sure.' The tone of his voice and his facial expression betrayed his disapproval.

'She's happy; enjoying herself.'

'And causing a shed load of frigging trouble,' Jean heard him mutter.

'Isn't it a lovely day?' Jean smiled, *and she doesn't suffer fools gladly, Mr Know It All.*

Jean paused at the entrance to the sunroom. Five tall armchairs faced the garden in a semi-circle. The top windows were open to let in the fresh air of an early May afternoon.

'...after my sixth, I told him that's enough, no more kiddies. I used to feel the bed jiggin while he gave it a good seeing to. He made a bloody mess of the sheets I can tell you…'

Jean coughed. Five white heads bobbed and nodded as they attempted to peer round the chairs' wing backs to catch sight of the interloper.

'Hello, love, we were just, erm talking over old times. This is our Jean, as is getting wed, again,' Mary said, leaving Jean in no doubt that the combined sexual knowledge of the group had been applied to an analysis of her and Ron's sex life. 'She's just turned sixty-nine,' Mary said with an exaggerated nod to her companions.

'I used to tell him to pull my nighty down when he'd finished,' said a dainty little lady whose bright blue eyeshadow and red cheeks gave her a distinct resemblance to a Dresden doll.

Amidst a wave of awkward shuffling and coughs, Jean suggested to Mary that they move into the dining room for a quiet chat.

'We could have stopped here,' said Mary, hoisting herself out of her chair and positioning herself at her walking frame; 'still, I can go to the lavvie, while I'm up.'

Jean started walking toward the dining room but aware of the handy man hovering she suggested they head for Mary's room. Looking up, Mary followed Jean's line of vision.

'He's a nosey bugger, if ever there was one,' Mary said.

No sooner had Mary settled herself in her judiciously positioned chair and Jean perched on the commode than Roza appeared with a tray of tea.

'I bring you this, to share with your daughter.' She smiled at Jean, 'Mary is good women, she look after me.'

CHAPTER FOUR

'I tell her not to take any messin from yon mon. The dirty bugger.'

Jean felt a niggle of a warning but didn't press her mother for further details.

'I've brought you some papers to sign, for the house sale.' Jean reached into her bag for the papers. 'And there's a letter for you. I didn't know you knew anybody in Leamington Spa.'

She moved to give her mother the letter.

'Leamington Spa? Is that Birmingham way?'

'Yes, close to Warwick.'

'I don't know anybody from round there. Must be a mistake.'

'The return address says it's from a C. T. Fox.'

'Fox! Must be summat to do with your dad, but I can't see how. Have you opened it?'

'No, it's addressed to you.'

'Open it and read it.' Mary flapped her hands, dismissing the letter. 'It'll be something and nothing.'

As she scan-read the letter Jean felt for the support of the commode arm. *Hell fire. I knew it was too good to last.* She couldn't believe her eyes. She read the text of the letter again. She shivered. *Dear God.* 'Mum...'

'What is it, love? You're as white as a sheet. What's up?'

'Mum, it's from...well should I just read the letter? It isn't bad news.' *Not so far, anyway.* Jean moved to crouch in front of her mother and took her hand. 'Mum, you seem to have a, prepare yourself, a grandson. Our Terry...'

'Terry? What?' Mary looked askance. 'Read it to me.'

Jean was aware of a threatening throb over her right temple as she focused on the embossed writing paper declaring itself to be the property of Fox – Design and Build

Partnership.

"'Dear Mrs Fox, I am aware that my contacting you in this way may come as something of a surprise. For that I apologise. My name is Charles Terence Fox and I am your grandson.'"

'Grandson! How come, Jean?' Mary's voice dropped to a whisper. 'I don't understand.'

'Let me read, Mum. "My mother was diagnosed with cancer earlier this year, and has since died. She was a wonderful woman, warm, generous and hard working. She led me to believe that my father's work took him away, abroad somewhere and that is why he didn't live with us much of the time. I admit she never said that he worked abroad. This was an erroneous supposition on my part. She was devastated when she heard he had been killed but his investments gave us a small income."'

'Investments! Abroad! Married! Why didn't she come to the funeral?'

'Mum, let me carry on. "In the days before she died, she told me the truth. My father was a dreamer, a vagabond, a bird of passage who she loved unreservedly. She accepted his strange ways and his strange love. She did not understand his desire to keep the two sides of his family separate, but she respected his wishes. With their deaths, I have presumed to contact you. I am an only child with no children of my own. If you feel it is presumptive of me to try to contact you, please ignore this letter. Or if it is your daughter, my aunt – Dad told us he had a sister – who opens this letter and is offended, I apologise. Yours sincerely, Charles Fox."'

'Well bugger me,' said Mary, shaking her head and looking dumbfounded. 'I'm flabbergasted.'

CHAPTER FOUR

'Me too.' Jean re-read the letter. 'There's contact details in the letterhead, as well as his home and email addresses and mobile phone number.'

'You'd best ring him then.' Mary sniffled into her hanky. 'Or do what you do on that pad thing.'

'Mum, are you sure?'

'Sure! Course I'm sure. He's flesh and blood. Fancy our Terry having a son.' Mary gave a deep sigh as she emphasised the word son. 'Your dad would have been pleased, what with the name carrying on.'

Jean felt her heart rate increase and her breathing slow, the raging bull in her stirred. *Bloody hell, Terry, what sort of a shitty mess have you left me with?* 'Why don't I go home and look them up on the internet and get an idea of what we're dealing with.'

'Dealing with, dealing with?' Mary's voice broke as she sniffed into her hanky. She raised her head to give Jean a doleful look. 'What are you saying?'

'Mum, we don't know him.'

'We didn't know Douglas when our Paula scarpered with him.' Mary gave an emphatic nod. 'And he's turned out all right. And that lad's my grandson, poor lad, no mam and dad.'

Jean gathered herself and reached for her handbag to retrieve her mobile. *In for a penny. Thank you, little brother.* Jean punched in the number on the letterhead. *Vagabond! If you weren't already dead...* Jean nodded to her mother to acknowledge that the phone had been answered. She listened.

'Hello, Charles, you recently wrote to my mother...'
'Yes, I'm Jean, her daughter...family history, I see.'
'Yes, she's well...living in a care home.'

'Retirement home,' Mary hissed, holding out her hand for the mobile.

'Would you like to speak to her?'

Jean felt a weight of unbearable sadness when she saw the look of rapture on her mother's face. *What would the loss of Paula or Izzy do to me? Poor old soul.*

'Hello, Terry love, is that you?' Mary nodded as she sniffed back tears. '…Charles, course it is – my Terry's boy. Who'd have thought it? …I'm pleased to speak to you too, love; a grandson at last. It's like our Terry's come back to me.'

Jean's head spun as the pendulum of her mood lurched in the opposite direction at the speed of a politician's U-turn. She suppressed the urge to scream. *No matter what I do I will never, ever, measure up to my BROTHER.*

Mary   *May 2017*

With her head lolling against the back of her chair Mary enjoyed the warmth of the afternoon sun on her face. She kept her eyes closed to try and focus on the thoughts that clamoured for her attention. She'd never been so busy, called on for her experience and expertise. The residents' group she'd set up with the help of Roza was really getting going. It was a proper group with minutes of decisions written down. Roza had suggested the residents had their weekly meeting without any staff and then invited the senior member of staff, on duty, along to discuss any issues. HIMSELF, the handy man was a bloody nuisance. He always managed to be hanging about the sunroom or, if the sun was too strong and the room baking hot, the dining room. Fred, who'd once been something important in the office at the hospital, when Jean had been training, and was good with words and savvy with computer stuff, had made a notice PRIVATE – RESIDENTS ONLY that they blue-tacked on the door before each meeting.

Mary was pondering on how to approach Audrey, the Senior Sister. It had been agreed that Mary and Fred should say something about HIMSELF but finding the right words wasn't easy. He was well in with the owners; reputed to be a relative. From the residents' point of view he was a creep, but Mary had inside information, from Roza, that he was more than creepy. Roza, and some of the other girls, were frightened of him. He rubbed against them whenever he could, touched their bottoms and gave them funny looks that made them feel dirty. Roza and the others wouldn't complain – they needed their jobs and it would be their word against his and they had no proof of his wandering hands, and neither did the residents. What a bloody mess. A mess that Mary relished. Thinking about the committee, HIMSELF and Roza's predicament provided a useful distraction from Mary's excitement about meeting Charlie.

Excitement was an understatement. Mary felt her heart bounce and her breathing take one of its wobbly turns when she envisaged their meeting.

'Mary, are you sleeping?' said Roza in a whisper.

'Dozing, love. Is it time?'

'Yes, do you want a wash down, before you put your new dress on?'

'Just under my arms and that, what with sitting in the sun.' Mary raised her arm and sniffed her armpit. 'I'm a bit sweaty.'

★

'Are you excited?' Roza helped Mary wriggle out of the dress she was wearing.

'I'm beside myself, if truth be told. Who'd have thought it, our Terry a dad?' Mary paused on her way to the sink. 'The daft bugger, I can't get over him never telling us. Do you think he were ashamed of us or summat?'

'You are lovely woman. Why would he be ashamed of you?'

'He were always very loving. I hope you have a lad when you have kiddies; they're more affectionate than girls. Although, I must say, our Jean does her best, and God only knows, with one thing and another, she hasn't had it easy.'

Mary propped herself against the sink to sponge herself down while Roza reached into the wardrobe to retrieve the new dress and release it from its plastic shroud. With her hair teased into shape and held in place with a dousing of hair spray, Mary was ready for the adventure of meeting her grandson. The sight of Himself hovering on the landing, contemplating a wall light, as they were leaving Mary's room, caused the women to exchange knowing looks with each other.

'I'm going to have a word with Douglas about you know what,' said Mary with an emphatic nod and wink. 'He knows what's what with most things.'

'Is he coming for you today?'

'Yes, Jean and our Paula will be busy interviewing Charlie and his wife – poor buggers They won't know what's hit 'em when them two get going with their questions. Still, they mean well. They'll know t'tale and t'tales master by t'time I arrive.'

'Mary, I love your old-fashioned way of talking. Even though I don't always understand what it is you are saying.'

CHAPTER FOUR

'What I'm saying, love, is that they should mind their own business till I get there; after all, he's my grandson, they're only his aunty and his cousin.'

'Perhaps they are worried for you, if he is not good person.'

Mary paused on the journey to the lift, to consider Roza's proposition.

'He's our Terry's lad, he'll be a good un.' She paused before stepping into the lift. 'Won't he?'

As the lift door opened Mary was surprised to see Douglas hovering in the hallway.

She'd given herself a good ten minutes to settle herself on the bench and get her thoughts in order. She liked to think through her anticipated conversations, to consider the questions that might be asked and practise her answers. Jean and Paula were sharp at questioning her about what she'd been up to but getting anything out of them about their goings on was like questioning the devil. Why had Paula given that good job up, where she was somebody, to work in a shop? Did Jean and Ron really sleep together and if they did, did Jean keep herself covered up? Mary shuddered at the thought of being stripped off in front of a man.

'Mary, you are a vision of loveliness, if I may say so.'

'Douglas, you're a right one with the flannel, but thanks all the same.' She took the arm he offered and gave Roza a cursory wave. 'You're early.'

'I am.' He led Mary to the bench. 'Let's have a minute, I could do with a word.'

'What's up? Summat's wrong,' said Mary lowering herself onto the seat. 'I thought it were all too good to be true.'

'Don't look so worried. Charlie's a lovely man, as is his wife, Naomi.' He paused to chew his lips.

'Spit it out then, summat's bothering you.'

Douglas opened his eyes wide, phewed and looked toward the ceiling.

'He's black, they both are.'

'Black! How's he managed that?'

'His mother, she was from Jamaica.'

'Jamaica! How did she get here, to our country?'

'I don't know.'

'You can bet our Jean and Paula'll know everything by now. We'd best be going then, he's met most of his family.' She pursed her lips. 'Well, all bar his grandma, that is. Black, you say.'

Mary looked Douglas in the eye. 'Why did you think that would bother me? I like blackies; especially them Gherkins. They were brave during t'war them lads were. They say t'Queen's very fond of em.'

'Ghurkhas.' Douglas swallowed a smile.

'That's what I said.'

Chapter Five

Izzy's Journal

It's amazing, we go back to school in two weeks, the summer has been really horrible with lots of rain and sadness but busy with lots going on as well. Some of it has been good though. I have been writing to you in my head all the time but not written anything down. I woke up early this morning and decided to write to you before I forgot everything, now I don't know where to start. I have some awesome news!!!!!! I will tell you later!!!!!!!

Everything is mostly good at home, with Mum and Dad. Dad is busy and swearing a lot and away from home — he says he is getting too (f word) old for the early train and the pain of hotels and London. By the way, the f word sounds really rude when my dad says it, but not when I say it in my head. I think it must be because he mostly shouts it out when he's angry. Mum says he should think of staying at home and writing stuff. It's good when he stays at home. Mum is a personal shopper now she passed that test — her probaytion. Well she's still not a personal shopper, all the time. She helps out when the other two ladies are busy or on a day off. She's learning about the clothes by working in the ladies' department at the store and then when they have a proper vacancy she can do it

CHAPTER FIVE

all the time. She is better, happier, even though she has stopped drinking — well most of the time. When she's with Aunty Sue she's like she used to be, but she's caring for Aunty Sue, helping her with her greeving, getting used to Uncle Bob being dead. She's worried about Dad since Uncle Bob died, she wants him to slow down and calm down. Grandma is having her cataract operations done next week, she is very, very, scared. She was a nurse on the eye ward a long, long time ago and keeps imagining what is going to happen to her when they are operating, even though she knows it's going to be nothing like it was in the olden days. Ron and Grandma are getting married when they have sold both their houses and bought one together. I'm being their bridesmaid. Grandma Mary is having trouble with her chest, she likes Charlie her new grandson, he is black, well nearly — a light shade - and she calls him Terry all the time. We all like Charlie, not just Grandma Mary, we've been to his house it is all glass with a truly awesome, ape-shit, I haven't found a new swear word yet, music system that plays in every room, you enter a song or singer and there it is. My friends at school have them but Dad says there is nothing wrong with CDs. He still plays records!!!!!!!!!! Charlie likes good singers like Sam Smith and Ed Sheeran. My mum knows I am a secret swearer, I was fuck-witted amazed when she told me she did it as well. She does it out loud sometimes, but I have to keep mine to myself.

Aunty Sue is doing very well, with Uncle Bob being dead and sorting out his scrap yard, his clothes and everything. She has lost weight and sometimes she looks as though she is far away, as though she is thinking about something else.

Becca and Mollie are mixed up. One minute they are falling out, more than they did before and the next minute they have their arms round each other. It makes me feel sort of hopeless and left out. I want to help them but, well, I am not sure what I am trying to say. I suppose I feel sorry and sad for them but useless because I can't do anything about it. The funeral thing was scary. I didn't like it when the curtains closed and Uncle Bob disappeared. Becca cried really hard, it made me cry as well. They had plastic flowers on a shelf, in the crematorium. Grandma says when she dies Ron has to insist that they move them. It's hard to think about Grandma dying. I lay in bed the other night and imagined being without her or Dad or Mum, or even Grandma Mary who is way past her sell by date — Dad says that not me. Anyway - I ended up crying myself to sleep. I don't think I have ever been as sad as at Uncle Bob's funeral, even after the big row when I was more frightened than crying sad or when Amy died.

We went on holiday, for a week — me, Mum, Aunty Sue and Becca. Mollie went to Spain with her friend's family. We went to Fowey which is pronownced Foy, like toy. Well it was more than a week because we stayed overnight going there and back. We had a lovely cottage overlooking the harbour. We didn't do much but Becca and me were allowed to go round the town on our own, even after eight o clock. We met some boys on the quayside, they were on holiday with their grandparents. This is the big, big awesome, double ape shit news. I have a boyfriend, so does Becca — a proper one this time, not one who is like a friend. The good news is they live near us, just outside Preston.

CHAPTER FIVE

My boyfriend is called Matt and his brother is Ralph, he is Becca's. We have met them in the caf at my mum's store in Preston. She "bobbed along" to make sure we had met up and to give us our orders to be back in time to travel home with her. I can tell she still worries about me but she is doing her mindful stuff and I don't mind as much — well I am trying hard as well. Here is some more big awesome news. Matt kissed me -lips but no tongue. It wasn't what I expected, nothing really happened except I got some of his spit on my lips. Ugh and double ugh. Becca is on to tongues and a bit of touching. I think she might have done more touching than she is telling me, she blushed and wiggled her shoulders when she was telling me — or not telling me — if you see what I mean. I wanted to ask about him splodging. Anyway, we are emailing now and planning to meet up when Mum is next working on a Saturday.

I have got all my stuff ready for school. Grandma and Ron took me to Manchester. We had to go to the clinic for Grandma to have tests before her operations then we went into the city centre. I think Manchester is awesome. Ron and I played a sort of poetry game using his iPad — oulipo. He talked to me about words, the sounds they make and how we decide meanings of words we haven't heard before. It was good fun. Why can't English be like this at school? I was fuck wit amazed that I enjoyed myself.

I'd better go now and get ready. Aunty Sue is taking me Becca and Mollie to Centre Parcs then when I come home its uniform shopping time.

See you soon.

Paula *August 2017*

Tilting the cheval mirror to get a different perspective on her body, Paula appraised herself.

I could do with losing a pound or two. I've lost a bit, with cutting down on the wine, but I'd show off the clothes better if I were half a stone less. That's it. I'm doing it. She clapped her hands, pleased with her decision and reached for the bedside phone.

'Sue, I've been thinking – Douglas, always groans when I say that – I'm coming to Slimming World with you. When's the next group?'

'Right let's do it, I'll call for you at quarter past five.'

'You said you were going to start again after Centre Parcs. No excuses. I'll see you later, hon.'

That's killed two birds – it will make me go and get Sue out, meeting people.

*

Paula glanced round the dingy church hall, the late afternoon sunshine all but obliterated by high windows draped with heavy red velvet curtains. The open fire door useless in its designated task of supporting air circulation. She was surprised to see two men, one in shorts and tee shirt, and in contrast one in suit trousers and shirt wearing a lanyard with a NHS logo. She didn't know him; he had the look of a pen pusher. Sue nudged her.

'Come on, I'll introduce you to Heather the consultant.' At the sound of her name a shapely woman, dressed in an outfit Paula recognised, turned toward them.

CHAPTER FIVE

'Sue!' Arms open, Heather strode across the room to envelop Sue in her ample bosom.

'How brave.' She stepped back, taking grip of Sue's hands. 'Welcome back.'

Sue flicked away tears and with a nod held out a hand to indicate Paula. 'This is my Paula.' She sniffed.

'I'd like to join,' said Paula.

'Hello.' Heather looked quizzical. 'I'm sure we've met before…Yes, I know, you helped me buy this.' She pointed her hands toward her body. 'You were brilliant.'

'She's a personal shopper,' said Sue.

'Well, training to be one.' Paula shrugged.

'Training my foot, you were brilliant.' She turned to walk toward two chairs set up in a corner. 'Come on, Paula, let's see what I can do to get you sorted. I'm sure Sue will save you a seat in the group.'

★

Paula was flicking through her Slimming World pack, weekly food diaries and exercise sheets, menus, healthy As and Bs as well as the photographs and stories of smiley-faced men and women who had changed their lives through sticking to the regime. She was in the middle of menu planning for the next week when she heard the creak of the garage door.

Douglas was home.

'Paula, love? Izzy?' Douglas said from the front door.

'In the kitchen,' said Paula.

A dull thud indicated Izzy's leap downstairs. 'I've joined the music club and been picked for the second-year hockey team,' Izzy announced to her dad as they made their way into the kitchen.

'And I've joined Slimming World.' Paula reached up to peck Douglas's lips.

Douglas stood back to contemplate Paula and Izzy. 'Well I'm not being outdone.' His attempt to change his warm smile into a mock rueful glace was undermined by the twinkle in his eyes. 'I've resigned, well from the end of this project and da da and drum roll,' he paused, 'I've written a novel.'

'A novel?'/ 'Why and When?' said Izzy and Paula simultaneously.

'To answer both your questions at once – to pass the time during that God-awful journey. And to stop me thinking about the state of the world, politics in general and the NHS in particular, especially when I'm stuck in another bloody, soul-destroying hotel room. It's not been the same since they cut expenses and put us in purple, plastic palaces.'

'What's it about, Dad? Can I read it? Have you told Grandma and Ron?'

'A murder mystery in a hospital. I'm not sure about you reading it, sweetheart.' Douglas looked sheepish and clasped and unclasped his hands.

'You mean sex, don't you? Don't bother about that, you should read some of Ron's stuff if you want to know about sex. What are you two looking at each other like that for?'

'Like what?' said Paula smiling and threading an arm round Douglas's waist and holding her other arm out to Izzy. 'We love you, little girl. Very much.'

'And yes, Izzy, I had thought of asking Grandma to have a shufty at it for me.'

'She'll have you signed up to that writing group in no time,' Paula said as she turned on the hob. 'Slimming World

CHAPTER FIVE

spag bol for dinner. Well, it's my usual recipe, it was already in the freezer, it's more or less the same, but theirs doesn't have red wine but it does have lots of carrots. They seem to put carrots in everything.'

'We'll be able to see better in the dark; it smells good?' said Douglas peering into the pan.

'I could do with losing a pound or two.'

'Will you go to university to learn how to be a writer, like Grandma did?

'You never know, love. Bob and Amy's deaths have been a wakeup call. Shall I open a bottle to celebrate – everything?'

'Not for me, hon. I'm determined to lose weight, get a grip on my life, to try and be content with...I don't know what I'm trying to say,' Paula twisted her lips, 'but, well the mindfulness course starts on Saturday,' She clapped her hands as though clanging cymbals.

'Izzy's growing up, making new interests and heaven forbid, meeting boys. You've seen the light about work. And a novel? I'm flabbergasted, Douglas. Who'd have thought it, a novel, and I thought you spent all your time arguing in bars.'

'I was arsed off with politics before Brexit and the election and Trump. The election of that idiot made my blood boil and now what with North Korea...'

'Dad, have you thought of being mindful, with Mum?' Izzy turned from laying the kitchen table.

'No, but I've thought of chasing you round the kitchen, young lady. You're not too old–' he wiggled his fingers– 'to be tickled.'

Izzy dodged out of the kitchen door and scuttled upstairs chased by Douglas.

Paula sighed. *I feel different; quiet, in control of myself. I want to be here, now in this house with Douglas and Izzy. Dear God, is this what it feels like to be happy and contented?*

Jean *October 2017*

The ringing of the phone shifted Jean out of her reverie. She'd been trying to get in touch with the sensations in various parts of her body as she lay on the floor in the sitting room, her head supported on a scatter cushion. An enthusiastic resume, by Paula, of her first mindfulness session had prompted Jean to try "body mapping" in an attempt to relax and empty her head of the tumult of tumbling thoughts competing for her attention.

'Hello, Jean Entwistle.'

'Mrs Entwistle, good morning.'

Jean balked at the false bonhomie.

'Jake, from Smith and Falconer. I've got a property I thought you and Mr Baker might be interested in.'

Jean's shoulders drooped, a shuddering phew escaped her lips. 'Where is it? Sorry, I didn't mean to sound so brusque. It's just that we've looked…'

'I know, it's a difficult time, there's not much about in the middling price range, well to be honest there's not much about in general, but this is a gem, only came in yesterday and I thought of you straight away. Duxbury Park – to settle an estate, needs some work but could be stunning. And Mr Baker said he was keen to do a bit of work.'

'Sounds great, if you email me the details we'll have a look at it and get back to you. Thanks for ringing.' Jean picked the cushion up from the floor and with a burst of energy whizzed it at the settee.

With Ron's barn selling within three days of being advertised and a steady stream of viewers for Jean's house resulting in two second viewings arranged for later that day, Jean was in a quivering state of readiness for something or other to happen. She was constantly tired. The sudden appearance of Charlie, and the to- and fro-ing to Warwick and then all the fuss at Fairhaven about that creepy odd job man harassing those girls. *Mum drives me crackers at times but once she gets the bit between her teeth there's no stopping her. Can I get a nonagenarian activist into my writing? What writing and when, chance would be a fine thing. Bob's death and above all...* Jean felt tears prickle as she perched on the edge of the settee cradling the phone. *Paula's what do you call it? Epiphany, that's it. I'm worn to a frazzle. I want to believe it will last. She's trying so hard.* The tears flowed. *I feel so humble, my mum standing by that girl.* Jean searched her memory – Roza. *And our Paula being so different, something I've wanted for such a long time. It's like all the tiredness I should have felt when I was dealing with it, her, everything she did has suddenly floored me. Get a grip, Jean, and ring Ron or the bloody house will be sold. If I don't get a decent night's sleep soon I'm going to scream, and I've forgotten to put my drops in, again. Nytol or Night Nurse? I'm going to have to take something. I'm losing it.* Jean rested her head against the back of the settee and closed her eyes. *What was that musical when I was a girl. I can still see that poster in Simmonds shop; a globe with a man sat on top of it. "Stop the World I Want to Get Off" that's it. Leslie Bricusse and Lionel Bart. Musicals, Jean? It's you that needs to be on a mindfulness course, not Paula. Why am I like this when I've so much to be thankful about? Then there's the WI Christmas lunch I need to fettle a menu choice sheet.*

The sooner I'm living with Ron full time the better. I need somebody to talk to. No, you don't, you've coped for years. Come on, pen and paper and make a list of what you've to be thankful for, then ring Ron and then treat yourself to a writing session.

★

My list

- Ron and love
- Paula, my lovely troubled child, fighting, as always, but this time for her salvation and Douglas for sticking by her despite her daft ways.
- Izzy, my darling girl. I adore her.
- Mum, long may she live, especially now she's in Fairhaven.
- Charlie, for giving mum a new lease of life, even though it's turned our Terry into more of a saint than ever.
- My eyes; vivid colours and safe night driving and only wearing glasses for reading and the computer.
- Val my friend who has always been, and will always be, there for me.
- Memories of a marriage to a true and honest man.
- Friends from nursing, the writers group, WI
- The strength to carry on. Go, Jean go. Get some Nytol, get some sleep and get on with your life.

Jean stared at the list. *Right, that's it, misery guts, get a move on. Ring Ron, then the estate agent.* She glanced at her watch. *Dear God, the first of the viewings, get some eye shadow and lipstick on and tidy round, they're due in twenty minutes.*

The viewing was completed with all the right noises being made by a retired couple who were moving back to the north-west from Scotland and had sold their house. Jean wandered round her house touching the furniture. *Perhaps we should have stayed here and made some changes, the upstairs bathroom suite, a new drive, bi-folding doors?* The phone rang.

'Hello, Jean Entwistle.'

'Mrs E. Jake here, they've offered the asking price if we take it off the market today.'

Jean paused.

'Mrs Entwistle are you still there?'

'Yes. Obviously, yes. Please tell them yes. What about the other viewing?'

'I'll cancel it. Did you and Mr Baker by any chance come to a decision about viewing the Duxbury house?'

'We did, thank you for reminding me. Book us in as soon as you can.'

Well things are moving now. I'd better start thinking about a wedding. What am I going to wear?

Mary   *October 2017*

Mary contemplated the vase of fresh flowers on her bedside locker. Every Friday a new lot appeared from Roza and the other girls. She loved the attention, the admiration and the feeling of having done something useful and special. Their admiring glances, the gentle touch of her hand when they were talking to her were enough thanks, and besides, she didn't care for cut flowers, she never had done. All that fuss and bother, changing water, picking out dead heads, cutting stems, for a bunch of flowers that was on its way to dying from the minute they'd been cut. She's rather have a box of liquorice allsorts or some of that posh chocolate that Jean liked. Mary paused to rack her brains – *Lint. Maltesers* "melts in your mouth not in your hand," she liked them as well. Her diabetes had put paid to toffee and chocolate. She'd tried the diabetic stuff and dismissed it as tasting like extra-gritty sandpaper.

'Come in,' Mary said in response to a sharp rap on her door.

A stranger, a tall woman in a Prince of Wales check suit, wearing bright red lipstick that matched her top hovered in the doorway. 'May I disturb you, Mrs Fox?' She looked posh but sounded ordinary.

'Come in, sit down, it's the commode–' Mary aimed a dismissive wave toward the corner of the room and then tapped the edge of the bed– 'or you can perch yourself here.'

The woman chose the bed. 'I'm Terry Mathews for the Care Quality Commission.'

'My lad were called Terry – Terence that is, was I mean. Will you be Theresa?'

'I am, but only my mother calls me that these days.'

'Have you come about that bother?'

'We've come to look at other things to do with Fairhaven, but yes I would like to talk to you about the incident that you brought to the owner's attention.'

'I thought it were all over and done with.'

'It is, but I wanted to know if you're satisfied with the outcome and the way your complaint was dealt with?'

'I am, but it's a pity that Sister had to go as well, she were good at her job, even though she were a bit sharp at times.'

CHAPTER FIVE

'It was a mutual decision between the owner and the manager. It turned out the man in question was harassing the Sister, as well as the care staff and she didn't do, or indeed, say anything – I've said too much. Let's just say it took your courage to bring the matter to light.'

'Ooh.' Mary's eyes lit up; she leant forward in her chair. 'Did he have something on her, blackmail, some funny goings on, I'll bet? He was always hanging about, round her office.'

'I'm afraid I can't comment on that.' She shook her head and smiled.

'You have your job to do, love. Were you a nurse?'

'A long time ago.'

'My daughter were a nurse, and my granddaughter's a physio.' Mary shook her head. 'Well, she is when she does her proper job, she's a shop girl till she comes to her senses. Her husband, our Douglas, he's a doctor, but he doesn't doctor anymore–'

The woman stood up.

'–it were him as told me what to do. But I wrote t'letter myself.'

'And a succinct, sensible letter it was. It's been a pleasure to meet you, Mrs Fox.'

Suck sinks I'd best write that down. 'Bye, love. Before you go will you pass me my pen and pad, they're behind them flowers.'

★

A car door banging shut startled Mary from her afternoon doze. She pushed herself upright then eased herself to the edge of her chair to get a better view of the road. She'd been offered a room, at the back of the house, facing the park, when her expose of the handyman coincided with the sudden death of Fred. Mary refused the transfer to Fred's room. He'd been a friend and he'd encouraged her with the letter, read it for her and suggested one or two changes.

She couldn't face having his room; his bed. Mary knew the girls disinfected everything and he hadn't died from anything catching, but it wouldn't be the same, and besides, all you saw at the back were trees and one or two people, and their dogs using the side entrance to the park. No, she was better with a view of the car park and all the comings and goings. Besides, she'd lived on a main road all her life and liked the noise of cars and traffic and folk milling about.

Our Jean and Ron? Summat must be up, her coming at this time, with him. She checked her watch. *Twenty to four. Our Terry, Charlie I mean and Izzy; a car accident??* Mary felt her heart flutter. Listening intently for the sound of voices she heard Mary talking to Roza. *What the dickens is she doing, dawdling and nattering when she knows I'm sitting here on my own, worried sick. How come they're laughing?*

'Mum, what's up? You look out of sorts.' Jean strode to her mother's side to crouch down beside her.

'What time–' Mary tapped her watch– 'do you call this? You're early. Hello, Ron.' Mary looked over Jean's head.

'Have we startled you?' Ron said, settling himself on the commode.

'What gave you that idea? I'm always glad to have company.' Mary forced a forlorn look. 'It can get very lonely in here, you know.'

'Mary, you old fibber, you are in your element, being waited on hand and foot and treated like The Queen.'

CHAPTER FIVE

'Less of the old.' She wagged a finger and smiled. 'Is summat up?'

Jean groaned as she stood up. 'Ooh that hurts.' She flexed her legs before sitting on the bed.

'Old age, it's catching up with you, love. You're no spring chicken,' Mary said.

'We've found a house, on Duxbury,' said Jean.

'Duxbury eh? That's posh.'

'And we've set a date for the wedding and booked a honeymoon.'

'Honeymoon at your age! There's no need to look like that, in my day a honeymoon was to get to know each other.' Mary nodded and gave half a wink. 'I keeps myself informed you know. These days they have a kiddie first. I check them birth announcements in t'Chorley Guardian. The mam and dad hardly ever have t'same name. Where are you going for your–' she gave a slight cough– 'for your honeymoon thing?'

'We've booked…'

'You'll not be having wreath and veil, will you?' Mary looking askance at Jean, shook her head and pursed her lips. 'Not at your age?'

Chapter Six

SNAPSHOTS

Izzy's Journal

October 2017

Hello it's me again. It's half term. It would be good if you could talk back to me. What would you say? Mostly I get on with what I'm doing — going to school and spending time with my friends. I like physics and chemistry and biology and maths, I like history but not geography so much. English is good but not as good as when Ron talks to me about words and how to use them like that oulipo I told you about before. Ron told me a French man invented it to combine art and science. I really like Ron I think he's like a grandad. I never knew my real grandads. What do you think about me asking him if I could call him a name for like grandad but not grandad, that doesn't seem right somehow. Its only just come to me to do that. Mrs Berry was right — putting thoughts on paper helps you think. Gramps? Gran? Pops, that's good Pops. It's like grandad but different. But how do I switch from Ron to Pops. I'll ask Mum, she's really, truly awesome these days with her mindfulness and new job and losing weight and hardly drinking. We eat a lot of vegetables, so I fart a lot. My dad's room smells, well it always did but it now

CHAPTER SIX

smells of whatever was there before and smelly old farts. Mum refuses to let Rita in to clean it because it's a HEALTH AND SAFETY HAZARD.

Dad is home more often now which is tremendously awesome, well mostly. The not mostly, is him wanting to check my homework and TALK IT OVER. What the fuck wit is it with my parents and their CHATS and TALKS I'm sure other kids don't have talkative parents. Perhaps I shouldn't say that because Becca and Mollie miss Uncle Bob to the moon and back. Becca worries me, I think she's gone too far with Ralph. Am I jealous? A bit I think because I don't see Matt any more we keep in touch with the odd text but its more or less fizzled out what with school, guides, music lessons and family stuff at weekends. Anyway, I checked on Zoella but I didn't find any answers but, to be honest, I'm not sure of the question either. What I mean is, I've seen love bites on her neck and near her bra even though she was trying to hide it when we had PE. Zoella is good for some things she has good sayings. One I like is "The secret of life is to focus your energy, not on fighting the old, but on building the new." She didn't make it up. It's from a man called Socrates. I showed my Mum she said that's partly what mindfulness is about, she gave me another saying. "Moving from trying to avoid, escape or get rid of unpleasant experience to approaching it with interest and curiosity." I like sayings, but how do I sort out Becca with interest and curiosity? I might talk to my mum. How awesome is that? Not long ago she 'd have been the last person in the whole wide world I would have confided in.

My family — Grandma has sold her house, so has Ron. They've found another and are talking to an architect about how it can be changed. Grandma Mary is happy. Her legs are not so good, but she can get about with her walking frame. She mostly uses it to go to the toilet, the lav she calls it. She can't "have a road through her", she means have a poo, unless she sits on a proper one. She's asked them to take the commode out of her room.

I forgot — I'm stopping going to guides. The church hall is going to be closed and I've lost interest anyway. Mum wants me to go until the end of November when it closes. She says its best to see things through!!!!!!!!!!!!!!!!!!!!

I think that's it. Oh, I know, it's my birthday next week. I'll be a teenager. I've asked if I can go to a personal shopper. My mum won't be able to dress me. That's what they say — they dress people. So Janey, the lady in charge is going to dress me. Next time I'll tell you some of her, my mum's I mean, stories from the store. Ugh some are very, very disgusting one lady didn't wear any knickers when Janey said she couldn't try on trousers without knickers she said her husband wouldn't let her wear any and he was sitting outside. They gave her a pair and she spent a lot of money. I know I'll ask Ron if I can call him Pops as his birthday present to me. I need to think about how I'm going to say it.

Bye xxxxxxxxxxxxxxx

CHAPTER SIX

Paula   *October 2017*

Paula pressed the start arrow on her iPad screen, wiggled her bottom and shoulders and closed her eyes. The low, mellifluous, mid-Atlantic, voice of the woman invited her to settle back and concentrate on her breathing. Paula manged to surrender herself to the seductive voice for a minute or so, before her restless mind intruded and reminded her that she needed to pick up the birthday cake and book the Tapas restaurant for Izzy's birthday treat.

Pulling her focus back to her breathing, she let herself experience the intake, holding and expiration of her breath to the background of softly lapping waves and bird song. As the ten-minute session ended, and the voice invited Paula to gently return her attention to her surroundings and open her eyes, she smiled. She was at ease with herself and looking forward to the late shift at the store. Izzy was travelling in to work with her, for her appointment with Janey.

★

'You go along and find Janey, she'll be in the women's department, while I drop my things in my locker,' said Paula heading toward the staff lift. Watching herself roll her lips together after touching up her lipstick, Paula was surprised to see Janey join her reflection in the mirror.

'Izzy? I sent her to find you.'

'I asked her to give me a minute. I need a quiet word.'

'What?' Paula's heart thudded. 'Why, is something wrong?

'Don't look so worried. I want you to do me a favour; something special.' Janey humped her shoulders and gave an exaggerated swoosh of breath. 'Let's say an interesting job.'

'R-i-ght,' said Paula.

'You don't have to do it. But I think you're up to it.'

'O – kay,' *What the hell's coming.*

'When you were a physio did you ever help someone, who was going through transgender transitioning?'

'Yes, a couple of times – post surgery.'

Janey sighed. 'Great. How do you fancy helping a regular customer of mine – Mike, to become Martha? He's lovely, one of my favourite clients. I've dressed him for years.'

'Why don't you want to work with him?'

'He needs, no deserves,' Janey sighed. 'Let's just say he's been through a hell of a lot and needs to have a fresh start and you can do that by starting off today with Martha. If that makes sense.'

'I'd love to. When?'

'Seven, this evening. The store will be quiet. Today's the day he becomes Martha, well more or less, if you know what I mean; the surgery is a while off.' She gave a wave in the manner of The Queen.

'Now, I'd better scoot along and see that lovely young woman waiting for her birthday appointment.'

★

Paula managed a quick peek at the treasures in Izzy's shopping bag before dashing off to help two friends who were personal shopper regulars to update their wardrobes for the winter, followed by a young woman wanting an outfit for a wedding on a cruise ship. In between clients she returned stock to the shop floor racks, unpacked new stock and supported her colleagues on the tills. Then it was

CHAPTER SIX

time for Martha. Paula was excited and anxious. *Slow down, breathe, be here, at this time and in this place. You can do this.* She looked up, from the departmental computer adjacent to the personal shopper suite, to see down the length of the store a tall person with short spiky hair, immaculately dressed, in a Theresa May type tweed jacket, wide legged trousers, and kitten heels walking toward her.

'Hello, you must be Martha.' Paula held out her hand. 'I'm Paula. Would you like a cup a tea or coffee?' She glanced at her watch. 'Or, perhaps a glass of wine?'

Paula placed the glass of chardonnay on the occasional table between the two, trendy easy chairs. *I could murder a drink.*

'Are you not joining me?' said Martha.

'I'd love to.' Paula gave an apologetic smile. 'But I can't be seen to be drunk in charge of a mobile clothes rack.' *Calm down, breathe. He – she – isn't going to bite.* 'I know you've seen Janey many times before.' Paula reached for the interview sheet. 'But would you mind if I started from scratch?'

'Mike was the person who saw Janey, but like you Martha would love to start from scratch. So please, go ahead, ask away.'

'Thank you.' *Phew.*

'Janey tells me that you were a physio before you came here?'

Paula noticed the deliberately modulated voice. 'Yes, I was, but I have to say I was a belligerent unhappy physio and now I've metamorphosed into a happy personal shopper.'

'Metamorphosis is my watch word.'

A split second of silence was followed by a mutual flash of recognition between Paula and Martha. The tense atmosphere in the small interview melted as they caught each other's eyes. Martha nodded to Paula. A professional friendship had begun.

Martha told Paula she'd sourced women's professional wear; a trouser suit, the tweed jacket, wide legged trousers and shirts from the internet to kick start her professional wardrobe. Her position as a partner in a local law firm dictated her work wear. It was the smart casual wardrobe that she was entrusting to Paula.

'I need pieces that will accommodate my current and changing biology. The hormones are doing their job but well, I'm sure you understand. Surgery is some way down the line?'

'Of course, we'll start off where we are today, and I'll give you my email address and you can contact me directly whenever you feel the need.'

'I'm sure that's above and beyond.'

'It's meeting your changing needs and–' Paula paused– 'keeping me busy and happy.'

'Physio to personal shopper?' Martha looked over the rim of her spectacles. 'I still don't understand.'

'Wrong job, self-loathing, stupid mistakes, miserable life, drinking too much, monumental fall out with my Mum – reality check.' Paula gasped, appalled with herself. 'Sorry, really, truly sorry I've gone too far.'

Martha tilted her head, a rueful smile played across her face. 'You've shown me your vulnerability. You can't know how much that means to me.'

'Let's get this show on the road then. Can I get you another drink before I harvest a rack full of gorgeous clothes for you?'

★

CHAPTER SIX

Paula crept into the family room. Izzy and Douglas were snuggled together absorbed in a dystopian shoot-shoot bang-bang film. Douglas looked up as Paula knelt beside him.

'You look happy, my love.' He squirmed round to kiss her, disturbing Izzy.

'Hi, Mum.'

'Hello you two. I am. Happy. I've just had the best day of my professional life.'

Jean   *October 2017*

As the dishwasher whirred into action ,Jean, hands on hips, cast a critical eye around her kitchen. *Be ruthless.*

'What are you thinking about, Grandma?' Izzy lolled against the oven housing unit.

'What I'm keeping and what's going to the charity shop.'

'Keep everything.'

'No, love. What isn't necessary–' Jean swept her arms wide– 'isn't necessary. Those cheese dishes for instance.'

'Those wedgy shaped dishes, is that what they are? Cheese dishes?'

'When I was as old as your mum, or even younger, I had a thing about collecting kitchen antiques.'

'Why?'

Jean lifted two of the dishes from one of the glass-fronted cabinets and held them in her hands, contemplating them.

'A good question, love.' She lifted down another two dishes and set them on the worktop with their mates. 'I suppose it was to do with a style: pine furniture and country kitchens. It was bit of a hobby, how it was at the time. How I wanted people to see me.' She shrugged. 'The house, funny how styles change.'

'Is that why you've got the kitchen roll on that thingy–' Izzy pointed toward a hand posser sitting next to a set of black balance scales holding a set of imperial weights, 'and the scales.'

'It is, my love.'

'Are they going?'

'No. Well I don't think so. What do you think? Perhaps I should ask Ron.'

'G-r-a-ndma.'

'Y-e-s,' Jean said in imitation of Izzy's tone.

Izzy shifted her position to move closer to Jean. 'Grandma?' Izzy clasped her hands together and lowered her head. Jean waited. 'Grandma?'

'What is it, love?' Jean held out a hand. 'What's bothering you?'

With a quick glance at Jean, Izzy gabbled. 'I'd like to call Ron, Pops. Instead of Ron I mean. Mum said it's okay with her, but I had to ask you about it. What do you think?'

Jean gasped and pulled Izzy toward her. 'He'll be over the moon, my darling, and so am I.'

'Why are you crying, Grandma?' Izzy stood away from Jean, her face wrinkled in concern.

'I love you so much, Izzy Quayle. I need a piece of kitchen roll.' Jean gave a hefty nose blow into the tissue and dabbed her eyes.

'Are you keeping Grandma Mary's coffee set and your grandma's tea set?'

'I am, love.' Jean gave another hefty blow into the kitchen roll. 'They're for you and your mum, but I think we'll pack them in labelled boxes and then when I'm gone you can sort out what you want to do with them.'

'Gone?'

'Dead.'

'Don't talk about dying, Grandma.' Izzy's voice quivered. 'It scares me, the thought of death, of losing people. Amy and Uncle Bob disappeared so quickly. I think about them and where they are; where they might be. Grandma, how could they be here one minute and gone the next?'

'Izzy, love. I'm planning on getting married, not dying. Come on, sweetheart, let's start the packing and talk about our dresses for the wedding. And you need to tell me about this Tapas restaurant we're going to for your birthday.'

★

The light and airy open plan design of the architects' office gave Jean a much-needed sense of calm. Izzy's talk of death and dying had thrown her, especially coming so quickly after her delightful request about Ron.

She smiled to herself; years of subscribing to *25 Beautiful Homes* and dreaming of clean open spaces was about to be realised. Over the years she'd rid herself of patterned wallpaper, each room now being a white box that acted as a canvas for her collection of paintings and books. Although she'd enjoyed changing the curtains and soft furnishings in one room each year, it always felt like a guilty pleasure especially compared to Val who had a taste for shabby chic and genteel decay. Living alone, any thoughts Jean had of taking on the job of major structural alterations to her already comfortable home had a hint of greed and obsession. Now, she had a soul mate and the chance of a fresh start.

Meeting Ron, becoming friends, tentatively exploring their similar interests and then the surprise that her deepening feelings for him were returned had led to being here in this architects' office. She felt young, giddy, enchanted with the world. *Am I sixty-nine or nineteen?* Her quiet reflection was interrupted by the companionable chatter of Izzy and Ron.

'What are you two up to?' Jean said.

'Nothing,' said Ron and Izzy together, laughing and looking at each other for confirmation. 'We're just playing with a few words,' said Ron, nodding and gurning as a plump man with mad professor hair approached them.

'Ron, Mrs Entwistle.' He smiled at Izzy.

'Please call me Jean, this is Izzy.' Jean glanced at Izzy. 'My – our granddaughter.'

'Bill. Yates builders for you.' A young man at a nearby desk held out a telephone. 'Sorry, but he says it's urgent.'

'Do you mind?' Bill shook his head, clearly annoyed as he moved to take the telephone call.

'Well, we are on mate's rates,' said Ron. 'Is something wrong?' He looked from Jean to Izzy.

Izzy smiled, suddenly shy. 'Ron.' Izzy licked her lips. 'I would like it if – is it alright if I call you Pops and you are my grandad?'

The pregnant pause was disturbed by Jean's need to harvest her tears.

'Lend me that, love.' Ron held out his hand for Jean's hanky. 'Izzy, I am overwhelmed, come here.' He held out his arms. 'My cup runneth over,' he murmured into her hair.

'I'm not disturbing anything?' Bill said, pausing and cocking his head before squeezing himself into a small chair.

'Our granddaughter…' Ron paused, licked his lips, gave a bewildered shake of his head and grinned. '…has just given me the best present ever. She wants me to be…excuse me, I need a minute.' Ron made to stand.

'Stay where you are; with your family. I'll organise some tea,' said Bill, struggling to push himself out of the tight fit of the tub chair.

Mary *November 2017*

Mary relaxed against the sensation of the hairdresser's fingers massaging her head. She looked forward to her weekly hair do. Roza, or one of the other girls, if Roza wasn't on duty, made sure that Mary had a bath before her weekly hair appointment. Baths and a wash down alternated daily. Mary had never been so pampered. Jean had arranged for a beautician to visit every three weeks to give Mary a manicure and polish her nails. She had six monthly visits to a chiropodist to check her feet because of her diabetes and regular trips to the GPs' surgery for blood tests. She kept a note of all her appointments in her diary.

Checking through her commitments, while she waited for the hairdresser to set up her temporary salon, she noticed it was Charlie's birthday later in the month. She'd ask Roza or Jean, if she wasn't too busy, to get a card but what would she do about a present?

Hair washed and in rollers, Mary closed her eyes to relax against the gentle heat and rhythmic whirring of the hair dryer.

'Here, love.' Mary wriggled her head out from under the hood of the hair dryer. 'How old is that lad of yours – the one with the kiddies?'

'Twenty-eight.' The hairdresser patted Mary's shoulder to encourage her back under the hood.

'What do you get him for his birthday?' Mary shouted over the noise of the dryer.

'I only buy for the kids.' The hairdresser raised her voice and gave a dismissive sniff. 'Not for our Jason and his so-called wife.'

'Miserable bugger,' Mary said loud enough to be heard on Chorley Market. 'What's up, what have I said now?' *She's got a face like a slapped arse.*

'We don't all have posh relatives with money to burn; chucking up good jobs and doing up their houses.'

Mary watched the hairdresser's mouth move. 'Well turn th'eat down if you think I'll burn. I don't want mi ears singed, and besides that, who'll do my hair if you chuck up your job?'

Roza's head appeared round the side of the dryer. 'I heard shouting, is everything alright for you, Mary?'

'I'm fine love, I ask her a simple question and she goes on about my ears burning and chucking up her job.'

Mary, ensconced under the dryer, watched the mouths of the hairdresser and Roza.

Somebody or other's aggravated her this morning. She's a flighty bugger, for somebody as does hair in a place like this. Alright one minute and then miserable as sin the next.

'What's up?' Mary watched the hairdresser huff and puff and then shimmy out of the room.

'She says–' Roza knelt in front of Mary– 'you called her name, and that she will not do your hair anymore.'

'Why would I do that? She were deliberately going to burn my ears. I ask you, what next?'

'I will finish your hair, Mary. Do not bother.'

CHAPTER SIX

'I've paid in advance and there'll be no tip. Wait till I tell our Jean, she'll be vexed.'

'I think it is storm in tea pot,' said Roza.

'I'm not one to make a fuss, am I, Roza love? But, thank you, I could murder a cup of tea after her taking against me. Am I dry yet and can I borrow the phone to ring our Jean?'

★

Cottage pie and carrots with thick Bisto gravy, Mary's favourite lunch. She was tempted with the offer of a second helping but the smell of baked apples, stuffed with juicy raisins and covered in lovely creamy custard made her mouth water. She sipped at her glass of water to settle her stomach between the two courses. Dinner at dinner time, she approved of Fairhaven's routine. Jean and Paula's posh ways of having their dinner for their tea wasn't proper. A warm homely dinner made for a good afternoon snooze.

'Armchair keep fit, this afternoon,' said Roza, collecting Mary's empty pudding dish.

Mary belched. 'I'd best have a dose of that Gaviscon when they come round with the medicines. It's that diabetic stuff they put in my food as makes me bilious.'

'I'll take you for your nap in a small minute. When I have helped Clarrisa to her room.'

'Take your time, love, I've all day. I don't suppose anybody will come to see me today. Out of sight out of mind.'

'It is workday, Mary. They all came last night, with cake from your pretty granddaughter.'

'As our Jean rung back? I left a message on that phone.'

'No need to bother, Mary.' Roza nodded toward the door. 'Look, she is here.'

Jean smiled at Roza and bent to peck Mary on the cheek.

'Did you get my message? You can never be sure with that flimsy phone thing.'

'Hello, Mum. How are you?' Jean said with a smile in her voice.

'You sound pleased with yourself, love.' Mary's voice softened, she relaxed. Jean would sort everything out. 'I don't want that hairdresser again, Jean. She's a real madam.'

'Was it the hairdresser that upset you?'

'That's what I phoned about, she was out of order.' Mary knitted her arms together in a gesture Peter Kay would have been proud of. 'One minute she's as right as rain and then before you know it, she threatens to burn my ears, chuck in her job and then storms out. Roza had to finish my hair.' Mary patted her white helmet. 'As though them girls haven't enough to do.'

'I'll go and have a word with Sister, while Roza takes you upstairs.'

'I'm that worked up, I'll never rest and its physical jerks this afternoon. I tell you, I'll be buggered by teatime. All because of that madam. They shouldn't let people like that in places like this.'

'Mum, take a deep breath, here's your chariot.' Mary and Jean watched Roza manipulate the wheelchair into the room, 'I'll call and see you when I've had a word. Okay?'

Mary eased herself out of her dining chair and made to move toward Roza and the wheelchair. 'You are a good un, our Jean, and when you've a minute will you get me a card and a present for our Terry.'

'Charlie, Mum.'

'That's what I said.'

Chapter Seven

Izzy's Journal

Sunday night again and time to think about school. We've had a lovely weekend me and my family and Becca. She had a sleep over on Friday and Saturday. She seems better, more like herself except she's ~~a bit,~~ extremely, excrutiatingly, agonisingly boring about Ralph especially when you consider that I have been dumped by his brother. I didn't want to admit it before, but it was him who finished with me. He sent me a text to say he was busy with his football team. To be honest I'm not really bothered, at least I've had a boyfriend. It wasn't what I expected, he didn't have much to talk about that I was interested in. Perhaps I'm not ready yet. Anyway, Becca is ready, and don't I know it. She's told me EVERYHING. How she like the kisses, cuddles and touching. I think I might buy her some mouth wash for her birthday, think of all the germs there must be on his tongue Ugh, Ugh, three thousand Ughs and worst of all she's touched his penis — through his clothes. Fuck wit, I'm still searching for new swear words. He wanted her to rub it, she says she didn't rub but gave it a stroke. He wants to feel in her knickers, but she hasn't let him YET. The reason I'm writing all this is I'm very, extremely worried about her. She says she knows what she's doing but I'm scared she's going to

CHAPTER SEVEN

end up like my mum was. Do you think I should talk to Mum or Grandma? I want to but what would could they do about anything and would Becca still be my friend if I told on her? It was much better when we crushed on boys in year 11. Is it because of Uncle Bob? I could go to the school nurse, she gives talks in PHSE. How would I manage that when Becca and me are always together?

I've done it, told my mum. I couldn't sleep and went down for a glass of milk. She saw the landing light on and got up. She was really, kind and lovely. Telling her was easier than I thought. She didn't go ape shit like she would have done before. She listened and said she needed to think things over. I think I might sleep now. I've had a dose of Calpol and a hot chocolate.

Monday night — Mum says I have to accept some of the responsibility for supporting Becca by telling her how her and Ralph and what they are doing is bothering me. Then she'll talk to Becca about the mess she made of things when she was our age, if Becca is willing to listen. Then and this is truly A. MAY. ZING (like the man says on Strictly) she said that what Becca and Ralph are doing is not necessarily wrong even though he is technically breaking the law but that it is dangerous to be playing with fire when they are not much more than children. She cried, then I cried. She's upset about LOST YOUTH. She might mean her own. I'm not sure. She's agonising about telling Aunty Sue. One minute she wants Becca to tell Aunty Sue herself, then she says she will tell Aunty Sue, then she thinks she should sort it out with Becca and leave Aunty Sue out of it. She cried most about me and her and us being able to talk. I'm dreading tomorrow but dreading Becca being pregnant even more. If she falls out with me but doesn't end up like Mum, then I've done a good thing. I wish we'd never met Matt and Ralph.

Tuesday night. I've told her. The best news is we are still friends. She still likes doing all that touching stuff even though she knows about the swimming strength of sperm. I told her about Mum, it was hard saying about the abortions and Mum being mixed up and sad and losing her way with Grandma. I love my mum more than ever. She's a brave woman. At first Becca didn't want Aunty Sue to know but she's going to practise with Mollie and then tell Aunty Sue. I'd go straight to Aunty Sue. Mollie is too unpredictable.

Paula *November 2017*

As she opened her eyes from her guided meditation session, Paula marvelled at the thought for the day. The leader had invited the group to consider the option of taking the time to stand back from situations and let events unfold rather than assuming the right to bustle in, organise and control. Paula sat in quiet contemplation. *I've been brilliant at telling other people how to live their lives, but crap at telling myself what's what. Nearly forty-three and I'm on the verge of growing up, being responsible for myself.*

'Find your breathing, be kind to yourself,' the leader counselled the hushed group.

Paula felt her iPhone vibrate in her trouser pocket. With a furtive eye on the leader, she surreptitiously inched the

CHAPTER SEVEN

phone into her hand, from her handbag. She glanced at the screen.

Sue. Get a grip, breathe, in one, her chest expanded *out one.* Paula braced herself to read the message.

Had a hell of a night with girls. Are you free to meet me in the coffee bar at college 12.30? x

Looks like Becca's told her. Some day off this is going to be. Breathe.

See you there. Xx.

'Sorry,' Paula mouthed to the group leader as she pushed the phone back into her pocket, 'emergency.'

*

The coffee bar was a place of bustle and noise. Students jostled Paula as she stood in the doorway, she stretched her back and twisted her head to peer, left, right, centre. Her shoulders slumped. *How the hell am I expected to find her in this scrum?* She edged forward to look round the tower of a tray holder piled high with trays of soiled crockery and cutlery.

'Sorry, a student.' Sue, appearing from behind Paula, leaned in to kiss her cheek. 'Trouble with an assignment.'

'You're here now.' Paula patted Sue's arm.

'I rang ahead and ordered us both a tuna salad.' Sue nodded toward a couple vacating a table. 'Grab that and I'll get the food.'

Paula shrugged off her coat and slung it on a plastic chair. The scene drew her in, *this'll be Izzy in a few years.* A group of girls with unlikely colours of hair, dragging what appeared to be overnight bags behind them, caused a jam in the traffic flow as they congregated round a table to shout, above the general din, to a bevy of girls already seated. Sue behind them with a loaded tray raised her eyes to Paula.

Dear God, let her be alright about me talking to Becca.
'Is it always like this?' said Paula.

'It's quieter after one, but I have a tutorial group at half-past. You don't mind coming here, do you? I really needed to talk about Becca, and him and what's been going on – away from home and the girls.'

'Course not. So, Becca told you?' Paula looked sheepishly at Sue.

'Paula there's no need to look like that. I'm grateful, really I am.' Sue glanced away to return her attention to Paula with a world-weary gaze. 'No. I got it from Mollie after I broke up the cat fight. The hair pulling, slapping and name calling was ugly, and frightening for all of us. But at least it's out in the open.'

'I'm sorry, Sue, I didn't want to interfere, but Becca, prompted by Izzy, came to me.' Paula pressed her lips together and shook her head.

'Don't be sorry.' Sue dragged her hands over her face. 'I'm worn out what with Bob's cousin – you've met him at ours; he's a know it all – pestering me about the scrap yard. He wants to buy me out. And this place and its endless mountains of paperwork.' Her eyes swept around the café. 'And now Becca. And Mollie's not much better with her moods and sulks. Some days, well most days, if I'm honest – well, there are times I wish I could swap places with Bob.'

'Don't say that.'

Sue pushed her plate of food away. 'I've made an appointment with the GP, but it's not for another two weeks, for me and Becca.' She reached across the table to take Paula's hands. 'What would you do if it were Izzy?'

CHAPTER SEVEN

'Try and talk to her, she already knows about me, the trouble I caused, and all that went with it.' Paula lowered her voice. 'And what a fucking mess I made.'

'Thanks for being so open with Becca. Telling her all that stuff can't have been easy.'

'How is she? What did she say?'

'She cried. She says she loves him. How the hell can she?' Sue's voice ratcheted up so that a couple at the next table intent on shuffling mounds of stodge in their mouths, nudged each other. 'She's only just thirteen?'

'Have you thought of contacting his parents, surely they have some responsibility?'

Sue glanced at her watch. 'I need to go, I'll think about it.' She stood up. 'And give you a ring, when I get a minute or two of peace.'

Paula finished her bottle of water. *My poor mother. What a toss pot I was chucking one shitty thing after another at her.* She rifled in her bag to find her phone. 'Mum, are you in this afternoon?'

★

Paula let herself into her mother's house.

'Mum?'

'In the bedroom.'

'This looks like a serious sorting out session.'

'I'm being ruthless, two categories: charity shop or keep, no in-betweens.'

'Can I help?' Paula paused.

'Let's put the kettle on. Is everything alright?'

'Yes, with me Izzy and Douglas, but Sue's having a rough time.' Paula smiled. 'And I've had an idea.'

'This sounds like a serious cup of tea.' Jean ran her hand through her hair. 'I'm dreading the kitchen sort out. Come on, let's attack a box of Florentines I've bought, to try for Christmas.' Jean smiled. 'Although they're not exactly Slimming World.'

As Paula reported on Izzy's worries about Becca and Ralph, she was conscious of her dry mouth and thudding heart. She swallowed. 'Pass me a tissue.' She wiped her eyes. 'Mum, how can I ever make up for what I've done to you; to us?'

Jean shuffled across the settee. 'Come here, love.'

'I'm sorry, Mum, truly sorry, I can never say it enough,' Paula muttered against her mother's shoulder.

'You've said it, love. Having you here, now, is all I ask. God knows, I've always loved you, even though–' Jean sniffed and reached for the tissue box– 'there were times, when I didn't really like you all that much – I think we need another brew.'

'M - um?' Paula smiled. 'Would it be alright – would you consider. What I'm trying to say is I'd like to buy your dress for the wedding, and can I be a bridesmaid, well matron of honour, with Izzy. A-n-d, will you let me organize the whole event?'

'Paula, my love, you never cease to amaze me.' Jean gave a carefree chortle. 'But now it's for the right reasons... Is that your phone?'

Tempted to stay in the warm glow of her mum's admiration and approval Paula let the phone ring.

'Check it, love, it might be important. I'll see to the brew.'

'Shit!'

'What?'

'Sue, school phoned her: Becca; something about a dissecting knife. She wants me to pick her up from college, her boss says she's not fit to drive, she sounds manic.'

'Ring her back and then shoot off. I'll leave a message on Izzy's phone to tell her to come here. She can come with me to see your Grandma.'

Jean *November 2017*

It was Jean's turn to lead her writing group's activity evening. In the aftermath of a charismatic speaker, who had accomplished the difficult task of keeping the disparate, nay eccentric, members of the group engaged for the best part of the two-hour workshop, Jean had somehow volunteered to follow up on his session. She was attempting to write a scenario in the surgery of a group of General Practitioners. The deadline was the following evening. Her thoughts crashed, meandered, dribbled and shouted to drag her away from her writing. She was caught up in other folk's troubles. She tried telling herself that Sue, Becca and Mollie were none of her business, but their friendship, or withdrawal of it in the case of Becca, was affecting Paula and Izzy. Then there was the two house moves, Christmas, the WI Christmas lunch food choices to sort out, the class of 66 Christmas bash to finalise and her mother's Christmas present shopping to sort out. Thinking about her growing list of jobs exhausted her each day before she'd finished her breakfast. Two nights of being awake and plagued with a bloated abdomen and farting told her that irritable bowel syndrome had the upper hand, and to top it all Ron was moving in, to live with her, over the weekend. Then there was the wedding. Although Jean was uncertain about Paula assuming command of proceedings, an inner voice whispered that Paula needed Jean to trust her…

'Grandma, where are you?' Izzy shouted from downstairs.

'Izzy?' *Bugger, where's the time gone?* Jean stubbed her toes as stumbled over the shoes she'd kicked off under her desk. 'Bloody hell.' Jean made for the top of the stairs.

'You look–' Izzy cocked her head on one side– 'as though you've just woken up. Were you having a rest?'

'No, love. I was lost in thought, mithered. Let's have a cup of tea and you can tell me about your day.'

★

'Becca's still not back at school.' Izzy opened the treats cupboard, on the hunt for biscuits. 'And she still won't answer my texts or talk to me.'

'Open that new packet. You mustn't blame yourself, love. She's taking her anger out on you, that's all. She'll come round; eventually.'

'She was going to commit suicide, that's why she stole the knife.'

Jean dithered, using the time, to reach into the fridge for milk, to think.

'Do you think she meant the teacher to see her put the knife in her backpack?'

'It was the technician who saw her. I saw her whisper to Mrs Marsh, then Mrs Marsh kept Becca back. I haven't seen her since. Aunty Sue told Mum she's best left alone for a while.'

'What about Mollie?'

CHAPTER SEVEN

'She says I did the right thing, telling Mum.' Izzy shrugged. 'She's staying with their grandma so that Aunty Sue can spend time with Becca. She says she's glad to be out of the way.' Izzy slurped her tea. 'Do you think I did the right thing, Grandma?'

'Yes, and I think you were very brave.' Jean linked arms with Izzy as they leant against the kitchen worktop.

Izzy laid her head on Jean's shoulder. 'I think about it all the time. I'm not jealous – that's what she said in the one text she sent me, that I was jealous and spiteful and the worst friend anybody would ever have. Lend me your hanky. I'm not. Am I, Grandma?'

'I would want you for my friend, because I know you are honest and kind and care about other people. Being a friend is a responsibility.'

'Have you and Aunty Val ever fallen out?'

Tell the truth. 'Once. Well, we didn't exactly fall out.' Jean reached out for the dish cloth, held it in her hand and put it down again. 'She wanted me to do something about your mum, when things were bad; to get her to see somebody. She was worried about me, and your mum.'

'Did you do anything?'

'No, it was too late: she was pregnant, yet again. She had another abortion, then she went to university, met your dad and you know the rest.'

'Did you fall out, you and Aunty Val?'

'No, I sulked for a bit. Perhaps because I felt guilty, for all sorts of reasons, and deep down I knew Val was right.' Jean released herself from Izzy's arm to rinse the dish cloth under the tap. 'It's out of your hands and up to Becca now, love.'

'Aunty Sue spoke to his mum and dad.' Izzy settled herself on a kitchen chair and, resting her elbows on the table, propped her chin in her cupped hands. 'He told them it was only a bit of fun and that he wasn't bothered about seeing her again.'

'Poor kid.' Jean hesitated. 'There was a girl who did her nurse training at the same time as us who got it very wrong about her friends.'

'Why?'

'She was the opposite of Becca; she was the one, in her group, who didn't have a boyfriend; bearing in mind they were older than you and Becca. She thought she'd been abandoned. She got pregnant. They all rallied round, did their best to help, clubbed together for a carrycot, if I remember rightly, but she pushed them away, no matter how hard they tried.'

'What happened to her and her baby?'

'She qualified with mine and Val's group, she failed her finals first time round, then stayed closeted in the operating theatres, out of the way. He grew up and became a surgeon. Your mum knows him.'

'Were you one of the friends she rejected?'

'No, she and her friends were senior to us. Come on, let's go and see Grandma Mary. You can help her plan her Christmas present list.' *God forbid that she wants me to take her Christmas shopping.*

Mary *November 2017*

Delighted as she was to see Izzy with Jean, Mary was flabbergasted at the pile of books they had brought with them.

'We've only just had Armistice Day, mi poppy's still on top of t'telly.'

'Christmas Day is five weeks today, Mum.'

'That's what I said. It's nowhere near time to think about Christmas presents, and anyway we usually have a ride out.'

Jean made a move to shift the poppy to the top drawer of the bedside cabinet.

'Here, leave that where it were. I like to think of them as is gone before; like your dad and our Terry.'

'Terry?'

'He were a good lad and would have fought if he'd been called on.'

'I dare say he would.' Jean lowered her voice. 'It's a pity he isn't here now.'

'Did you say summat?'

'Grandma said it's a pity he isn't with us now.' Izzy raised her eyebrows to Jean; they both smiled.

'You two are up to summat. Coming to see me and then messin' with mi stuff.' Mary tutted. 'Show us them books then, or I'll not get a minute's peace.'

Izzy spread the catalogues out on the foot of the bed, within Mary's reach.

'It'll take us weeks to go through this lot and I can't read that small print.'

'Izzy could make a list of all the people you want to buy presents for and then we can brainstorm ideas,' Jean said, trying to smile.

'Brainstorm. What's that when it's at home?'

'Suggest ideas,' said Izzy.

'The world's gone mad.' Mary gave an emphatic nod. 'Did you see yon mon, t'other day? ...President Fart, he needs his hair cuttin' good and proper and that Mrs May looks buggered and that German woman's as bad.'

Izzy snorted.

'There'll be no decent world left for you to grow up in, our Izzy. So, we'd best get goin' and sort out something from Father Christmas for you.'

'I don't believe, Grandma Mary, I haven't done for ages.'

'What did I say, the world's going to hell in a 'and cart. Our Terry allus believed.'

*

Mary checked her watch: half an hour until Emmerdale. She rested her head against the back of her chair to settle herself for her thinking time. She liked to reflect on goings-on, in the family, in the Express, on the telly and in Fairhaven. Jean and Izzy's visit had given her an agenda.

Our Izzy's upset about that kiddie of Sue's. She's not going to be like her mam then, nowt but trouble for years on end. It beats me why our Paula give up that good job to be a shop girl. They can't fool me by dressing it up in with a fancy name, she's a shop girl. Although, she looks pleased with herself for once in her life, I'll give her that. What the hell folk'll think about a candle for Christmas, God only knows. But, as usual, our Jean knows best. She means well, she likes helping, doing jobs and that, must come from her nursing. She were no trouble as a kiddie, always liked being with posh folk, like Val. Still, she's made her way in t'world, with being serious and reading a lot. Not like our Terry, full of fun, and generous, he never appeared but what he had a bunch of flowers in his hand. That lad of his is the same. Nobody'll call black people to me. According to our Jean I'm buying him a Chorley football

CHAPTER SEVEN

club mug for Christmas. I should think they have all the pots they need. But what do I know? Then they're buying a job lot of book tokens for everybody else except Paula who's having one of them CD things that plays nowt but bells. I'd best tell em to get something for Roza and t'other girls. A tin of Roses or Quality Street or a box of hankies, or bath salts or is it them what's gerrin candles? I'll leave it to our Jean. She likes deciding things...

Mary roused to the reassuring homely sound of the Emmerdale theme tune. She focused on the telly screen in eager anticipation of her programme.

'Bugger,' she said at the sight of the rolling credits, 'I've missed it.'

Chapter Eight

Izzy's Journal

Everything's gone topsy turvy and mixed up. I told my dad that, and he said the whole FUCKNG WORLD is confused so I was perseptive to feel the same way. I'm not sure about the world, my dad means Brexit and President Trump and Prince Harry being engaged to Meghan Markle and all the fuss, although he calls it "bloody tarradiddle" about it on the telly and in magazines and newspapers, but for me every day seems to mean something different happens, nothing stays the same, not like it used to. I used to get up, go to school — enjoy being with my friends, go to Grandma's, do my homework and then perhaps have my piano lesson or go to guides and go to bed and then the same the next day and the day after that.

Now????? If this is growing up I'm not sure I like it. Perhaps my mum was right wanting me to be a little kid for ever.

School is still good, most of the time but it's hard work now Becca's back. We've had loads of talks because of what Becca did — the school nurse talked about relationships and something she called heavy petting. It made me think of children pressing down hard when they

CHAPTER EIGHT

stroke baby animals at a petting farm. Then our form teacher talked to us about on-line harassment and bullying. What he meant was that we hadn't to post anything about Becca and sex and suicide. The mums who are friends got together, they didn't tell us they had but we all got LITTLE CHATS about friendship and boys and sex. Anyway, Becca is back at school, she's quiet and looks tired and fed up. She trails about after me but doesn't join in. She doesn't come round to ours much so I'm spending more time, after school and at weekends, with Olivia. Being at Olivia's is a bit scary, her brothers are noisy and their room smells of something funny — farty yet a bit sweet and sour at the same time. They swear all the time except at the meal table. Their mum and dad are lovely and mostly ignore the boys when they are being silly except they are strict about technology at the table and manners at family meals. They're a happy family. We are happy, well most of the time. Mum had too much to drink on Christmas Day so she was in bed most of Boxing Day. She's never drinking again??????? Yesterday she got up saying she was bursting with energy and "resolve" — she kept saying it all day. She has RESOLVED everything. We are starting with Grandma and Pops' wedding. She wants it to be on a cruise ship and coinside with Grandma's 70th birthday in April. We spent most of yesterday on the phone. Aunty Val, Charlie and Naomi are on board. A pun!!!! And this is the big news: so is Grandma Mary. Me and Mum went to see her last night. She wasn't happy that the television people have "buggered up" the times of her television programmes, because of Christmas, but she was glad to see us. At first, she said it was a crack pot idea and the wedding wouldn't be proper and legal. Then when

161

SNAPSHOTS

Mum told her Charlie and Naomi were coming and asked her if she wanted to come, she cheered up and said she'd always wanted to go on a cruise, the people who ran the youth club used to go on them all the time and then she said what did it matter if it was a sham there'd be no children involved that would be bastards!!!

Then she had one of her favourite rants about checking how many couples in the Chorley Guardian were married when they announced the birth of their babies. There were three this week, and she doesn't like the names they choose. She nearly choked when I told her that Nevaeh was heaven backwards. So, she's coming and bringing Roza. Mum suggested she and Aunty Val would look after her, but she said she wants Roza to go as her companion and that she's reckoned up and when she's put money on one side for her funeral she's still enough to pay for Roza. Pops is up for it. We are going to keep it a surprise from Grandma until it's all booked. Charlie is giving Grandma away. She still calls him Terry all the time, but we don't bother anymore. Dad is being best man and me and Mum are being bridesmaids. Pops says we are his family and he doesn't need anybody else to be there. Mum is very excited and RESOLVED to make it very, very, very special for Grandma.

Back to school tomorrow. I'm looking forward to it. Christmas has gone on a long time. I got a fitbit and makeup and smelly stuff, a new case for my phone, money and a toilet bag. Our English teacher didn't give us homework but said we had to read, read, read. I was reading Little Women, so I finished that and watched it

CHAPTER EIGHT

on the telly. Dad says it's "PATERNALISTIC CLAP TRAP" and that I would be better reading about the work that Louisa May Alcott did as a nurse during the American civil war. He thinks Grandma has a book I could borrow. She collects books by nurses who are writers as well.

Grandma has read Dad's book and made some suggestions, something about showing not telling. When he's redrafted it she is going to mention it to her publisher. Mum and me were very, very surprised that he listened to what Grandma had to say and then set about re doing it!!!!! Grandma is looking for an agent for her second book because it is too literary, something to do with it being about the characters and not about a plot. Perhaps it would be better if she started again.

Back to going back to school. I hope Becca has cheered up. I heard Aunty Sue telling Mum that she was thinking of sending her to a boarding school to do with Uncle Bob being in the Masons. That's a secret society, that everybody knows about, for men. Mum thinks Aunty Sue should make her stick it out at Parklands. I want her to stay and be cheerful and for us to be how we were but somehow, I don't think she'll ever be my best friend ever again. It makes me sad and a bit frightened that I tried to do good and ended up making things bad between us.

Anyway, my New Year resolution is to be happy with my family and not be frightened of growing up.

Paula *January 2018*

Paula paused in the middle of footbridge that spanned the Chorley to Preston railway line. She gazed to the distant mound of Rivington Pike sitting on top of the summit of Winter Hill. The turret and the mound of the Pike always reminded her of a single breast wantonly exposed to the elements. *This is where being mindful gets you, thinking about breasts instead of food, school uniform, Mum and Ron's move, the wedding and the mess with Sue and Becca, Douglas and his novel, and I need to make an appointment for a smear test.*

Relaxing into the moment and the splendour of the rainbow reflections in the puddles at the side of the railway line she was startled to hear the gentle thrum of the train as it slowed to approach the station. *Bloody hell.* She skittered down the steps and lurched towards the nearest carriage door. Panting slightly and feeling a twerp, Paula glanced round the carriage – the other passengers were caught up in the stupor of their daily commute, nobody was interested in her ungainly dash across the bridge, down the steps and onto the train.

During her quiet day at work Paula had time to think about her mum's wedding. The enormity of the task she'd voluntarily taken on clog danced around her brain with bells and whistles and ribbons flying so that she couldn't catch her thoughts and hold them still. How did she book a cruise? Would the wedding be on the ship or on shore? How would she arrange everything: flowers, photographs? Had she left it too late to book for April? How would she pack all the wedding clothes? Where would her mum sleep the night before the wedding? Did it matter when you were

CHAPTER EIGHT

seventy, hardly a blushing bride? What was it all going to cost? Trundling a rail of clothes toward the stock room as she cleared redundant stock left over from the sales she stopped, the clogs stilled, the bells and whistles quietened.

I'll text Douglas and ask him for the name of the man he knew who sold cruises. Surely, they'll know what to do. Be in this moment here, now. Breathe, observe yourself, be curious and carry on.

*

As Paula made her way to the cruise company to talk to a specialist wedding cruise concierge, she gazed around at the industrial units on the business park tucked away in the foothills of the Pennines. The familiar and reassuring edifice of Rivington Pike, with its light covering of snow against a gathering orange and crimson sunset, momentarily took her breath away. *I'm doing the right thing, at last, doing something for my mum, instead of the other way round. Please, God, let me get this right. Sod the cost.* She clicked the lock of her car keys and made her way to the building that had been pointed out to her by the guard staffing the barrier entrance.

*

A smell of burning fat hit Paula as she opened the front door, a smoky haze swirled around the hall. Douglas and Izzy were in the kitchen, the sharp, cold air from the open bi-folding doors and open windows told its own story.

'I told him the temperature was too high.' Izzy's voice held a smile as she rolled her eyes at Paula and moved around the island unit to peck her cheek.

'They're only burnt on one side,' said Douglas, peering through the glass in the oven door at the sausages resting in the oven. 'Charcoal's good for the stomach. How did you go on, love? Was it worth it?'

'Very much so.' Paula reached up to kiss Douglas. 'I like burnt sausages. What are we having with them?'

'Shit! Mash.'

'Dad?'

'Not literally, you cheeky little madam.' Douglas lobbed a wobbly silicone oven glove at his daughter. 'Sometimes I think you're not as innocent as you let on.'

'I'll mash the potatoes,' said Izzy, lobbing the glove back at Douglas.

'And to think I look forward to coming home to this, burnt food, shit mash and oven glove catchers.' She shook her head. 'I love you both so much.'

'Skedaddle and get changed, we want to hear what Captain Bird's Eye, and his team, had to say.'

Gathered around the kitchen table the family interrupted their careful dissection of the charcoaled sausages to consider the cruise ship wedding.

'They are lovely people, who really know their stuff,' said Paula.

'The proof of the pudding, and all that,' said Douglas holding up a fork full of sausage and mash.

'I trust them, they've got a trophy cabinet, they win prize after prize for customer service, the size of a green house. Shelley, our concierge…'

'Concierge?'

'Yes, our dedicated person. Douglas, are you going to keep interrupting?'

CHAPTER EIGHT

'Who me?'

'Shelley, our concierge.' Paula raised her eyebrows at Douglas. 'She liaises with the wedding coordinator on the ship and Bob's your uncle.'

'How will we get to the church?' said Izzy.

'We don't. It's all done on the ship, when it's in international waters.'

'What about the bans. Will it be legal in this country?' Douglas said.

'Grandma Mary says it doesn't matter if it's legal or not because there won't be any kiddies that'll be bastards.'

'See. I knew you knew more than you let on. Shit and bastards in one night.'

'Dad!'

'Anyway, it's all going to be sorted, and best of all, Roza goes free.'

'They'll have built the cost in somewhere, but well-done, love. Does anybody want another sausage?'

Paula excused herself to make phone calls to the rest of the wedding party. The cruise Company had promised to hold the booking for twenty-four hours. Two hours later she'd spoken to everyone except her grandma, who she would need to visit. The family knew that Emmerdale, Coronation Street and Holby City took precedent over anything other than a visit from Izzy or Charlie, and even they would be required to sit in companionable silence for the duration of the programme.

Ron's enthusiasm and heartfelt thanks had Paula cursing herself for the valuable time she'd wasted doubting and mistrusting him at the start of his relationship with her mum. She reminded herself that dwelling on the past had the potential to push her to the edge of her comfort zone of self-loathing which would be quickly followed by a glass or three of wine. Her mum's serendipitous absence at the WI gave them opportunity to discuss in detail Paula's visit to the cruise company, transport to the airport, and Ron's outfit. He readily agreed to a visit to see one of Paula's colleagues with Jean, when she was let in on the wedding arrangements.

Val, who saw wonder in almost every situation, and her husband, signed up without any qualms other than the luggage allowance. Val had a reputation for her inability to travel lightly.

Charlie and Naomi suggested that, if possible, they fly from Birmingham. Everything was in place for the booking to go ahead. Then Paula would tell Jean. Paula felt giddy with excitement. She licked her lips, she could taste the lemon and melon overlaid with the crunchy green finish of rhubarb that was her favourite rosé wine. Throwing her shoulder back, she turned her back on the wine fridge, mounted the stairs and ran a hot bath. She was feeling a touch queasy despite what Douglas said about charcoal being good for the stomach.

Jean *February 2018*

Jean and Ron waved goodbye to the removal van.

'At last.' Jean slipped her arm around Ron's waist. 'Our own home.'

Ron pulled Jean toward him and bent to kiss her.

'I think we'd better close the door, before we go any further,' said Jean nodding toward the road of detached houses.'

CHAPTER EIGHT

'Sod the neighbours.' He kissed her again. Jean gave him a gentle push as she reached for the front door. 'And bless the family, here's Paula come to drop Izzy off.'

Jean gave Paula and Izzy a tour of the refurbished house. The architect had suggested some basic alterations – knocking through a small room next to the kitchen to make an open plan kitchen and snug. Refitting the kitchen and en-suite bathroom and dividing the attic space that had previously been a playroom into two studies. Fitted bookshelves lined each study and the wall of the living room. All Jean and Ron had to do now was unpack the collection of cardboard packing cases that cluttered each room.

'It feels so spacious after that lodge,' said Paula.

A friend of Val's had loaned her holiday lodge in Garstang to Jean and Ron for the duration of the work on the house.

'I'll be eternally grateful to Myra, but it's good to be back in Chorley and in our–' Jean squeezed Ron's arm– 'very own home. I feel giddy, excited, daft, happy – I could sing.'

'I like your singing, Grandma. What are you laughing at, Mum?'

'Grandma got the music prize at school, surely she's told you. Uncle Terry used to complain of earache and beg for mercy even if she sang along to a jingle on the telly.'

Jean sniffed the air, in an attempt to appear snooty, and smiled. 'Well, Izzy, me and you can sing all we like while we make up the bed and set up the kitchen.'

'I'll see you all later, about six?' As Paula moved toward her to kiss her cheek, out of the corner of her eye Jean saw her wink at Ron. 'Don't eat too much – you need to save yourselves for your dinner.'

They're up to something. The wedding! My money is on a Lake District hotel. 'See you later, love. And what are you two looking so pleased–' Jean gave Izzy and Ron a lopsided look– 'and shifty about?'

'What, us? Let's find the kettle and have a brew before we start,' said Ron busying himself peering at box lids. 'One of these boxes should be labelled "brew stuff".'

★

The table in the dining room was set with Paula's best cutlery, dinner service and wine glasses.

Huh oh, prepare yourself. 'This is lovely, for a Wednesday,' said Jean nodding toward the dining room as she found space for her coat in the cloakroom and made her way into the kitchen. 'Champagne as well.'

'Well, it's Valentine's Day,' said Douglas, intent on his task of coaxing the cork out of the bottle. 'And a celebration for your new home and life and family, and anything else that takes your fancy.'

The atmosphere in the kitchen sparkled and fizzed with suppressed excitement.

Whatever it is, they're all in on it. Jean swallowed; her lips were dry. She felt her breathing stutter, her legs felt wobbly. She reached for one of the high-backed chairs tucked under the breakfast bar.

'And we've booked the wedding,' said Paula, glancing round at Ron, Izzy and Douglas.

'You're shaking, love,' said Ron putting an arm round Jean's shoulder. 'Don't cry, you'll be thrilled.'

I truly hope so. 'Go on then.' Jean reached out to take a glass of fizz from Douglas. 'Tell me.'

CHAPTER EIGHT

'We're going on a cruise, Grandma,' Izzy said, breaking the miniscule vacuum of silence. 'I love you, Grandma and Pops. This is going to be the best wedding ever.'

Jean felt the suppressed tension in the room shift and slacken. While her family smiled and nodded at each other, she felt a commotion of thoughts and feelings ooze and run together.

'What about, Mum?' The champagne in her wine glass slopped as her hand shook. *I'll be a bloody carer on my wedding day.*

'She's coming – with Roza. Me and Val offered to help look after her, but she insisted she wanted Roza. Don't cry, Mum.'

'My God.' Jean's free hand covered her mouth. 'Paula, what can I say?' Jean shook her head as a fresh cataract of tears poured down her face.

Her face dried and her glass refreshed, Jean listened, flabbergasted at the level of arrangements Paula had made with the help and support of Ron, Val and Charlie. All that was left to do was to choose dresses for herself, Paula and Izzy at the personal shopping appointment, for the three of them, that Paula had made with her boss.

'And this is the best bit, Mum, Ron and Douglas have got a personal shopper appointment as well.'

'You are joking?' Jean looked flabbergasted. Douglas was well known for his lack of anything that smacked of modernity and style. So long as his clothes were moderately clean, he was sartorially satisfied.

'I'm sorry to repeat myself–' Jean held her arms out in an attitude of supplication– 'but what about Grandma? I'll need to take her shopping.'

'She and Roza are shopping on-line – apparently stuff arrives most days, gets tried on and then either bought or returned. It's safe to say Grandma is a QVC junky with a wardrobe to rival the Queen.'

'I wondered why she got shirty when I offered to go through her wardrobe. You've thought of everything, love. How will I ever thank you?'

Paula shuffled up the settee to take Jean's hand. 'You gave up large parts of your life to love and support me and got nothing but crap back…'

'No more tears, you two. I'm opening another bottle of bubbly.' Douglas reached into the fridge. 'Save them for when I've been to the personal shopper and end up looking like Elton John on a bad day.'

'There is one more thing, love – wedding rings. Charlie and Naomi have invited us to stay with them and suggested we have a trip to the jewellery quarter in Birmingham,' Ron said.

'I am truly blessed.' Jean took a swig of her champagne. *I truly am.*

Mary *February 2018*

Mary held up one of the pairs of knickers from the pile scattered at the bottom of her bed.

'These can go, elastic's buggered.' She handed the offending underwear to Roza who was standing by with a black bin bag. Mary rummaged through the pile until she ended up with four pairs of knickers that had passed the inspection. 'You'd best get me six pairs, what with what I've got on and them on t'bed and them in t'wash I should have

CHAPTER EIGHT

enough. Let's do t'vests next. I don't want be looking powsey with them all being in their finery.'

'Mary, what is powsey? I think it might mean downtrodden. You should not fear as you will look exceptionally smart with all your new clothes.'

'Go to him on that second stall up, next t'cheese counter. He's Indian, but nice with it.'

Mary was mentally cataloguing her cruise wardrobe when she glimpsed Jean appearing at the top of the stairs. 'As it got to that time? That black skirt will do a time or two.'

'Sorry, Mum.' Jean shrugged off her coat and untied her scarf as she entered Mary's room. 'What were you saying, something about a skirt?'

'F't cruise.' Mary winced. 'Bloody hell, I've put my foot in it.'

Jean smiled as she bent to kiss her mother. 'It's alright, Mum, they've told me.' She settled herself on the end of the bed.

'I must say, I'm looking forward to it. It's years since I had a decent holiday,' announced Mary. When Jean and Terry were children, Mary had put money aside each week for an annual holiday. She had a tin for everything – gas, electricity, coal, Christmas – and whatever she had at the end of a week went in the holiday tin. Unlike many of her neighbours, who if asked about their Wakes Week's holiday plans replied, "we're just going for days," Mary was proud to announce their travel plans, to places as far afield as Blackpool, Morecambe, Fleetwood and, when the tin had a good year, the Isle of Man. Her husband wasn't one for being away from home, but he joined in the holiday festivities by tying knots in the corner of his hanky, settling it on his head and alternated dozing in his deckchair with picking horses from the *News Chronicle*. Mary remembered the holidays as a golden age when the days were sunny, and her children made sandcastles on the beach. With neighbours from down the road in the same guest house, the week at the seaside was a splendid home from home. She'd been "abroad" twice, and wasn't over keen on it. The sun was too hot, and she couldn't trust the food and there was no proper beach. On a holiday after Jean's husband had died, she and Jean had sat by the pool in Tenereefy with Jean mithering herself about what Paula was up to. Mary had to see the doctor with midge bites and her nose and shoulder had peeled like an onion. Then she'd had a long weekend with Jean in Barcelona looking at funny building and drinking pink pop with fruit in it. The pop had given her a banging headache and the queues for the ugly church thing were a mile long. That Gaudy man had been building the thing for years and even though he was dead nobody had finished it off for him. It still wasn't done with. No, abroad wasn't all it was cracked up to be, but, a cruise? Well, who'd have thought it?

'Our Paula says it'll be like being in a posh hotel with that there air conditioner on all t'time. And there'll be no midges.'

'Are you sure you'll be alright with the flying and everything?'

'Our Paula's got it all sorted. My passport and me being helped at Ringway.'

'Manchester Airport.'

'That's what I said. And besides we're only flying to Rome, our Paula says it'll not take more than a couple of hours.'

'You and Paula have got everything sorted then?'

CHAPTER EIGHT

'I'll tell you what, she's a different girl since she went to work in that shop.' Mary nodded emphatically as she knitted her arms across her chest. 'It's a crying shame she's wasted all the education but, so what, you say it's done her a world of good chucking that proper job in.'

Jean examined the pile of knickers next to her on the bed.

'I'm having all new.' Mary pointed. 'Well apart from them knickers and a couple of vests.'

'Are you sure you're alright for money, Mum?'

'I've plenty, especially since our Paula's insisted on paying for you, and Roza's going free.'

'I didn't know that, Mum.'

Mary contemplated Jean. *I'd best be careful, she gets peeved if I say owt.* 'What made her go–' Mary hesitated and tapped her fingers together– 'off rails in t'first place? I never had any of that sort of trouble with you and our Terry.' Mary watched Jean's face. *I'm safe.* Jean's lips twitched. *No, spoke too soon. I'm in bother.*

'Mum, no matter how many times you ask me, the answer's the same. I don't know.'

'There's no need to get shirty with me, lady.' *She bloody well knows but won't let on.* 'Well, she's turned out decent in t'long run and our Izzy is a real treat.' Mary fought to control her voice. 'And our Terry's lad's a real gent.' Mary felt a sense of calm when she thought of her grandson and great-granddaughter. 'They're the light of my life, them two.'

Mary caught a glimpse of Jean's lip twist. 'And you as well, you does your best for me, when you can.' *She'll have them lips sticking like that if she doesn't watch it.*

'Has she been for that smear thing?' Mary made a pointing motion toward Jean's crotch. 'I'm glad I had everything taken away.' She shuddered and shook her head. 'What's private down there, should stay private. If you ask me.' Mary watched Jean's lips twitch in a half smile. 'Now what've I said?'

Chapter Nine

Izzy's Journal

Hello Journal, I think of you as sort of a person now, someone I really like but who is far away. Perhaps that's what Mrs Berry meant when she told us about the power of writing stuff down. It means I can tell you secrets and thoughts I maybe shouldn't say out loud. The most awesome thing has happened. My mum is pregnant — with TWINS — BIG SHOCK. It is utterly, stupendously, brilliantly amazing. Mum went to the doctors for a smear and came out expecting twins. Well we didn't know about the twins straight away just that she was pregnant. She didn't know because she has funny periods and she thought Dad had poisoned us with his cooking. The big surprise for me is that my parents still do sex. Yuk, double yuk and bugger. I am cutting down on swearing. Olivia's brothers do it out loud all the time and it doesn't sound good.

Back to the twins, we're working on names, Mum and Dad are pleased now they are over the shock and are not stunned. They are due around the 30 August. They didn't tell me at first. Not until the next day when Mum had a scan that's when they heard two heart beats and saw them in their sacks. It all happened very quickly because Dad has a friend who is an obstetrition. Anyway, everybody knows now. Pops cried. Grandma was flabbergasted. Grandma Mary said, "bloody hell fire, I hope they're lads because you get more back from a lad with them being a lot more loving and affectionate". Mum said not to mention the bit about lads being more loving and affectionate to Grandma. Aunty Sue asked if Mum was having an abortion. She's still not coping well, with Uncle Bob being dead and Becca and Mollie are still being mean to each other.

Anyway, back to names. Dad explained that they will not be identical because Mum is older she shot out two ova (Dad likes me to use the correct anatomical terms). So, we are looking for two boys and two girls' names. Dad says we have done the Manx connection with my name. His aunty, who brought him up, was called Marjorie Isaleen, her brothers called her Margarine. Mum likes Isaac and Charles and Fleur and Jasmine. Dad likes Mary and Catherine, his grandma's names as well as Grandma Mary, of course, and James and David. I'm not sure but definitely not Matthew or Ralph, and not Polly. A girl in my maths group is called Polly she's clever but stuck up and smells of dirty knickers. I like flower names, Lily, Daisy, Heather, Rose and Jasmine. Bruce is good for a boy, and Max. Olivia says that I've only picked them because I've got crushes on Bruce Roberts and Max Seddon.

Other stuff. Grandma doesn't want a white dress for the wedding because Grandma Mary will sulk and harp on about wreath and veil all the time. I think she should have what she wants. When you think about it, Grandma Mary can be mean to Grandma. I don't think she does it on purpose, but it hurts me to see Grandma looking sad and upset. Grandma Mary loved Uncle Terry the most. I can understand why Grandma doesn't always want Grandma Mary to come out of the home for family get togethers but she is part of the family and anyway she's probably going to die soon. I've had a strange thought — Are mothers and daughters always sometimes mean, or tetchy or cross with each other? I don't know the right word. I've looked up synonyms for tetchy there are some corkers — irascible, crotchety, cantankerous, pettish, crabby, waspish, peppery and crusty are my favourites. I think English Language is my favourite subject. I might be a writer. Mr Coupe says if I slow down and check my spellings and punctuation I would be an excellent student. If we ask to have the window open because we're sweaty, he says "horses sweat, young men perspire, and young ladies go all of a glow". We tell him he's sexist and he says he's too old for sex. He thinks he's being ironic, but he is very old but nice, like a saggy old armchair.

We are still going on the cruise although Mum isn't going to be matron of honour. She's stopped feeling sick, she's given up drinking but she can't stop eating Jaffa Cakes. Dad says pregnancy cravings are a myth, Mum tells him to "bugger off", but nicely. They are very happy, everybody is except Aunty Sue.

Friends news. Becca is better when she is at home or round at ours. I think I should tell our form teacher that Amber and Lucy are bullying her, they sneaked sugar on top of her bread, before it was baked, in food technology and then offered her a sharp knife and whispered, "try a bigger blade this time". Nobody likes them and their mums are not friendly with our mums, so they haven't had the chats we've had. If it keeps on I'm going to ask my mum's advise. She's very wise because of all the trouble she had. I love her loads. It seems a long time since we had our row and she had hers with Grandma. I want to be the best big sister I can be. Do you think I'm right to try and do something about Becca being bullied, or will it make things worse like last time?

Time for hot chocolate and a dose of Calpol.

Paula *March 2018*

As Paula heaved herself out of the low seat of her car, she heard a rat-a-tat. She glanced up to see her grandma standing at her first-floor bedroom window, balanced against her walking frame. Paula had taken to visiting at least once a week, she enjoyed listening to her grandma's stories and her jaundiced view of life. Politically correct was an alien phrase to Mary, and Paula was left in no doubt that her grandma's definition of "a foreigner" was anybody with the misfortune to have been born outside Lancashire. At the sight of her grandma's beaming smile, Paula felt a cosy blanket of warmth and love for her.

'You'll soon need a crane to get in and out of that posh car. Come on, get yourself settled on that commode.'

Paula dumped her coat and scarf on the end of the bed and pulled the commode out of its usual resting place to be nearer her grandma's chair.

'There's summat as is always puzzled me,' said Mary.

The look of resolve on the old lady's face told Paula that she was about to be subjected to an Inquisition.

'What's that, Grandma?'

'Well, it's like this.' Mary rubbed her hands together, paused, touched a finger to her lips. 'Why, when you'd everything a child could ever want, did you turn awkward like you did? It nearly finished your mam off. She were that proud of you passing for Bolton School. Then you went and buggered it all up.'

Paula sighed. *If only I knew.*

'I happen shouldn't have mentioned it with you expecting but–'

'Was she proud of me?'

'I'll say she were. You made up for us, me and your grandad and our Terry.'

Paula felt the air shift, she had a vague feeling of Christmas morning, pleasant anticipation of a gift to be revealed: her mum *had* been proud of her and Grandma was about to reveal family gossip.

'She were always drawn to posh folk. Val's a grand lass, no airs and graces but her mam and dad were a cut above. She always fetched folk t'house though. I'll give our Jean that, she weren't ashamed of her home.'

'But you've always been close?'

'We have, and we haven't. She'd do owt for me, I know that, but it's as though it's her duty. Now our Terry he were a different kettle of fish.'

'You said she was proud of me.'

'You were the sun and moon to her, what with your dad working all hours of t'day and night.'

Paula felt light-headed. A half-remembered sense of being held close, a tender stroke against her cheek, a gentle

CHAPTER NINE

scent of spring flowers – Blue Grass her mum's favourite perfume.

'I'd forgotten about us always being together.'

'Your little friends would call for you and you'd send em away because you were doing summat or other with her.'

'I remember, we read and baked, and she taught me how to play the recorder.' Paula caught her breath. 'I'd forgotten.'

'Don't take on, love, spilt milk and all that.'

Paula shifted from the commode to perch on the end of the bed. 'I'm trying to understand, Grandma.' She reached to the side table and helped herself to a tissue. 'Like you said, I've made a real bugger of my life, up to now, with one thing and another.'

'That's true enough, but you've come to your senses and our Jean's happy for the first time in a long time. Although, your dad were a grand lad, a real grafter and he left her well provided for.' Mary glanced round and indicated for Paula to move closer. 'There's another thing that's been on my mind.' She dropped her voice. 'Do you think they've commiserated it?'

Paula sat back, puzzled.

'Anticipated being wed.' Mary gave a vigorous nod. 'You know, done stuff together – in bed?'

'Bonking? Grandma!' Paula laughed, she felt a sense of joy, sharing memories and juicy gossip. 'Course they have.'

'You waited until you were wed in my day. All a lot of fuss about nothing, if you ask me. My mam told me to keep the light off and my nightie on, that's all I knew on my wedding night. The rest, well, let's just say it weren't anything like I were expectin.'

'Did you get on with your mum?'

'I don't know about gerrin on, it were more about gerrin through t'days with enough food in our bellies and clothes on our backs. There were no real childhood in them days, you know. Not like now.'

'Yes, but did you fall out?'

'No, well not much, not when I were at home. Once we were wed, she thought I were yessy with housework. She were allus neat and tidy, kept the house like a little palace.' Mary's eyes twinkled, her face enigmatic. 'She were more like our Jean, and you,' she winked, 'are more like me.'

'I'll take that as a compliment then.'

'I you want. But you've still not answered my question. Why did you turn like you did?'

'If only I knew, Grandma, I'd tell you. I regret a lot in my life...' The sudden tears overwhelmed Paula. Image after image and sensation after sensation flashed around her head; choking on a cigarette, the pain of the first penetration, her legs in stirrups and the push of fingers in her vagina, her dad turning his head to hide his tears, police interviews, humiliation after humiliation and the sure knowledge of knowing that she was rotten confirmed over and over. Lost in the deluge of tears, she was unaware of Mary struggling out of her chair until she felt the bed shift and a bony arm link through hers.

'I'm always saying summat I shouldn't.' Mary laid her head against Paula's shoulder. 'I'm sorry, love.'

'Don't be. It helps facing what I've done but still doesn't answer your question, Grandma. I've decided what's done is done and I must accept being here, now. And do you know what?'

Mary shifted her position to sit upright. 'What, love?'

'At long last I feel happy. Over these last few weeks I feel different, clean and fresh and whole.'

'You won't tell your mum I've upset you, will you? She'd be vexed with me.'

Paula shepherded Mary back to her chair, pinched a tissue to give her nose a honking blow and sat back on the edge of the bed.

'Can I ask you something, Grandma?'

Mary nodded.

Paula sighed as she struggled to catch the right words. 'Why are the four of us, you, Mum, me and Izzy a bit – sensitive with each other?'

'It's not with each other, it's mothers and daughters as is the bother. Happen it's because life moves on and we want to stay the same and our young uns want summat different, summat they think is better. One thing I do know is over the years our family's got better off. Although thinking about it now, we'd best watch out. My dad used to say, "rags to rags, in three generations". Happen you were having a go at going back to rags.'

'I love you, Grandma.'

'Now then, don't take on, especially in your condition. Why don't you see if you can find us a cup of tea, and then I'll show you my new clothes.'

Jean *March 2018*

Who'd have thought my seventieth birthday, a bride and a new grandma? Jean reflected on the profound changes that a year had brought. Catching sight of Paula in one of the many photographs she'd displayed throughout the house now brought a sense of quiet joy, rather than the disquiet and sadness that had lurked for so long. Her reformed daughter, who now smiled at life and walked with her head held high, facing life with a new honesty and frankness, instead of hunching her shoulders and scurrying and searching like a rat in a maze. Paula and Izzy's new-found closeness had left Jean with a feeling of release and a vague yearning. She was no longer the first-person Izzy sought out for love, comfort and reassurance. It was Paula, Izzy now snuggled up to on the settee, scouring the iPad for a special dress for a school party, or casually nattering together about school and work. Jean scolded herself for the occasional, fleeting pang of jealousy, reminding herself that she had been privileged to be the woman Izzy had turned to for so long. Izzy had Paula now, and Jean was in her rightful place as a loved, but more distanced grandma. It was how it should be.

Her mum settled in Fairhaven, a nephew from out of the blue, and a new home with a man who loved her. How long can it all last? How many more good years? The morbid thoughts, that crept up on her with increasing frequency, perplexed her, yet she knew that thoughts of mortality were natural at her age. Jean and Val had taken to discussing the preparation for the inevitably of ageing and death as the years flew by. The joke, with their nursing friends, was that they would all find themselves in the same nursing home, unaware that they knew each other but surprised to share the same reminiscences of hospital life.

The impact of Amy and Bob's deaths had brought deep and significant changes to the lives of Jean's family. The row to end all rows after Amy's death had given the event a poignancy. The young woman's legacy, in death, had set Paula on a long road back to Jean. While Bob's death and Becca's grief had been a catalyst for Izzy to begin to push open the door that led to adulthood. And her mum, a political activist?

Get a grip, Jean. Edit yesterday's writing. Jean flicked on her laptop, rolled her shoulders and stretched her arms. She was saved from her editing by the beep of a car horn and the sound of Ron opening the front door to Val. 'Put the kettle on, I'm on my way down,' she called as she danced her feet under the desk to locate her slippers.

'I was just saying to Ron, the place looks stunning.'

'Is everything alright?' Jean voice held a note of scepticism. As close as the two women were, it wasn't their habit to call at each other's homes unexpectedly.

'I'm on my way to Preston so I thought I'd call in.' She sighed, pulled up the corner of her mouth and hesitated. 'Maggie Smithfield died last night.'

'Never. What? When?'

'She was walking up her path, with a bag of shopping, collapsed, a neighbour saw her, went to help. An ambulance came, took her to hospital and she was BID.'

'BID?' Ron looked over the top of his specs.

'Brought in Dead,' Jean and Val chorused. 'She died in the ambulance,' Jean clarified for Ron.

'Who is she? Not one of your nursing gang?'

'She took her finals with us, her second time around,' said Val.

'And she'd tagged on to our outings this last year or so. She was always a bit of a lost soul, poor Maggie.' Jean patted Val's arm.

'Seventy, it's no age. Just shows you have to make the most of–'

'Don't. I was paddling through the doldrums when you turned up. Now I feel really miserable.' Jean resented the feeling of despair and dread that swirled around her. 'Look at everything I've got. What the hell do I have to feel down in the dumps for?'

'Because you're a miserable bugger, with death around the corner and nothing to live for.' Val plonked her mug on the worktop. 'You daft bat, you always did think too much. Come on, I'm going to collect some shoes I've ordered. Wait till you see them, they're corkers.'

Jean turned to Ron who had his head in the dishwasher. 'Do you mind, love?'

'No, go and enjoy yourself, I'll try and get this leak sorted while you're out.'

'That reminds me of a story Anne Tyler repeats in a couple of her novels where families use the dishwasher as their pot cupboard. They take the clean pots they want out, use them and then put them back dirty and then set the thing going without ever emptying it.'

'It's a pity you didn't tell me about that when I lived on my own.' Ron hoisted himself to his feet. 'I'm making a chilli for our meal; you and Vic are welcome to join us.'

'Brilliant, idea. Why don't one of you give him a ring while I smarten myself up?' Jean said, heading toward the door.

★

Once they had chewed over all they could about the life and times of Maggie Smithfield – her surprise pregnancy, her single state, the rumours about her sex life with various overseas housemen and the way she'd hidden herself away in

CHAPTER NINE

Bolton Royal operating theatre – they'd arrived at the park and ride for Preston. Having decided that they'd done what they could to make Maggie welcome on their occasional lunches, they'd concluded that their lives were more blessed than dammed, that they were going to live every day to the full and attend Maggie's funeral.

'Let's call and see if Paula's free for a coffee, she thought a lot of Maggie's son,' said Jean.

Val's shoes were indeed corkers. Jean noticed that the shoe box described them as multi glitter, cross strap platforms. The platform was an inch high and the heel four and a half inches.

'It's a good job you saw them before I did,' Jean's eyes glowed with envy and admiration. 'They're a bit tight on your right foot. Are you sure you can walk in them?'

'Absolutely, and by the time of the wedding they'll be wide enough–' Val gave a teetering demonstration– 'once I've worn them with my hiking socks.'

'You didn't say you'd got your wedding outfit.'

'I haven't, just these bloody gorgeous shoes. Come on, let's go and see if Paula's free.'

Jean and Val hovered outside the entrance to the personal shopper fitting rooms. They could hear Paula and another person laughing behind a closed door. The door opened as Paula announced, 'I'll see you outside.'

'We can see you're busy, love,' Jean said.

'Give me a minute or two, to sort out–' Paula nodded to the changing room and with slight emphasis added, 'Martha.'

'Martha?' murmured Jean as a statuesque woman stepped out of the cubicle. 'Ah, Martha.'

'Martha.' Paula turned her head to give her mother a surreptitious squint. 'This is my mum and my Aunty Val.'

'Paula's told me all about you.' Jean felt heat suffuse her neck and face. 'You're her favourite customer.' She closed her eyes to the image of Val, goggle eyed, her mouth agape with incredulity.

'And she's told me what a wonderful mother and grandmother you are.' Martha nodded and smiled.

'She is – definitely, she is. Would you like to see the shoes I've bought?' Val spluttered.

The shoes examined, and Martha on her way to the till with Paula and her purchases, Jean and Val could relax.

'Well, we made a bugger of that,' said Jean.

'I'll say, we're supposed to be liberal minded and the first time we're put to the test we act like two gauche kids. I wish the ground had opened up and devoured us.'

'Here's Paula, now we'll cop it.' Jean gritted her teeth and looked askance in anticipation of Paula's reaction.

Paula paused, arms akimbo, face impassive. She grinned. 'Martha says, that'll teach her to wipe her thick foundation off before she tries on clothes.'

'Sorry, love, it was unexpected, meeting her like that. Have we let you down?'

'You could see his – sorry, her – bristles,' Val said.

'Why don't you sit down, and I'll make us a cup of tea, or perhaps a glass of bubbles.' She paused. 'We always offer prospective brides a glass of fizz when they try on wedding dresses.'

'Have they come?' Jean clasped her hands in glee.

'This morning. I meant to give you a ring, but the time ran away.'

CHAPTER NINE

'Before we do, I've a bit of bad news.' Jean hesitated, touched her mouth and pursed her lips.

'What is it, Mum? Not Grandma?'

'No, nothing like that. We–' Jean waved her index finger between herself and Val– 'heard that Maggie Smithfield; your friend's mum, died yesterday.'

'John's mum?' Paula's gave a tut, her head on one side. 'Poor man. I'll send a card. Now fizz or tea?'

'Weren't you very fond of him?' Jean was puzzled at Paula's dismissive attitude.

'In another life, Mum; everything's different now. I'm sorry about his mum though.' Paula moved toward her mum and to Jean's surprise bent to peck her cheek. 'Are you crying, Aunty Val?'

'Touch of sinusitis,' said Val, helping herself to a tissue from the box on the side table, 'we'd best have the fizz, for medicinal purposes, you understand.'

'I love you as well, Val. Thank you for everything you've done, standing by us, well me despite all the stupid stuff.' Paula blew Val a kiss as she turned to move toward the door.

At the door she stopped and turned. 'Mum I've been meaning to ask you, why does Grandma push us away if we say anything about loving her? I've noticed she screws her face up when any of us try and kiss her.'

Jean and Val exchanged looks.

'What?' Paula looked mystified. 'What have I said?'

Jean shrugged. 'Paula, love, I would give anything for her to write "with love" on a birthday card instead of "best wishes". And as for her telling me she loved me, or even our Terry, she never has, and I don't think she ever will. It just isn't in her vocabulary.'

'She does though, doesn't she, love you – all of us.'

'I presume so, love. Who knows. Perhaps it's the way she was brought up; how things were in her family. How it was at the time; the depression and then the war. Perhaps survival was more important than sentiment.'

Mary *April 2018*

Mary had an adversarial mindset toward the weather. Her long life had taught her to be ready for its malign intent. As a housewife she'd noticed that it chose to rain on days when she had a big wash of bedding or towels. She'd struggle all day to dry damp bedding over the maiden, with the house like a Turkish bath, the windows steamed up and the next day the bloody weather would be dry and bright and breezy. The school holidays were the bane of her life, especially after her husband's death – he'd made himself useful and been around to amuse Jean and Terry during his annual Wakes Week's holidays. The rest of the school holidays her kiddies were either stuck in the house bored, watching the rain sluice down the windows or slutched up to glory. All the result of rotten bad weather thwarting her every step of the way. If it wasn't rain it was the wrong type of sun.

She couldn't abide hot weather – it dried the clothes to a crisp so that she had to drench the buggers to get the iron to glide over the creases. Her clothes stuck to her and if she was out for any length of time, she turned blotchy red and had a rash in every crease of her body; she went through gallons of calamine lotion. She liked spring best, but not early spring like now with showers one minute and bright beams of sunlight the next. Her husband had been unpredictable like early spring; she never knew when she had him. He'd be talkative and having a laugh one minute and then dark and broody the next. She blamed the war. Late spring was best, pleasant, warm and calm, with colourful plants and flowers, with longer days when you could sleep without sweating cobs. She'd like to die in spring, with lovely flowers like daffodils and tulips and perhaps bluebells for her coffin. But not this year, she was too busy what with the cruise and the wedding. Paula's twins were due in August. She'd plenty to live for, but it would be as well to make one or two plans, just in case.

The wedding cruise and her death had given her something to muse on. Now she needed a talk with Jean and Paula. Mary reached over the arm of her chair to retrieve her portmanteau of a handbag.

'Can I get that for you, Mary?' said Roza, appearing with her arms full of clean towels.

'Please, love. I were just thinking about washing day, all the bother of drying stuff when it were cold and damp. They shove 'em in a drier these days, don't know they're born half the time.'

'This is a great weight, Mary,' Roza said, hoisting the handbag onto Mary's knee.

'All my important stuff's in there, but it's that phone thing I want now.'

'Do you want me to find a number for you?'

'No thanks, love. I'm determined to do it myself. If you don't mind though, you could hang off though, just in case.'

Mary stared at the phone in her hand. She would manage it even if it killed her, the little bugger would not better her. She gripped the plastic adversary tight in her left hand and turned it slightly to the left. Which was the on switch? She startled when the face lit up, bingo, now what?

'Swipe up,' said Roza.

'I were going to.' With an exaggerated sweep of Mary's hand the keypad appeared. Her birthday; but how did the 8 October 1924 fit into four numbers?

'It is your birthday, Jean told me,' said Roza as she turned to leave.

'I know that, but how the bloody hell am I supposed to remember which numbers?'

'Is it not in your diary?'

More fumbling in the bag produced Mary's diary. But where was the number written?

'Try looking on the page with your birthday.'

'I've remembered.' Mary poked 0824 onto the phone and hit the little blue square that said Jean.

'It's me. I've come through on that phone thing. I've done it myself.'

'Brilliant. Is everything alright, Mum?'

'I want to talk to you and our Paula.'

'I'll be in, as usual, in about half an hour. I don't know about Paula. Do you want to give her a ring?'

Mary prodded the side switch and the screen went dead. What a palaver.

'Here, Roza love,' Mary called as Roza appeared from the next-door bedroom. 'Can you find our Paula on this thing for me? I'm blowed if I can face going through all that bother again. It were a lot easier when you walked to end of t'street and pressed button A.'

★

As luck would have it Jean, Paula and Izzy arrived at Fairhaven together.

CHAPTER NINE

Mary endured them each pecking her cheek before they settled themselves; Jean on the commode, Paula on the edge of the bed and Izzy on the floor.

'Is everything alright, Mum?'

'Course it is. Why would it not be?'

'The phone call. Are you upset about something?'

'Why would I be? You always did meet trouble half-way, Jean. If you must know, I wanted to talk to you both about summat; the cruise and that.'

Jean and Paula exchanged worried glances.

'There's no need to look like that.' Mary shook her head. 'Like I said, you always did see bother round every corner.' Mary chirruped a tuneless whistle for a second or two as she gathered her thoughts. 'If I die while we're on yon ship I don't want any fuss. Roza looked on that pad thing so I know what happens.'

'Mum!'

Mary held her hand in a stop gesture.

'Let me have my say. They have fridges, but they sometimes end up full, especially if there's a lot of old folk on board. That pad says they can bring you home but if it's all the same with you two I'd rather be cremated and left where we've landed – it 'ud be like the war years. I'd be in "a corner of a foreign field that is forever England". It's a poem.' Mary sighed, contented that she'd pulled off her rehearsed speech.

'Rupert Brooke,' said Jean.

'That's what I said.' Mary pursed her lips. 'Anyway, I'd like spring flowers. And while we're on about it, if I die here at home I'd like *Praise My Soul the King of Heaven,* we used to sing it at school, and for t'end, when they close them curtains, I want *Crazy* sung by Patsy Cline.'

'Why *Crazy?*' said Jean.

'We were all young once, you know.' Mary's eyes fixed on the top of Izzy's head. 'I remember what it were like; it's not only young-uns and them there celebrities as have feelings you know. We kept thing like that to ourselves; private like.'

Chapter Ten

Izzy's Journal

I'm fed up. What is the point of school? I know the answer, I've heard them say it enough at school and from Mum and Dad, get qualifications, go to university and get a good job.

All the stuff about jobs is a load of old tarradiddle (My best word — for now) look at Mum. Options, frigging Options. I'm taking Maths and English and perhaps Biology a year earlier. So what? I'm glad I'm clever and all that because I want to be the same as my friends but I'm mixed up because I'd like to be really good at something as well. When I feel snuggly with Mum and Dad, they tell me over and over BE YOURSELF, DO YOUR BEST and BE PROUD OF YOURSELF. How the hell am I supposed to be myself when I don't know myself who I am? It scares me when I think of Mum she didn't find out she was herself until a few months ago — It took her thirty years!!!!!!!!!!! And she still sees dangers where there aren't any. I'm not stupid. But I do think I'm turning out to be more like my dad than my mum. I get angry about things like that Mark Zukerberg, he made zillions of money but betrayed people and Jeremy Corbyn and Jewish people, and the NHS. That's one thing I want to

CHAPTER TEN

do — save the NHS so that people don't die on corridors and they get the operations they need, when they need them. And my room. Well it is my room and if it's a mess that's my choice. So back to options, and why are they called that? There are hardly any. There is no way I'm doing geography. The teacher, Mr Eccleston, is mean and if you ask me, he's pervy.

I feel a bit better now. The mixed-up feelings come and go. I know I like feeling loved by my family and Olivia and Becca. I love them, my family as well even when I think I might hate them. I want them to be there but I want to be free of them as well. It's good that we will be getting the twins, perhaps the grown-ups will relax a bit when they come. We've decided on their names Mary Elizabeth. Grandma Mary is very, very pleased. Elizabeth is after Dad's grandma to keep things even. And Max James, after nobody. Grandma Mary suggested Terrence, but dad told her she was pushing her luck.

One thing I am looking forward to is the cruise and the wedding. I've got my dress. It's gorgeous - very pale pink, with flowers sprinkled around it. It has a round neck with bows at each side. I'm not a pink person, but it is so pale it's hardly pink. Best of all the waste skims over my podgy belly. I hate my little fat body. Why can't I be perfect then boys might like me? I've been practising make-up to cover my acne — my eyes are still watering from poking myself with the mascara brush. My mum says "the odd spot does not acne make". At least I don't need braces. How do people kiss each other with braces? I don't think I could fancy anybody who had them. What if my tongue got stuck!!

Family news. Mum is getting hughmungus so she's getting her outfit at the last minute. Grandma's dress is lovely. It's pale grey and flowery with a big hat like Duchess thingy - Prince Charles wife wears.

Grandma Mary has sorted out dying. She's being cremated and left behind if she dies on the cruise. If she dies at home, we've to sing her favourite song — I'd never heard of it. Mum and Grandma think Grandma Mary has secrets, about a boy, from when she was young. Pops says Grandma Mary is enjoying tormenting them and being enigmatic. I don't understand why they just ask her if she had a boyfriend before Great-Grandad?

I need to sleep now, well after I've done my skin routine. It's really hard work getting through everything. School, parents, clothes, homework, friends, chores — I'm now in complete charge of table clearing and the dishwasher.

I've remembered something Grandma told me. When it was my third birthday I told my mum "yesterday I was a baby now I'm three." That's how I feel, today I'm one person but who will I be tomorrow?

Paula *April 2018*

Paula sat back on the settee, her eyes closed, her head cosy against a cushion, her hands rested on her abdomen. Mary and Max were tumbling and turning, jostling for position

CHAPTER TEN

in the ever decreasing space in her uterus. At twenty-one weeks she and the twins were over the halfway mark of the adventure of pregnancy. It was her weekend off and she was taking time to relax. Paula was blissfully happy and contented.

'You must be awake. I never seen such a beatific smile,' said Douglas.

Paula felt the settee sag and then the warmth of Douglas's hand over hers. She shifted her hands so that he could feel the babies through her clothes.

'Never in my life have I felt like this.' She opened her eyes. 'It's wonderful.' She stroked his face. The warmth of his kiss added to her joy. She felt utterly secure and loved.

'Yuck, get a room you two.' Izzy hovered over them. 'It's Sunday afternoon.'

'I thought you were doing your homework,' said Douglas as he fiddled with his trousers.

'You know what thought did?' Izzy tapped her temple and winked at her parents. 'Followed a muck-cart and thought it was a wedding.'

'Cheeky madam.' Douglas stood and put his arm round Izzy. 'I see you've been talking to Grandma Mary, and besides that, what do you know about getting a room?'

'Duh, Dad. I'm thirteen–' Izzy gave her father an emphatic nod– 'and a half. I do know which bits go where, you know.'

'It's only five minutes since I was changing your nappy, and now look at you, worldly-wise, little monkey that you are.'

'Whatever,' she sighed and shrugged. 'What's for dinner?'

'Meat as is never been eaten before,' said Paula repeating Izzy's earlier gesture of a temple tap and a wink. 'Lamb shanks, they're in the slow cooker.'

'Why does Grandma Mary keep going on about dying?' Izzy plonked herself next to Paula and reached to feel her brother and sister. 'I can't wait for them to come.'

'Birth and death, it's all going on here?' Douglas lifted the lid on the slow cooker and sniffed. 'Perfect' he announced. 'To answer your question, love. After the cruise and the wedding, it's the next big thing that's going to happen for her.'

'Dad!'

'Well, you should know, Izzy, at your advanced age, the older you get the more you think about death.'

'I think Izzy spends most of her time thinking about how exciting life is. Don't you, love?' Paula said, stroking Izzy's arm.

'S'pose so.' Izzy gave a desultory wave. 'Best get back to my homework.'

Douglas opened the fridge. 'I'm going to have a beer; can I get you anything, love?'

Paula shook her head and made to relax back into her doze. She was in a grove with bright sun sending slats of sunlight into the dim space. She was aware of the rasp and prickle of leaves against her legs and the uneven texture of the bark at her back as she leant against the trunk of an ancient oak tree. She saw the girl she had been, small, and curvaceous with her hair scraped back into an untidy ponytail. She could hear the voices of other girls and boys. She cocked her head and listened; there were two groups. She was simultaneously alone and with first one group and then the other, so that she was part off and apart from

CHAPTER TEN

each group. One group of kids were swigging booze from what looked like bottles of whisky and smoking while they smooched to music round a campfire. They held out their cigarettes and bottles of booze, inviting her to join them. She made a step forward, her hand stretched out to enjoy their bounty only to find she was walking toward the other group. They had a solitary bottle, but it looked more like cider than whisky, that they were eking out into plastic cups. They were mostly girls, with one or two boys all dressed in full school uniform. They turned to wave to her and the girls sitting on a tree trunk hutched up to make room for her. She glanced back at the group around the campfire. She made to move toward them, anticipating the peaty taste of the whisky and the nicotine hit of a cigarette. As she turned, her face and clothing altered. Paula had morphed into Izzy who shouted, 'No thanks, enjoy.' Izzy strode toward the girls sitting on the tree trunk. She held out her hand to accept a plastic cup.

Rousing to consciousness Paula was aware of the thud of the fridge door. She opened her eyes to see Izzy stood at the kitchen island drinking a glass of milk. Paula yawned and stretched. 'I don't know what's come over me today, I could sleep for England.'

'It's what you need,' said Douglas, appearing from behind *The Observer*. He folded the newspaper into an untidy parcel. 'Don't shoot me down in flames, love, but do you think you should think about giving up work?'

Paula shuffled toward the end of the settee and levered herself to standing. 'I might see if I can reduce my hours, but I'd like to work on as long as I can.'

'How long will you stay at home after M and M are born?' said Izzy, giving Douglas a quick glance.

'You two are up to something.' Paula reached for the kettle. She tried to look stern as she scrutinised her husband and daughter through half closed eyes. 'Spill, come on, or I'll do–'

'We love you.' Douglas stepped behind Paula as she stood at the sink filling the kettle, his arms round her abdomen. He kissed the top of her head. 'But with work, organising the cruise and the wedding and looking after us – well, we're worried about you.'

'You think I'm going to lose it again. Don't you?' She pushed back against Douglas. 'I know you're all watching and waiting. Wondering when the crash will come.'

'Paula, my love.' He reached out. 'Give me the bloody kettle and sit down.' He shoved the kettle onto its base. 'Listen to yourself, deciding what we think. Who mentioned losing it?'

Paula huffed; her heart was racing as she bustled into the pantry to retrieve potatoes and broccoli. *Breathe, hold it together, think, breathe, calm down, breathe.* She leant against the worktop, her heart rate pounding; she took deep breaths until she felt the thud of her heart quieten. Izzy appeared in the pantry doorway looking sheepish.

'Mum, we didn't want to upset you.'

Paula opened her arms. 'Come here, we won't be able to do this much longer with these two between us,' she whispered.

'I can feel them kicking. Come on, Mum. Come and sit down. I'll do the veg.'

Paula linked her arm through Izzy's. 'I'm sorry, really sorry.' She hoisted her bum onto a bar stool at the breakfast bar. 'I obviously need more practice at being the new me.'

CHAPTER TEN

Jean *May 2018*

Jean put aside the *Guardian* review supplement. She turned toward Ron who was immersed in the main newspaper. 'Would you mind if I invited the women in the family round to watch the royal wedding next Saturday?'

'Why would I mind?' He lowered the newspaper and peered over the top of his specs.

'I didn't think you would, but I wanted to check; as well as Paula and Izzy, I'll ask Mum if she wants to come for the day, and perhaps Val and Sue and her girls.'

'Douglas could come round.'

'To watch the wedding! It would offend all his sensibilities.' Jean's voice ratcheted up. 'And the air would be blue.'

'That wouldn't be anything new, but I meant to go over the edit I've done, after his revisions of your edit.'

'What do you think of it?'

'Great, if he can find an agent or a publisher. It should be a winner.'

'The operative word being IF, I'm beginning to wonder why I thought I could write.' Jean shook her head. 'What is it Vanessa Redgrave says at the start of *Call The Midwife* – "Why did I start all this?".'

'Less of the miseries, woman. Get on the phone and get your party sorted. Tell your girls I'll make a lasagne for lunch and buy in a crate of Provencal rosé and then, my love, you can buzz off into the office and construct yet another submission.'

'I really am disillusioned, fed up, pissed off, even. Why didn't I stick to a genre novel about nurses? Finding an agent who's in tune with a novel set in an industrial northern village in 1954 is like plaiting straw.'

'It's how it is, too many manuscripts chasing too few agents and publishers. Literary inflation.' Ron picked up his discarded newspaper, opened the page then peered over the top. 'What made you think about having a wedding party?'

'I want to look after Paula. Since her Quo Vadis moment, she's trying so hard to be the best daughter, mother, wife, friend and well to be honest I think she might collapse under the strain of it all, especially with her insisting on organising our wedding. And, on top of it all, the babies and work.'

'Sweetheart, don't you think you might be being a bit hard on her?'

Jean was flummoxed to find herself overcome by tears. 'Pass me a hanky.' She waved her hand toward the man-sized box of tissues sitting on a side table near Ron.

'Come here,' Ron said, pulling Jean toward him. 'What's all this about?'

Jean sniffled; gently pushing herself out of Ron's embrace, she snorted into the tissue. 'For so long I've wanted what I have now.' For a second or so the room dipped and swirled; she shook her head. 'You, us, being together, and Paula, how I've longed for her to be different; at peace with herself.' Jean was aware of herself sobbing, yet felt disconnected from the sounds she was making and the distress that swirled around her. She snuggled back into Ron's side, her head on his shoulder. He held her. Minutes passed. Her pounding heart slowed, the tears slackened to occasional escaped drops that trickled down her cheeks. 'I love you, and Paula and Izzy, and Mum of course, so much,' she whispered to his chest, 'but I am so frightened that I will be lonely again, lonely and bereft. I don't want to die on my own like Maggie Smithfield, poor girl, not found for two

CHAPTER TEN

days. And I'm a crap writer.' She glanced up at Ron.

'Now I know you're feeling better if you're harping on about your writing.' He stroked her back. 'I promise that I will do all in my power to stick around and love you and, Jean my love, you need to remember that that brave daughter of yours firmly believes that she has put the past behind her. You – we all – need to believe in her. Now go and make the phone calls and there's no lunch for you, until you've emailed at least two submissions.'

Jean made her phone calls. Paula and Izzy were delighted, Val suggested that they all wear wedding hats and nominated herself to bring a couple of puddings. Sue and Becca made an offer of contributing chocolates and nibbles. Mollie, who was currently exploring politics to the far left of Trotsky, refused, stating she would rather eat her own vomit, and anyway, she was spending the day revising for her GCSEs. After the usual pantomime with her mother's mobile phone, Jean established that her party was second choice to Fairhaven's celebration, and her mother's attendance at the family party depended on her establishing whether she could bag a good seat in front of the telly, and whether Ron would go easy on the garlic in the lasagne and if he would be serving fucker bread with it.

'It's focaccia bread, Mum,' said Jean.

'That's what I said,' replied Mary. 'It's my favourite.'

Mary *May 2018*

Inside information, from Roza, that the royal wedding day lunch would be sandwiches and biscuits, and that seats in front of the big telly in the lounge would be first come first served, had Mary reflecting on her options. She could stay in her room, on her own, and watch the festivities on her little telly and eat in solitary confinement, or she could go to Jean's and join the party. She thought carefully. If she stayed put, she might get a glass of sweet sherry with her butties, but at Jean's they'd be having that nice pink wine and a proper dinner. And she'd see Izzy and Paula. Her mind was made up. What to wear? It wouldn't have mattered if it had been herself and Jean and Ron, she would have worn her comfy beige trousers with the elasticated waist that gave her room for expansion after her dinner, but with Val and Sue going to the shindig, a bit more of an effort was called for. Val was always immaculate with her hair and nails done and make-up on. Her clothes were top class, course she came from money. Sue dressed to kill as well, even with them jeans they all wore she'd have a tailored blouse and them big fat pearls she liked and smart shoes. There was nothing for it, Mary decided, she would sacrifice one of her cruise outfits.

'I'll have that flowered skirt and blue top.' Mary nodded to the open wardrobe.

'That is a good choice,' said Roza, easing the skirt away from its neighbours in the tightly packed space.

'What do you think of her, that Meghan?' said Mary, pushing herself out of her chair and shuffling toward her wash basin. 'I'll just have a bit of a swill.'

'Let me help with your nighty.' Roza lifted the skirt of the nightdress. 'Oh you've already got your knickers on.'

'I've started wearing em in bed since that fire alarm went off, during t'night, last week. You can't be too careful.' Mary attended to her swill, patting under her arms with her flannel then giving her face a good rub. 'They'll all be dressed up to the nines at our Jean's.'

'You will look lovely as well. What do you think The Queen will be wearing?'

'She has to wear bright colours then she stands out in a crowd, that's what our Paula told me.'

'And Ms Markle, what do you think her dress will be like?'

'So long as it's better than his mam's. That poor girl were made to wear that creased up meringue of a frock. She had a rough time of it, she did. And then her dying like she did.'

'That sounds like Izzy and her parents. You are ready just in time.'

*

The telly was on when Mary arrived at Jean and Ron's with Paula, Izzy and Douglas. Mary headed for the comfy, wing back chair that Ron always insisted on giving up for her. Paula and Izzy disappeared into the kitchen to see Jean while Ron and Douglas settled on the settee, across the room from Mary, to exchange information on some noisy motor race. Mary was not pleased to be left like Piffy on a Butty, with the men, while her daughter, granddaughter and great-granddaughter were ensconced in the kitchen laughing and talking. *Out of sight, out of mind, that's me. I'd have been better off on my own in my little cell.* The doorbell heralded the simultaneous arrival of Val, Sue and Becca who went straight through to the kitchen. Mary was vexed. *I'm not wanted.* She glanced at the telly, her heart quickened, there was David Beckham and his wife. *He's a handsome lad.*

'Grandma Mary, look, I've made you a snowball.' Izzy held out a tall glass holding a pale yellow liquid with a cherry on a cocktail stick sitting across the foam at the top of the glass. 'And a macaroon, Aunty Sue brought them because I told her they were your favourites.'

'You're a love. Look, there's David Beckham, he's a nice lad, who thinks a lot about his kiddies, and he's well in with the Royals, even though they've not given him a knighthood.'

Mary sipped her drink. Pleasure oozed through her. 'By God, love, that's strong, but never mind, I'll drink it.' She smacked her lips and took another sip.

As the other women settled into their seats with drinks in hand, Ron and Douglas excused themselves.

'Are you alright, Mum?' said Jean settling herself near Mary.

'I am now,' hissed Mary, 'why did you leave me in here with only men for company?'

Mary watched Jean chew her lips. *I've spoken out of turn again. I don't think I'll go on that cruise.*

'Come on, Grandma, tell us who's arrived?' said Paula easing herself down onto the settee. 'I've been stuck upstairs phoning the cruise company. What've I missed?'

Mary readjusted her sulk to exclude Paula and Izzy and include Victoria Beckham. 'She looks as though she followed a muck cart and thought it were a wedding. I thought she were supposed to know summat about clothes.'

All eyes turned to the television, the personalities arriving, their clothes and the women's capacity to walk uphill on vertiginous heels.

'She's on her way.' Mary sat forward and waved her hands at the telly. 'In that car.'

The room quietened as commentators speculated on the dress and hairstyle of the bride before switching back

CHAPTER TEN

to consider the outfits of the congregation who were now taking their places in St George's Chapel.

'You see, Queen'll be wearing a proper hat, like that there Mrs Major, not one as looks as though it's a flying saucer, or a television aerial or one as has dead birds nestin' on it.' She picked up her glass. 'Izzy, is there any more of this before that Meghan arrives at church?'

'Do you like hats, Grandma Mary?'

'In their place. Weddings and funerals and that. I'm not keen on them fascinating things.'

Ron appeared with a platter of assorted canapes and a pile of napkins. 'I thought these would put you on until after the service.'

Mary screwed up her nose as she inspected the morsels of food. 'Is this all we're having for our dinner?' She reached for a miniature spear of asparagus wrapped in prosciutto ham. It was something she recognised from Jean's previous posh parties.

'We'll eat later, after the service; have another couple, Mary,' said Ron.

'My stomach'll think my throat's been cut,' she muttered, reaching out for a piece of salmon on a stick and a piece of white cheese wrapped in a leaf.

The television showed The Queen and Prince Phillip arrive and then switched to the progress of the bride, then back to a sweep of the congregation.

'I like our Queen, but she doesn't half an' look miserable, and he looks like death warmed up. Course I expect they'll be wanting their dinner as well. Which reminds me, I need the lav.'

'Mum, it's nearly time?'

'I'll help you, Grandma Mary,' said Izzy, squirming to her feet, 'come on lean on me, we'll soon be there and back.'

By the time Mary had sorted herself out in the toilet, wiped round the seat, just in case she'd dripped, and rinsed her hands and hobbled back with Izzy, the bride was ready to walk herself down the aisle.

'Them kiddies look like a rag, tag and bobtail outfit, straggling behind her,' said Mary, shuffling her bottom toward the back of the chair.

'I think she's so brave, walking on her own,' said Sue with a catch in her voice.

'Well, she's used to making an entrance,' said Mary, lifting her glass to find there was nothing but a smidge of froth lurking at the bottom. 'Do you think it'll last, or go the way of all them others?'

'Mum, let's listen to the service.'

Mary huffed and examined the contents of her glass. *That's you told, Mary.* She pressed her lips tight shut and closed her eyes. She registered a choir singing and then a hymn being sung and then a sticky feeling on her leg. She opened her eyes; her glass lay on its side in the well of her skirt, the Snowball foam had trickled through the fabric. She licked her fingers and dabbed at the gunge with half an eye on the telly. She watched nonplussed as the vicar, in the pulpit, waved his arms about, nearly shouting. *What's up with him?*

'What religion is he?' she said.

'Episcopalian,' said Sue.

'I thought he must be something foreign, going on like that.'

'It's the American equivalent of C of E,' said Jean.

'That's what I said.'

CHAPTER TEN

Mary shook her head. 'I don't know what the Queen Mother would have said. I'll tell you now she wouldn't hold with Americans joining our Royal Family. There's no good comes of mixing with folk as don't understand our ways.'

'What makes you say that, Mary?' said Sue.

'That Wallis woman were a low unto herself and mark my words–' Mary flicked her hand towards the television– 'she'll be no different.'

'Where does that leave Prince Phillip,' said Douglas.

Mary bristled. 'He defended our country like a good un during t'war. And weren't his Queen Victoria his grandma? He'll do for me despite his philandering ways.'

'And what did the Queen Mother say about him putting it about?' Douglas looked at Mary over the rim of his glasses.

'That poor woman had a life of trial and tribulation, just like me.' Mary indulged in a melancholy smile. 'But I'll say this for the Queen, she knew how to give her mam a right good send off when she died.'

Chapter Eleven

Izzy's Journal

I love weddings. I love my family and I love Adir. I don't know his surname, so I've been practising calling myself Mrs Adir. He's our cabin steward and he comes from Kerala in India.

It was the wedding yesterday and we're all having a quiet day today. Only me and Dad were at breakfast. Mum's fingers and legs are swollen so she's resting. I saw Adir in the corridor, he gave me a wave. I felt fluttery and sick at the same time. It was hard work making myself eat the pancakes and maple syrup. Me and Dad are in the library now. He's doing the crossword and sudoku.

The wedding

Mum is brilliant at organising. It was better than the royal wedding, nothing went wrong, it was perfect. Journal, please notice I'm not swearing, I do not need to swear. I am happy, sublimely happy.

Grandma, me and Mum got ready together. We had our makeup and hair done in our cabin with mocktails. I have never felt so cool in all my life. I got ready, in my dress

CHAPTER ELEVEN

first, then Grandma in her gorgeous swirly, netty dress, it is pale grey and white with a bit of black with a humongous hat. Mum was last, poor Mum she did her best with turquoise baggy drawstring trousers and a blue overdress and a big silver necklace and silver earrings. Mum and Grandma had to have their eye make-up touched up with crying. Adir and all the other stewards and maids on our corridor were lined up outside when Charlie knocked on the door to escort her to the wedding room. They all clapped as we walked to the lift. Adir touched my arm. When we got to the wedding room Mum slipped into her seat next to Grandma Mary. Then the music changed to Grandma's favourite part of Rhapsody in Blue and Ron turned and looked at Grandma, he was crying. There have been lots of tears, even Grandma Mary, although she said she had "a stinking cold coming on". I had to blink and sniffle because I didn't have a hanky. Dad slipped me his while Ron was folding the veil on Grandma's hat back. Grandma Mary dropped her handbag and swore then apologised just as the Captain was starting the service. When Grandma and Ron walked up the little aisle Grandma Mary walked with Charlie. Tears were rolling down her lovely old face. Charlie wiped her eyes and kissed her on the cheek. It was really, really, lovely. I didn't notice anybody cry like we did, at the royal wedding. Perhaps that's why they have long boring services with classical music and mad vicars so that people can gather themselves. The Queen and Prince Phillip looked bored stiff, not like Grandma Mary.

The wedding breakfast was scrumptious, although Grandma Mary said the salmon tasted off, we think she didn't appreciate the caviar. Best of all Adir was serving. I felt hot and sticky. Charlie said nice things about how Grandma and Pops made him feel part of the family and then Dad rambled on about how special Grandma was and how Pops had taken us all on board. Pops just said he loved Grandma, and all of us. Grandma Mary said Terry's speech was the best!!!!!!!!

What do I do about Adir? I'm not stupid I know it's a crush. But when and how do girls stop crushing? I think I'm going to be a kid forever, some girls in my class have real boyfriends and one girl says her mum has taken her to the doctors for the pill!!!! Then there are the others who still haven't started their periods. I suppose I'm somewhere in the middle. My shape is changing. I've not got a floppy belly anymore but I'm not sure what I'm trying to say other than I'd like to be more mature, but not one of those girls who boys like because they let them do stuff. I think about kissing and touching a lot. I've practised with making a mouth by pressing my finger and thumb together and sticking my tongue in the space, what a waste of time. When I swapped spit with Matt it was gross. I didn't feel anything other than yuk. Perhaps I'm frigid. I looked it up on the internet. I think I may be "lacking in sexual arousal." I like the idea of having someone special and holding hands and that but I'm not sure I want all that touching like Becca had. I'm fourteen in November. I think I'm going to be an old maid. The website told a woman of twenty-two who felt like I do that her mind wasn't fully turned on to sex yet. Perhaps that's me??????

Anyway, back home tomorrow, after the most fantastic time of my life. I wonder if Adir might be on the corridor near our cabin? I'll just go and check on Mum.

CHAPTER ELEVEN

Paula *July 2018*

The task Paula had set herself on concentrating on her breathing was futile. The sounds of the ward – voices, telephones ringing, curtains swishing, and trolleys squeaking – mingled with her jangled thoughts. She was comforted by her shifting abdomen. At least one of her babies was alive. She gave an answering rub and a tentative prob. She was thirty-five weeks pregnant and waiting for an elective caesarean section. The itching had started in earnest after the cruise. The mild irritation she felt on the ship she'd blamed on a new brand of suntan lotion. When the itching became exacerbated Douglas had diagnosed intrahepatic cholestasis of pregnancy, contacted her obstetrician, who was an ex-colleague, and now here she was gowned, socked and waiting to be taken to theatre. She couldn't concentrate on reading. She was tortured by thoughts of a dead baby despite the contortions of her abdomen. Her attempts to practise mindfulness defeated her. She glanced at the clock, one-twenty, she was due in theatre at two. Thank God, Douglas and Izzy would arrive any minute to accompany her as far as theatre doors and then wait for her to deliver Mary and Max. Paula kept her eyes on the ward clock willing each minute to hurry up. Douglas and Izzy's arrival coincided with the large hand shifting to six. Douglas looked ashen, strung out and his flies were undone. In contrast Izzy was fizzing. Her eyes were everywhere, tracking the midwives and health care assistants as they went from bed to bed carrying out routine observations, checking monitors, and straightening bed covers while taking the time to talk to the women waiting to deliver their babies. As Douglas turned to admire the view out of the window and fiddle with his flies, Paula felt herself relax. They were together, a family of three for the last time. In a matter of minutes, she would be off to theatre and then three would be five. She reached for Douglas's hand and kissed it, then reached out her other hand for Izzy.

'Don't cry, Mum,' Izzy said. 'I feel sick, I'm so excited.'

'Not long now,' said a midwife appearing behind Izzy, closely followed by a porter with a wheelchair. 'You'll soon be able to see your brother and sister.'

Paula shuffled off her bed and into the waiting wheelchair. The midwife helping her gave her shoulder a squeeze and passed her notes to Douglas.

'I could have walked.'

'Rest while you can, the twins will soon be running you ragged,' said the midwife.

Paula forced a smile, and as she gave a cursory wave to the other women in her bed bay the attendant porter released the brake on the chair, and she was on her way to theatre. Paula, Douglas and Izzy were met at the theatre doors by her consultant, the anaesthetist, a paediatrician and two specialist SCBU midwives. Paula reached for Douglas's hand.

'Why so many of you?' Her voice trembled.

'It's normal practice for an older mother with twins,' said Douglas, giving her hand a tight squeeze.

'And a geriatric father.' The obstetrician smiled at Douglas. 'Still got what it takes, Dougie.'

'Cheeky sod,' said Douglas. 'Although, we can't thank you enough for all you've done for us.'

'Got to look after our own.' He turned to Izzy. 'Now, young lady, what are we calling these two little ones?'

'Mary and Max,' Izzy spluttered and licked her lips.

CHAPTER ELEVEN

'Well, Paula, let's put this team to work and get you in theatre and then we can get Mary and Max delivered and in the arms of their dad and sister.'

In theatre Paula shuffled onto the lowered theatre table. She caught sight of the clock: two-twenty. She watched the anaesthetist insert a canula in her arm and let herself relax into the welcoming arms of the drug as it took her towards oblivion.

★

Paula was aware that her lips were dry. She swallowed. Her arm felt stiff, the bed was slippery under her bottom. *Hospital bed.*

'Dad, look – Mum's awake.'

'Douglas? Izzy?'

'Hello, love.' Douglas's face loomed above her. 'Well done, my darling.'

'The babies?'

'Here's Mary.' Izzy appeared next to Douglas cradling a bundle.

'Max?' Paula croaked. 'Where's Max?'

'He's having a rest in SCBU,' Douglas said.

'SCBU? Why SCBU?' Paula's hands shook as she reached out toward Izzy and the bundle that was Mary.

'He's just a bit small: 4lb 8oz but he's going to be fine. You can see him soon.'

'Help me sit up, Douglas, then Izzy can sit on the bed next to me and show me Mary.'

'She's a little fatty, 5lb 10oz,' said Izzy, holding her sister out to Paula.

Izzy first, Paula told herself. 'Give Mary to Dad, love and then you can give me a cuddle.' The smile on Izzy's face was a glorious reward for Paula.

Paula and Mary stayed on the post-natal ward while Max was in SCBU for five days to establish feeding and have phototherapy for jaundice. The family of five arrived home to a mountain of greetings cards, gifts and balloons.

Jean   *August 2018*

Summer was flashing past. The blistering heat of early July had given way to days of rain and grey skies. Jean was thankful for the respite of cooler nights and more settled sleep. In previous hot summers she'd enjoyed the luxury of spreading out in her double bed; now she was wrapped in the arms of a sweaty Ron, albeit in a king size bed. When sleep eluded her, she chastised herself for longing for a snore-free, sticky-less night. When a bout of IBS threatened, she was conscious of the need to trudge to the ensuite. Risking a dainty fart had not yet reached the marital bed.

Although the hustle and bustle of the cruise and wedding had been extra special and, as Izzy would say awesome, the week on the ship seemed to have happened in another time frame. Her memories had a delicate, ethereal quality like a photograph slightly out of focus. The birth of the twins and the ensuing grandma responsibilities, she had assumed so soon after the wedding, left Jean with a dazed, yet exhilarating sensation that she had never been as happy or as busy. The glow and happiness that had surrounded the wedding party had continued with the addition of Max and Mary to the family.

CHAPTER ELEVEN

Ron was a revelation. He'd been jittery at the thought of holding the tiny babies, his hands shaking as he held them out to receive a sleeping child. Five weeks later, he changed nappies and bottle fed without a qualm, usually under the supervision of Izzy who was now an expert in everything to do with her brother and sister.

As she set the table for the evening meal at Paul and Douglas's house, Jean watched Izzy sort Max and Mary's laundry that she'd retrieved from the utility room and piled on the settee in the family room.

'Are you okay, Grandma?' Izzy smiled at Jean as she placed a blue garment on one pile and reached for a pink babygro. 'They have to share the other colours,' she said, nodding to a third pile of clothing.

'I'm fine, love, if a bit perplexed as to when you changed from a child into the stunning young woman I see before me.'

'You see me every day.' Izzy split the coloured pile of clothing that threatened to topple over. 'I can't have changed all that much.'

'I'll swear you've changed shape overnight.' Jean reached for a tea towel to give a fork a polish, she cocked her head to one side and narrowed her eyes. 'You've lost your puppy fat, and emerged as a beautiful butterfly. You even walk differently.'

Jean watched Izzy dip her head and give a shy smile. 'I feel a bit different,' she whispered.

Dear God, Boys! Jean gulped. 'How's that, love?'

'I've decided what I'm going to do, when I'm older.'

Phew. 'That's good.' Jean nodded in encouragement.

'I'm going to be a nurse, I've not decided what sort yet.' Izzy settled the piles of folded garments into a large wicker basket. 'Dad suggested I read about Louisa M Alcott as a nurse and do you remember I borrowed that book of yours *The Language of Kindness*...

'What are you two up to?' said Douglas appearing in the doorway, cradling an infant.

'Grandma thinks I've grown up overnight.'

'That's remarkable, I was only thinking the same thing myself the other day. You are a treasure, a wonderful young woman.'

'I'm just telling Grandma that I've decided what I want to do – for a career.'

Jean inwardly gritted her teeth in preparation for Douglas's reaction. She stood still – waiting.

'I'm going to be a nurse.'

'A NURSE! I take back everything I said.' Douglas grinned, peering over the top of his specs at Jean. 'That's fine with me, love. So long as you're happy.'

Jean shook her head, amazed.

'Tell me one thing though, and I know Grandma is dying to know–,' he peered at Jean– 'why not medicine?'

'Don't look at me like that, Douglas. It's not my idea,' said Jean.

'No, Dad, it isn't. It was you who told me to read more about Louisa May Alcott and I did, then I read that book of Grandma's about the *Language of Kindness*. I've decided I want to do what nurses do, be more intimately involved with patients, not what doctors do.'

'Which is?' said Douglas.

'They are more distant, deciding what the disease is and what the medicines should be. It's nurses that do the real caring, helping the patient get better, or have a peaceful death.'

CHAPTER ELEVEN

'I'm impressed, young nurse Quayle, you've done your homework, I'll give you that.' At the sound of an infant's cry Douglas handed his bundle to Izzy. 'Feeding time for my other daughter.'

Jean wiped away a tear with the tea cloth. Douglas's response to Izzy added to the feeling of life being a kaleidoscope of shifting colours and hues, although the patterns changed, they were still vibrant like the glory of sun casting multi-coloured shadows through stained glass.

I've been sleep walking for so long. Getting through the days. How do I hold on to this new life? Why do I always expect the worst?

'Grandma, what are you looking at?' Jean roused herself, conscious of Izzy standing at her side.

Jean put her arm round Izzy's shoulder and pulled her toward her. 'Don't waste your life, Izzy.'

'Are you thinking about Mum?'

Jean was nonplussed. Tired and overcome with her new-found tranquillity and peace, her sense of joy churned against her old feelings of remorse, dejection and sense of failure that as a mother she'd let Paula down. 'No, love, your Mum is better now. We all are.'

'You are the best Grandma in the world.' Izzy kissed Jean's cheek.

'Because of you, my darling.'

Perhaps that's it, thought Jean. It's the other person, in any relationship, that helps make us who we are. It wasn't just me. It was Paula as well. But it was mostly me. I know that now.

Mary *September 2018*

The first Sunday in September heralded Autumn. Mary felt a nip in the air as she manoeuvred her walking frame toward the front door of Paula and Douglas's home. She glanced at the trees that surrounded the house; there was a definite golden tinge. A feeling of intense joy at the sight of the tress, the crisp, earthy smell and the feel of the nip in the air. She felt at one with the world, suffused with a second or two of intense joy, followed by a fleeting sense of yearning for her life to last a while longer. She hesitated and glanced around, *bittersweet that's how I feel. There were a show called that. I saw it in Manchester.*

'Come on, Grandma.' Izzy was striding through the porch door holding a drink. 'See, I've made you a snowball.'

Mary peered at Izzy then stopped, taking in the young woman's shapely figure, her eyes; they were bigger, rounder. It was a week, give or take a day or two, since she'd last seen Izzy and yet in that short time all signs of her being a kiddie had disappeared. *How the bloody hell's that happened. She favours a Fox now, wi them eyes.* 'Hang on, I don't want to clutter or your Grandma'll be on at me. She nodded toward the drink. 'Put it in't front room, love, where I usually sit.'

Established in her usual chair, with her snowball in her hand, Mary scrutinised the assembled party or at least those who kept still for more than ten seconds. She treasured her time with her family but their inability to settle in one place made her head spin.

'How's the snowball, Mary?' said Douglas, sticking his head round the door of the sitting room. 'You haven't seen Izzy, have you?' He disappeared before she could answer. Mary was left open mouthed, her answer aborted.

CHAPTER ELEVEN

Izzy appeared with a turquoise bundle under each arm. 'Have you seen Dad? He wants us to have our photograph taken with you.'

'Camera.' Douglas bounced into the room holding up a complicated looking camera. 'How shall we do this?'

The settee flashed into Mary's head.

'The settee.' Douglas advanced toward Mary, relieved her of her snowball and offered his arm. 'Steady as you go, Mary.'

'Douglas!' Jean stood in the doorway, 'Mum can manage on her own, well with her frame she can.'

It's like Casey's bloody court in here. 'I'm here, you know, there's no need for talking about me as though I were a parcel. Let me get sat down and then give me them babbies.' Mary huffed. 'I haven't seen 'em for over a week.' Keeping a grip on Douglas's arm Mary gingerly lowered herself onto the settee. She usually avoided any contact with it. It looked comfy and firm, but Mary didn't trust the bugger. She waited for its whoosh sound and the ensuing feeling of sitting on a meringue as she was swallowed up in its seat cushion. Leaning back was out of the question. She had once chanced it and ended up feeling as though she was being drowned in a feather bed with her little legs straight out in front, her frock rucked up and her knickers on show.

'Dad, pile the cushions behind Grandma Mary then she can rest back.'

Mary leant forward anticipating the piling up of cushions. *They've more money than sense buying summat as is as useless as this. Fur coat and no knickers, if you ask me.*

'It's no wonder you live in that back kitchen,' said Mary, wriggling her bottom against the mountain of cushions.

'Family room, Mary. And by the way I agree with you.' Douglas winked at Mary. 'Give me substance over style any day. 'Izzy give Grandma Mary a child and you sit next to her with whoever it is you're left with.'

Mary held up her arms to receive the infant. She swallowed, her mouth was dry, she felt a slight tremor in her arms.

'Are you alright, Grandma Mary?' Izzy said as she dipped down to extend her arm and deliver her sibling. 'You're trembling.'

'I'm fine, love. Let's have a look at this lovely babbie.' Mary peered at the child. 'Which one is it?'

'Mary – I've colour coded her in a pink Babygro. Although you can tell without undressing them, she's bigger and has more hair,' said Douglas.

'And she looks less like a gremlin,' said Paula, bending to kiss Mary. 'I'm sorry I was asleep when you arrived, Grandma.'

Mary shook her head. It was true the babies weren't the bonniest that Mary had ever seen but she'd kept her thoughts to herself not wanting Jean to have one of her faces on. Trust Paula to spit out the truth. Still, they were her flesh and blood and she needed to talk to Jean about money. Izzy hadn't been a bonnie baby and look at her now – like a picture.

'Come on, Mary, Izzy, smile for the camera.' Douglas fiddled with the camera.

Mary forced a smile. She hated having her photograph taken. 'Where's our Jean?'

Her money and Jean's assumed control of it rattled Mary. She'd not given permission for one of them enduring powerful things and it was her money to do with as she

CHAPTER ELEVEN

pleased. Jean meant well, but she overstepped the mark with her organising and planning. She wasn't the only one who could make a good job of sorting stuff out; look at Paula and the wedding. She'd done all that and been expecting as well.

Mary decided to change her will.

Chapter Twelve

Izzy's Journal

I've had an awesome summer. I feel grown up, adult. Everybody says I've changed. They mean outside. I'm still short, but I don't mind that. After all Grandma and Mum are tidgey. I have a proper bust now. Grandma took me for a bra fitting. It's one of her things - wearing a WELL-FITTING BRA, that and LOOKING AFTER YOUR SKIN. I love my family.

What I meant to say was that I feel different, inside. Grandma talks to me like a grown up. She went to a fund-raising do with Aunty Val and some of their old nursing friends, something to do with wildlife. It was a ladies evening. Grandma thought she'd be sipping sherry with the lady mayoress and only noticed just before she went that the electronic ticket mentioned topless waiters — men not ladies and a male stripper. She tried to get out of going but Aunty Val told her not to be a prude. Grandma couldn't speak the next day from shouting over the music and laughing. She told me that if I go to see a stripper I should avoid one with red hair, and a white puny body. They saw EVERYTHING.

CHAPTER TWELVE

School on Wednesday, year 9. I will really, really, miss Mary and Max. Because of them, and the reading I've done and the talks I've had with Dad and Grandma I have decided what I want to do. Grandma thought Dad would go off on one when I told him I wanted to be a nurse but after a bit of a grump he's been awesome and said so long as I go to a top university, he's okay about it. I wonder if he's so worn out with lack of sleep he'll agree to anything. He's coping very well considering he's old enough to be the twins grandad, if not their great grandad. Max and Mary can go five or sometimes, well once, six hours at night.

I've tested myself and waited with some brilliant news. Please note I have not used any swear words. Although my heart is beating really fast as I write this. A family have moved in next door but one AND they have a son - Joel, who's my age and a daughter Ana, who's two years older. Well, somehow Pops knows the Mum and Dad. Ana is staying at her old school to finish her GCSEs but Joel is swapping to Parklands. He's gorgeous, and I'm going to walk to school with him — to show him the way. School is five minutes round the corner!!!!! Olivia who is crushing on him is fizzing. She's gone back to swearing at the thought of me being on my own with him. She offered to call for me and I told her to bugger off. - my only swearing lapse all summer!! I have a mega, awesome crush and go funny at the thought of walking next to him. I'm going to wear one of my new bras and I'm practising how far to roll over my skirt, so it looks awesome with my long black socks. Thank God I won't be on a period, so I shouldn't have any spots. Just thinking about him has given me a headache. I might need a dose of Calpol. Should I chance some mascara?

I'm not looking forward to seeing Becca. I've not seen her much over the holiday with being busy with Mary and Max and she's been at her grandparents. I get a knotty feeling because I feel responsible for her.

Paula *September 2018*

As she swung her legs out of bed Paula was sensitive to the bulge of her abdomen; the way it filled the space between her splayed thighs and dangling boobs. She rubbed her wobbly, crumpled belly. It was encased in a pair of Douglas's boxer shorts and one of his long-forgotten tee shirts. Think positive she told herself. *At least I can sleep on my stomach and walk without having to hold up my bump.* She hauled herself off the bed and shuffled to face the cheval mirror, closed her eyes for a second and dared herself to stand naked and face her reflection. She opened one eye as she pushed down the boxers, closed her eyes again and lifted off the tee shirt. *Go for it.* She opened her eyes. *Bloody hell.* It was seven weeks since the twins' birth and the day of her post-natal examination. In the days following delivery she'd accepted her distended shape. The joy of being able to get in and out of the bath on her own and to feel the hot water, covered in bubbles, slosh between her spread legs was almost orgasmic. Fleeting glances of her belly had brought vague pictures of sheets of tripe that, as a child, she saw on display in butchers' shop windows. Today was the day of reckoning. Paula perused her body *diastasis recti?* She

CHAPTER TWELVE

palpated her abdomen, *no just good old-fashioned flab.*

'Mum.' Izzy appeared, reflected in the mirror dressed in her school uniform and holding a steaming mug, her head on one side as she observed her mother. 'What are you doing?'

Paula pulled up the boxers and reached for the tee shirt she'd thrown on the end of the bed. 'I'm facing facts, my love.' She took the mug that Izzy held out to her. 'What will I do without you?'

Paula looked sideward at her daughter. She looked and then looked again. 'Is that a touch of mascara I see before me?' She smiled. 'You look lovely, best not let your dad know you're wearing make-up to school though.'

Izzy stepped back, surprised.

'Come here, my beautiful girl.' Paula held out her arms. 'You are the best, the very best, thank you–' Paula sniffed back tears– 'for being you.'

The doorbell rang. Izzy flustered, turned toward the door. 'That'll be Joel.' She turned back and kissed Paula. 'Bye, Mum.'

Paula heard Douglas say goodbye to Izzy, the front door clicked, followed by a heavy tread on the stairs.

'Did you know about that; her walking to school with that boy?' Douglas stood arms akimbo in the doorway. 'I didn't like the way he looked at her, or she at him for that matter.'

Paula shuffled to Douglas, put her arms round his waist and nestled her head on his chest. 'Don't grump, they're only walking to school and she's worked hard this summer with the twins.'

'Twins, there'll be more on the fucking way, if we don't watch out. Have you had a word?'

'Douglas, calm down.' Paula stood back, her hands resting on Douglas's arms. 'After the row; she knows all there is to know.'

'Well, we both buggered up our early lives, me with Amy and you…' Douglas nodded vigorously '…with everything you put yourself through. I just don't want Izzy to be like us.'

'She won't.' Paula pulled on her dressing gown, alert to the sound of one baby crying, followed shortly by the answering call of another infant. 'They won't. Come on, let's feed the twins and then I'm off for my post-natal and then it's back to Slimming World.'

'Paula?' Douglas sat on the end of the bed and pulled Paula toward him. 'I love you so very much. You, and our beautiful children.'

★

Paula was seeing her consultant obstetrician in his private rooms, a perk of being the wife of Professor Douglas Quayle.

'Paula. Do come in,' he said from his consulting room door.

Paula took a deep breath and with a mighty effort attempted to draw in her abdomen. Even though the pendulous flesh of her abdomen was supported by huge, reinforced knickers, Paula felt a freak. She was all too aware of the scrutiny of the professional, urbane man, who was dressed like Prince Charles on a meet the people tour.

'You're looking well,' he said, standing aside to let Paula pass into his domain. 'Is Douglas well?'

'Yes, he's with the twins.'

'I do admire him, at his age. We were at medical school together you know.'

CHAPTER TWELVE

Stuck up twat, he means poor Douglas, stuck with a frump like you.

'Toddle behind the screen. Sister here–' he indicated a short, stunning looking girl, beautifully made up with her hair in some complicated pleat– 'will help you get ready for the examination.'

Paula contorted her face into the grimace of a smile. The Sister's smile lit up her face. Paula relaxed a smidgen. 'I'm sorry about the knickers,' she whispered, as she peeled off her tent like top and eased herself out of the elastic bondage encircling her abdomen.

'Par for the course with twins; use the step.' She nodded toward a step poking from beneath the couch. 'Us little 'uns have to stick together. Ready?' she asked as Paula settled back on the narrow couch.

Watching the obstetrician don his gloves and hold out his fingers for a squirt of jelly, Paula prepared herself for the inevitable.

Breathe, in out, in – ouch, bloody hell that hurt.

'Everything appears to be in good working order.' He pushed up Paula's gown to scrutinise her abdomen. 'No diastasis, but then I understand you are a physiotherapist, well done, my dear.' He peeled off the gloves. 'I'll see you when you are dressed.'

As the Sister absented herself, Paula rolled up the knickers and stuck them in her roomy handbag. She dragged on her tights, and lugged on her top, ran her hand through her hair, slipped on her shoes and presented herself on the other side of the screen.

'That was quick,' said the consultant.

If only you knew. As Paula eased herself onto a chair at the side of a mahogany desk, she was conscious of the splodge of KY Jelly against the seam of the crouch of her tights.

Jean *September 2018*

A dull ache in her neck was the first sensation Jean was aware of, then a slight draught over her legs. Without opening her eyes, she was aware it was morning: bird song and the swish of car wheels. Where was she? Through bleary eyes the pattern of abstract flowers on the window blind told her she was in the spare room designated as Izzy's bedroom. She adjusted the quilt to cover her legs, manipulated the pillows and snuggled down into the warmth of the bed. The pattern of hands on her watch told her it was ten past seven. Perhaps she could manage another hour? The next she knew was the notion of someone by her bed. She opened her eyes. Ron with a mug of tea.

'Bad night, love,' he said, proffering the mug.

'I couldn't get off.' She pushed herself to a sitting position and took the tea. 'Didn't want to disturb you.'

'Was I snoring?'

'A bit. I'm sorry, love, it's not just the snoring.'

Ron settled himself on the end of the bed. 'It's getting to be a problem. Isn't it?'

It was, but Jean was reluctant to admit it. 'I'm fine, so long as I wear my ear plugs and get off to sleep before you come to bed.' She gave a weak smile. She knew it was a daft notion, but she wanted them to hang on to the post wedding glow for ever, well for as long as possible. But how could they do that when she couldn't stand the sound of snoring? It had been fine when they spent the odd night together – she could

CHAPTER TWELVE

make up for the lost sleep with naps and sound nights of sleep when she was on her own. The bed she kept made up for Izzy had been a God send from the snorts and whistles of Ron's snoring. Most mornings she managed to creep back into the matrimonial bed before Ron woke.

'Shove up,' said Ron, 'let's have a cuddle.'

★

Showered, dressed and breakfasted, Jean opened her computer and braced herself for a morning's writing. She needed to get her head into the life of a working-class, British girl in the textile mills of post WW1 North America. She was writing a novel based on her maternal grandma's experiences. Her head refused to make the transatlantic journey, it insisted in staying in twenty-first century Chorley. Ron had announced he was making an appointment to see their GP. Not only was he concerned about his snoring – apparently, it had been on the long list of irredeemable sins his previous wife had identified as evidence of his unsuitability as a husband – but he had trouble with peeing. Based on evidence, from Val, about her husband's dormant prostate cancer, Jean was letting her imagination run away with her. She was preparing herself to nurse her husband, of less than four months, through terminal cancer of the prostate before becoming a grieving widow. Tears pooled, as she imagined herself bereft and alone.

'What's up, love?' Ron cluttered into their joint study carrying an armful of magazines. 'Are you alright?'

Jean whisked the tears away. 'Thinking about my grandma.' She waved her hands in dismissal. 'Just being daft.'

'I've got a cancellation at the surgery for ten-thirty. So, I'll be back to go to the solicitors with you and Mary.'

Jean swivelled her chair and stood up to make a clumsy attempt to put her arms round Ron and his pile of magazines. Ron overbalanced and, in his attempt to right himself, dropped the magazines, causing them to skitter across to the floor where the glossy covers slid over each other to form a multicoloured pathway across the study floor.

'I've spent ages putting that lot in date order,' he said. 'It crossed my mind, when I was doing it, that it was a waste of time and effort.'

'Leave them, love, we need to get off to the doctor's,' said Jean.

'I'm okay on my own, you get on with your writing. I won't be long.'

A fleeting sense of being affronted, not wanted, dismissed was supplanted by a rapid realisation that it was she who had worked herself into a lather and that Ron was putting himself out for her sake. As a single man, snoring had not been an issue for him; it still wasn't – he was putting himself out for her sake. And what was that statistic about enlarged prostates? She couldn't recall her redundant knowledge but in the fleeting time she thought about it, realised she was being absurd and over dramatic. *Meeting trouble halfway, my mother would say.*

'Let's take my mum for tea and cake after the solicitors,' Jean said as she bent to pick up the magazines.

★

Jean supported Mary's weight as her mother shifted her balance from one leg to another to mount the well-worn

CHAPTER TWELVE

stone steps leading to the popular café in Heapey.

'I thought they were supposed to have ramps and stuff.' Mary hesitated. 'For cripples.'

'Disabled people,' said Jean.

'Cripples? Disabled? Doesn't it all mean t'same thing?'

'I suppose it does, words change.' Jean held the front door while Mary shuffled into the café.

'Where are we sitting?' Mary glanced round. 'Not up them steps, I hope?'

Jean gave a weak smile to a man and a woman draining their cups. They took the hint and signalled for their bill. 'I've been there, love,' the woman whispered as she edged out of her seat.'

'What did she say?' Mary's voice boomed out.

'She said you'll be comfortable there,' said Jean, smiling with relief as Ron pushed open the café door.

'You parked alright?' Mary shuffled her bottom toward the back of the chair. 'Me and our Jean were just talking about words.' She picked up the menu. 'What do we call darky boys, these days?' She looked over the top of her glasses at Jean. 'Before you say anything, I know that's wrong, but so's black.'

Jean saw the twinkle in Ron's eyes and quickly looked away.

'It's all that Jeremy Corbett's fault. He's ruined the Labour Party and he doesn't like Jews.' Mary took a breath. 'I'll have tea and a scone – with cream. Did I ever tell you your dad had a friend who were one.'

'A Jewish person?' said Jean.

'Yes.'

Jean reached for her handkerchief and spluttered into it. 'Mum, you are worth your weight in gold,' she said, reaching to squeeze her mother's hand.

'You're not so bad yourself, love.' Mary gave Jean a beatific smile. 'You need to take two Panadol if you've a cold coming on. I don't want you ill because you've been running about after me.'

Jean felt loved and secure.

Mary *September 2018*

Mary switched on her telly. *Homes under the Hammer*. She'd expected Gloria, that friend of Cliff Richards, and that posh Angela woman, the one who did the high kicks with Morecambe and Wise and the other one who once read the news. While *Homes under the Hammer* concentrated on the auction of a seedy looking two-up two-down, in somewhere she'd never heard of, Mary reflected on telly programmes. Dixon of Dock Green, she'd liked that and The Sweeney but not Morse. He were too stiff, full of himself with his posh car and serious music. And why didn't he have a proper name? Morecambe and Wise were a case, they had good turns on with them and they were funny without being crude, although they always made daft comments about lovely Val Doonican. Steptoe needed a good wash and she could never understand why Harry Secombe didn't stick to singing instead of messing about with them Goons. Hey up, somebody had bought the house. This was the part that Mary liked best when they talked about what they were going to do and how much they were going to spend doing it up. Mary had never believed on spending much on her house, above what was necessary, not like Jean throwing good money after bad.

CHAPTER TWELVE

'Hello, Roza love. What's up?' Mary was pleased to be distracted by the unexpected appearance of her favourite carer who always made time for a chat. Mid-morning was a busy time in the Fairhaven, with baths, bed making and other palaver. Once she was settled in front of her morning telly it was unusual to see any staff again until nearer dinner time.

'I need to draw curtains.' Roza shimmied behind Mary's chair making for the window. 'For a minute or two.'

With a quick flick of her head, Mary glimpsed a black van outside.

'Who's gone this time?'

Roza pulled the curtains together. 'Agnes.' She gave a sad smile.

'Agnes! She can't have. It's her birthday tomorrow and she'd ordered a lemon drizzle cake. Bloody hell, I were looking forward to that, I can feel my mouth watering just thinking about it.'

'Mary!'

'I'm sorry, love.' Mary pursed her lips and shrugged her shoulders in a vain attempt to look crestfallen. 'It'll be me next,' she sighed, 'but I'm ready. All my arrangements are in order.' Mary hesitated and gazed into the middle distance. 'My mam were called Agnes, she were a lovely woman, very caring and kind, although she were house proud. Woe betide you if you left your finger marks on her dresser when you opened a drawer.' She sighed again as Roza peered between the curtains. 'She were more like our Jean, in that respect, than me.'

Roza drew open the curtains.

'She's gone then, Agnes?'

Roza nodded. 'What do you mean, Mary – arrangements?'

'Well, I've sorted my will, last week with our Jean and that solicitor woman, then Ron treated me and our Jean to afternoon tea. Can you remember them prawn sandwiches made me go? Still, I needed it, I hadn't had a road through me for three days. What were we saying?'

'Arrangements?'

'My will, like I said. And I've got my hymns and Patsy Cline sorted in my head.'

'Patsy Cline?'

'For t'end, when t'curtains are closin' and–' she smiled as she crossed her hands over her chest– 'and they're all upset.'

'Mary, please do not talk like that.'

'Hey, love, don't upset yourself, it should be a good do.' Mary waved her hand toward her bedside table. 'Help yourself to a tissue, and while you're over there pass us mi pen and note pad. I'll make a few more notes for our Jean. Just in case she's forgot what I told that solicitor woman.'

Roza settled Mary with her pad and pen and made for the door. 'I'll leave you with your television.'

'Thanks, love, and, Roza, don't forget that lemon drizzle, that's a good girl.' Mary licked her lips and switched her attention back to *Homes under the Hammer* to watch a woman estate agent in a tight red frock, announce how much the renovated house was worth. 'She's no better than she should be,' Mary said to the television screen as she knitted her arms across her chest in disgust at the dress taste of young women who appeared on the telly. The sight of the pen and pad on her knee reminded her of the urgency of making a few notes.

CHAPTER TWELVE

Hail the conkering hero,
Praise my soul the King of Heaven
Crazy
Lemon drizzle cake
All things bright and beautiful
Orchids in wreath
scatter me at the creamatorium

Chapter Thirteen

Izzy's Journal

I took Joel to see Grandma Mary today, on the way home from school. I didn't ask then Mum couldn't say no. Grandma M loved him. She likes men. She told him all about her brothers who died in the war. Anyway, when I told Mum it led to one of our CHATS. I understand why she's concerned with how she was and everything and Dad coming over all Victorian and protective. If he mentions a chastity belt once more I'll tell him where to get off. Then there's Becca's legacy: suicide attempt and now eating problems. Ugh I really am tempted to start swearing again. But why can't they see that I'm like me not like them? Us kids can't win. There's Becca who doesn't want to grow up and Aunty Sue has her seeing a counsellor who works at her college and me with Joel for three weeks and four days and Mum suggests I go on the pill!!!!!!!!!!! I am worried about Becca though, she's lost stacks of weight and sicks up her school dinner — We've all heard her in the toilets. She looks minging, her hair's greasy and her acne has joined up in one big mess and she smells, but only if you're close up. She still sits next to me, when she comes to school, in the sets she's still in with me. Aunty Sue is thinking of moving her. I wish she would. I should feel bad about what I've just written but I remember what Mrs Berry told

CHAPTER THIRTEEN

us about writing things down to help us face growing up. I should have stuck with her way of writing a journal, but I'd rather write as I think about stuff.

Joel makes me fizz all over. We hold little fingers when nobody's looking while we walk to school. We kissed lips, no tongues. I felt his penis against my leg!!!!!!!!!!!!!!!!!!!! Even so, I think Mum's going off on one talking about the pill. I don't think, in the history of the world, that anybody got pregnant through their leg. We are allowed to do our homework together but not in bedrooms and we can go into town in a group but not on our own. Same for the cinema so long as a parent drops us off and picks us up. Dad is so obvious, hanging around. He'd be a good character on the telly — Douglas the overprotective Dad. It helps that Joel is really, really clever and wants to go to medical school.

I looked back over my journal for stuff for a homework assignment on adolescence. It helped. I've changed. I decided that the whole emphasis of my life has shifted. My family are important to me but it's my friends that really, really, really matter. I said in my conclusion that I was immature for a long time and questioned if that was because I was an only child and an only grandchild for a long time, before the twins were born and Amy didn't live with us, and asked if it's because my parents are older especially my dad, who saw the Beatles live!!!!!!!!!!!!!!!! I didn't put this in my homework, perhaps I should have done but the stuff with Amy dying, and Uncle Bob has made me realise that death is real. Grandma Mary was fed up when I saw her, another of her friends died and she didn't get a piece of lemon drizzle cake?????????? Is lemon drizzle cake like a funeral Christmas cake? She told us she won't be "caught short by going sudden". Joel thinks she's lovely. He doesn't have a great-grandma. She showed us her list of songs for her funeral. I am teary thinking of being without Grandma Mary. Although she seems really cheery when she talks about her funeral. Dad says I'll be the richest kid at Parklands with Amy's ~~legasy~~ legacy and the money Grandma M is leaving me, and Mary and Max and Charlie and Naomi's baby — if they have one. I don't mind if she lives a long time and her money runs out. I love her very, very much.

I'd better go and get on with my homework. We get loads this year. I'll see if anybody has said anything about the video I put on the group chat of Max and Mary smiling at each other and then start.

Paula *October 2018*

Her first day on her own with Mary and Max. Well more or less, if Paula didn't count Izzy's usual help with feeding and nappy changing before she went off to school. She'd been up with Douglas, showered and dressed before he left for the train to London. Her intention to Zumba for half an hour, to a DVD she'd borrowed from her mum, she decided was too ambitious; pelvic floor exercised in the shower would have to do for now. After all, she was back at Slimming World – not bad when Mary and Max were only eleven weeks old. She'd had a tubal ligation during the caesarean section. When her consultant suggested the procedure, she hadn't hesitated to accept his offer; her previous attempts to control

CHAPTER THIRTEEN

her fertility had been questionable and although Mary and Max were welcome and loved, another child at forty-three with a sixty-two-year-old father would be a disaster. So here she was sorting washing – not that she intended to iron it, she had the *Iron Maidens* and their efficient home collection and delivery service to help her with that. Then it was on to preparing a Slimming World slow cooker casserole for dinner. A happy housewife and mother. Who would have thought it? And daughter and granddaughter and stepdaughter, she added to her list of happiness – and cousin, she added to her family inventory. Call in and see Grandma, she reminded herself.

Her mum and Ron were away, on their annual writers' retreat in mid-Wales. Paula had been trusted with complete command of the family in their absence. Not the onerous task she would once, and not so long ago, have resented.

On tiptoes Paula ventured into the nursery. Max was awake. She lifted him up, held him close and kissed his scrumptious bald head.

'Now, little man, let's enjoy a cuddle on our own.' Paula smiled down at the child in her arms as she jiggled him in the way that mothers through the ages have instinctively cradled their babies. His answering smile filled her with intense awe and bliss. She felt she would remember the moment for the rest of her life. As she bent to kiss her son, the blast of the ring tone of her mobile phone, in the back pocket of her jeans, clattered into the moment.

'Bugger.' She reached into her pocket, flicked open the phone and glanced at the screen. 'Shit, Sue. I knew it was too good to last.'

The upshot of the phone call was that Sue was, yet again, excitable, strung out and weepy.

Paula groaned inwardly and promised to be round at Sue's within the hour. With Max in her arms, she crept past a sleeping Mary to gather a change of clothes for each child, crept downstairs, retrieved two bottles from the fridge and pushed them into the baby bag. Upstairs once more, she eased a smiling, gurgling Max into a tiny quilted jacket. 'We've no time to play, sweetheart,' she murmured. 'Aunty Sue's losing it again and your mummy owes her big time.'

Mary announced her presence with a snuffle and sneeze from the near-by cot.

'Mummy's here, darling,' she said raising the cot sides of Max's cot, who howled in protest as Paula turned to her daughter. 'Baa baa black sheep,' she sang in a jazz rhythm to the apparent disgust of both her children.

★

Ten bin bags lined the hall at Sue's. Bob's clothes, that Sue had suddenly come to terms with relinquishing, had been sorted and were waiting to be taken to the charity shop.

'I don't think I can do it,' said Sue; she closed her eyes and shuddered. 'It seems so final. All his clothes given away.'

'You look after Mary and Max, they should sleep for another hour, and I'll ship this lot into town, if you're sure that's what you want.'

'Yes. No. I'll come with you.'

'It'll take longer.' Paula looked at a quivering Sue. 'But what the hell. We'll make more than one trip.' *Baked chicken and Slimming World chips for dinner then. Sod the casserole.*

And I need to see Grandma at some stage.'

During the long afternoon Paula drove to town and back three times listening to the miseries of Sue's life with

CHAPTER THIRTEEN

her warring daughters, her worries about Becca and the inevitable diagnosis of anorexia, the ensuing family therapy and Sue's decision to hand in her notice after her protracted period of sick leave. On her way home from Sue's, Paula called to visit her grandma. Her luck was in – there was a parking space close to the entrance. She hoisted the twins and their baby seats out of the car, trundled into Fairhaven, upstairs to her grandma's room to find Mary ensconced under a hair dryer. With a promise of visiting the following day, Paula retraced her steps, fastened the babies into the car and breathing a sigh of relief she headed for home to face three raw chicken breasts and a pile of vegetables

★

'Peace perfect peace,' said Douglas as he opened the fridge. 'I still think they are young for a bedtime story.' He held up a bottle of beer. 'Want one, love?' He held the bottle up to Paula.

'No, I'm fine.' Paula licked her lips. 'I can't say I'm not tempted, but get thee behind me and all that. Izzy–' Paula raised her voice to shout– 'dinner.'

Izzy meandered in from the sitting room. 'Smells good, Mum.'

'A bastardised Slimming World recipe. I should try it before you decide it's good or not.'

'Bastardised?' Izzy paused on her journey to the dining table. She shook her head at her mother.

'Corrupted, spoiled. How would you define bastardised, Douglas?'

'I agree with you, love. And to take the analogy further–'

Paula and Izzy chortled and rolled their eyes at each other.

'–I was going to say, before you two so rudely interrupted. That bastardised is not something you could say about you, my darling daughter Well both of you – my wife and daughter, there's nothing corrupted or spoiled in our family.'

But there was. Corrupted, spoiled and poisonous, but never again.

'Mum, Mum–' Izzy pointed to the plate her mother was holding– 'there's sauce dripping off the plates.'

Recovering from her flash of thought, Paula bent to her side and emulating Julie Walters' Mrs Overall announced, 'two soups'.

Jean *October 2018*

Jean stretched her back as the boot of the car clicked into place. She felt a quiet yearning for home, yet a reluctance to say goodbye to the golden hues of the Welsh valley that had been their home for a week. It was the fourth time she'd enjoyed a writing retreat in this beautiful, tranquil spot. The group had talked last night over their usual, final night Indian banquet, about next year's retreat. Dave, the secretary, had been up early to catch the owners of the accommodation to secure next year's date and agree a price. Ron had been keen to get himself and Jean signed up to secure their place, yet Jean felt this would be their last visit with the group. She couldn't catch why she felt subdued; a quiet melancholy. Was it a premonition, a foreshadowing of events? She shivered; she was being daft after eating too

CHAPTER THIRTEEN

much food, too late at night, not to mention too many gin and tonics. It was probably a dose of IBS, the bloody disease had a way of hijacking her entire body.

★

Home again, Paula had been in and picked up the post. She'd left a vase of five sunflowers in the middle of the dining room table, providing a dramatic and cheerful welcome.

'What's this?' said Paula, leafing through the pile of envelopes. 'It's a letter, from Euxton Hall Hospital, for you, Ron.' She held the envelope toward him as she cocked her head in a questioning pose.

At the sight of his sheepish and apologetic posture, Jean felt a resurgence of the disquiet she'd felt in Wales. 'What's the matter?' she said.

'I didn't want to spoil the week away.' He took the envelope and slit it open with his thumb. 'It's an appointment to see a GU specialist.'

'Why?' Jean pulled out a dining chair and sat down. She felt out of time and place.

'I've got an enlarged prostate.' He moved toward Jean, holding out his arms. Enfolded in his arms, Jean felt Ron shaking.

'I've been trying to ignore it, but the back pain got worse.'

'Back pain.'

'And not being able to – make love.'

'Dear God! Why the hell didn't you say something?' Jean's voice quivered. 'I should have noticed but we've been so busy and tired, what with the wedding and the twins and everything else. I didn't think. When's the appointment?'

Ron's hands shook as he consulted the letter. 'That's been quick; it's on Tuesday.'

Jean teased the story from Ron. He'd consulted his GP before he and Jean were together because of difficulty with urination. He'd been examined, and his PSA tested and told there was nothing to be worried about. Ron had accepted the explanation, got on with life, met Jean and put up with the odd niggle of back pain and peeing during the night. After their initial passion, life had settled down. Ron admitted that Jean's intermittent vaginismus had come as something of a relief and that their preference for mutual masturbation had satisfied them both. Jean had noticed the length of time it took for Ron to have a pee. She'd checked on the salient facts on the internet and discussed it with Val, and reassured herself all was well. And now she knew; she'd been a selfish fool only too happy to close her eyes to the obvious.

★

Visiting her mum and catching up with the trivialities of life at Fairhaven provided a hazy background to Jean's yearning that Tuesday arrive and a new and different version of the future be faced. Her mum's verbal montage left Jean and Ron nothing to do but nod and smile in their roles as human blotting paper, absorbing Mary's review of her immediate life events. A new care assistant who "was no more than a kid" had had the audacity to suggest that Mary needed help wiping her bum. The flu injection nurse had used a blunt needle and the new cook hadn't used beef skirt to make a potato pie and "that Mrs May looks jiggered" and "Duchess Mee Gan looks as though she's expecting twins". And then the ultimate crime, Anton had been knocked out of Strictly the first week dancing with a woman "as looked like a fairy elephant".

Sunday lunch with Paula, Douglas Izzy, Max and Mary wasn't easy. Paula had sensed her mother's disquiet and while Douglas and Ron were absorbed in a review of Saturday's sport while playing with the twins, Jean couldn't escape Paula's scrutiny.

'Is everything okay, Mum?' Paula peered in the oven. 'Cassoulet, a new recipe. I made it yesterday.'

'I'm a bit tired – not sleeping. Did you confit your own duck?'

'No, it's tinned, like we used to bring back from France.' Paula looked dubious; she paused, scrutinising her mother's face. 'Ron looks knackered as well. Come on, Mum, something's up?'

Jean momentarily hung her head. 'He's got a raised PSA as well as back pain and an appointment at Euxton Hall on Tuesday morning. I'm worried sick.'

Mary *October 2018*

Her birthday cards lay on her knees. Mary had been appalled that the young girl who called herself a carer had chucked them in the litter bin. They were kids at sixteen, she was not much older than Izzy, and here she was pretending to be something she wasn't. She was common as well, with all them piercings and that muck on her face. And she'd had a tattoo. A girl from a decent home wouldn't have a tattoo. Mary dismissed a mithering awareness of Paula and some animal or other on her shoulder. She'd had it done after her dad died, that time when she were all mixed up about being a doctor, so it didn't count. Roza had gone home to Poland to visit her mother who was poorly, so Mary had been allocated the new girl as her main carer. The Sister had explained that Chantelle – "a name says a lot about a person," Mary muttered frequently – could only work under supervision given her age.

"Well that was all my eye and Fanny Martin," Mary told anyone who would listen. Fairhaven was short staffed, what with holidays and folk off sick. Mary had noticed that when anybody from that agency that was in charge of learning the girls how to do their job, put in an appearance, it was all sweetness and light and more staff than you could shake a stick at.

Next time that QVC lot came round she was having a word.

'Here. What's your name?' Mary called to Chantelle who was passing her door.

'Yes, Mary.' Chantelle hovered at the door.

'It's Mrs Fox to you.' Mary smacked her slack lips together. 'Where's my teeth?'

'In the bathroom, I've not had time to clean them.'

'Bring 'em back. It'll be the tea round soon and at ninety-four–' she patted her birthday cards– 'I refuse to suck my biscuits like a babby. Our Jean'll have something to say about all this. She were a proper nurse, you know.' Mary glanced at Chantelle's waist. 'Silver buckle and everything.'

Mary heard Chantelle mutter something under her breath.

★

CHAPTER THIRTEEN

The day dragged on; other than mealtimes, Mary was on her own, with few comings and goings to watch and listen to. She reviewed the lives of her family. They were all well off and busy; wrapped up in their lives. They only told her what they wanted her to know, when she knew very well that there was plenty going on that they could tell her. How come Ron had never taken up with another woman; his wife left him years ago? What did he see in Jean? What did she see in him? Mary could see he had summat about him, charming without being smarmy, even if he were on the thin side. And he had money.

Douglas; he's a rum bugger. Clever, full of himself; always sure he's right. He'd argue with Jesus himself, or that Jeremy Corbyn. He'd been good to Paula, put up with a lot, course it must have suited him having a bonny young girl on his arm. He'd made a mess of things in his young life with that poor Amy. Then running off with Paula. He likes a bit of bother. What was he doing now, having a tale about a murder in a hospital published? Makes you wonder what goes on in them places. I could tell a tale or two about here.

Our Izzy, God bless her. She's turned out grand. Like a little mother to them babbies and she thinks the world shines out of our Jean and that Ron. She needs to be careful though – going with that lad. Still, she knows what's what with all that sex and that, they all do these days. I knew nowt, well not really, till my wedding night. It turns my stomach thinking about it.

Jean's landed on her feet with yon mon. Except she looked worn out yesterday. I knew it ud be too much for her living with a man after all these years. But would she listen? She's another as is always known best. Not like our Terry. A lad as were the salt of the earth. He'd do anything for me he would, except tell me about his wife and child. Still, he must have had his reasons. I can't see as it were because they were a different colour. He knew I were broad minded. Madge's son married a Catholic, but I still sent 'em a pair of pillowcases as a wedding present. It weren't worth going to watch ceremony on account of he wouldn't turn. Can't say as I blame him. Our Terry, I mean Charlie, he's a rum un. Spectaculates in property. And he's made a bob or two.

Mary closed her eyes and dozed for ten minutes.

Now, where were I? Before Mary could settle to recap her meanderings and reflections of her family, she heard the lift stutter into life. Craning her neck – the daft girl always left the door half-closed instead of leaving it wide open – she anticipated the lift's thud and bump as it landed. She clapped her hands in glee as Paula stepped out backwards, pulling the double buggy toward her.

'Paula, and the little uns.' Mary leant forward in her chair. 'I didn't expect you today.'

'Mum's held up – well she might not make it.'

'Out of sight out of mind.' Mary forced a dejected look. 'That's me.'

'Is it alright, if I lie them on your bed?' Paula knelt to unbuckle a child.

'Let me have one of em.' Mary held out her arms.

'They're getting heavy, Grandma.' Paula advanced toward Mary. 'Are you sure?' She bent to settle a little body in Mary's arms.

'Hello, little lad.' Mary smiled at Max resplendent in a blue coat. The little boy beamed at his great-grandma.

'Where's your mam then?' Mary bent her head to plant a slaver kiss on Max's head. 'Off galivanting?'

CHAPTER THIRTEEN

Mary watched Paula pause as she searched for something in the baby bag.

'What's up? It's not like you to dither about.' Mary shivered. *Her's come to tell me summat.* Mary's voice quivered. 'Jean!'

Paula picked up Mary from the bed and held her close.

'Has there been an accident?'

'No, Grandma, no accident. Mum's gone with Ron to see a doctor about a swelling in his prostate.'

'Swelling in his prostrate,' Mary mumbled. 'Is that what men wee through?'

Paula shook her head. 'No, well it, the prostate, is involved in…well it's like a traffic policeman. It makes sure urine and semen–'

Mary nodded to encourage Paula to carry on. It all sounded interesting if a bit mucky.

'–don't get mixed up during sex.'

'Really! And you say he's got a lump mixed up with all that? Poor bugger.'

Chapter Fourteen

Izzy's Journal

October 2018

Half-term. What is it with parents? I'm fourteen next week, the age Grandma M was when she left school and started work at the Co-op. In medieval times girls had babies at my age. (Well when you think about it my Mum almost did.) Which, when I think about it is why I'm stuck here at home and Joel is stuck at home round the corner. It's a known fact that sperm can't fly. We only want to be together to talk and listen to music. Well and hold hands and kiss. I remember that saying, something about the sins of the fathers being visited on future generations. When I have children I'll trust them. Honestly, I can be trusted to care for Max and Mary, make a meal and be told about Pops but - well I'm buggered if I understand parents. They're all the same.

Pops! He has cancer of his prostate and some in his bones. He's having treatment - chemotherapy and pills. He's determined to be positive so Grandma and Mum say we've got to do as he asks and be positive as well. Mum says nothing is likely to happen for a year or two. That's

CHAPTER FOURTEEN

another thing I've noticed about adults they avoid saying what they mean. She means he's going to die in a year or two. Dad says prognosis are always on the pessimistic side. I don't think he was saying that because I cried. I don't want any of my family to die. Pops joked and said he intends to see me through GCSE and A level English. He's a brilliant grandad. We are trying to keep Grandma and Grandma M apart or make sure one of us is with them when they are together. Grandma M asked one of her carers, who she doesn't like and who, according to Grandma Mary, 'isn't a full shilling,' to print off stuff on the internet about prostate cancer. Dad says Grandma M has as much sensitivity as that bloody oaf Boris Johnson because she keeps asking Grandma questions. Mostly about 'that there prostrate what acts like a policeman'. She actually said the word sperm. Although she calls a penis a man's thingy and when she says it she moves her lips but no words comes out. We think sperm and prostate is new to her vocabulary.

Anyway, what else. My friends are all good, well except Becca. She's started to bunk off school, first she said she felt poorly, now she just disappears. Aunty Sue's been into school. I wish she would leave school or they would move house. I don't want to be her friend but I'm stuck with her because of our mums.

Mary and Max can smile. I love them so much. I definitely want to work with little children. Dad keeps talking about when me and Joel are at university, he means medical school which just shows he's not cool about me being a children's nurse. Which makes me even more determined to be one because I know in my heart that it's right for me. Mum says I have a vocation.

I'd better go and get ready I'm going shopping for a Halloween costume. Dad says it is BLOODY AMERICAN RAMPANT CONSUMERISM but when Grandma and Pops brought Pumpkin outfits for Mary and Max he was the first to take their photographs!!!!!! The party is at Joel's. His parents are really, really cool, about most things????????????

Another thing I noticed when I read my journal for that assignment was how much I went on about Zoella. I've seen her on Strictly, watching her brother. She looks nice but not like I thought she would even though I've seen her photograph on the website. I don't follow her now. I talk to my friends and Joel if I want advice and need to think out loud, but she and her brother have made gazillions. He's a good dancer though.

See you soon.

Paula *October 2018*

As she punched the Buy Now Amazon button for the CD *A Jazz Portrait of Frank Sinatra* Paula felt a vague stirring of guilt. There was a specialist music shop in Chorley, she should have made the journey into town, not only for the CD but other stuff she was buying for Christmas presents. She agreed with Douglas that they should buy goods and services locally if they wanted town centres to survive. Yet

CHAPTER FOURTEEN

internet buying was easy and trouble-free, unless items needed to be parcelled up and returned to the supplier; a job Paula despised because of the faff of going to the post office, particularly with the twins in a pushchair. It was only one CD, after all, one that Ron would enjoy, so there would be no returns. Still her job as a personal shopper depended on the survival of the department store. Rumours abounded that the chain she worked for was in trouble – she'd noticed two, thirty percent off, vouchers in the post and on the internet in the last two weeks. Her iPad inbox was full of discounts and sales. Would she have a job to go back to after her maternity leave? Pushing the iPad behind a cushion she smiled. *Duh, as though that will solve anything, out of sight out of mind. What will that achieve?*

'Smiling to yourself?' Douglas stood in the doorway, his eyebrows lurched as he peered over the top of his specs. 'I'm making a brew.' He pointed toward the kitchen. 'Do you want one? And, by the way, what were you smiling at?'

'My self-delusion. I thought you had a deadline to meet with that report?'

'I do, my brain's addled looking at graphs and pie charts. What self-delusion?'

Paula waved away his question. 'What do you think I should do about work?' She walked toward her husband and they headed for the kitchen.

'Whatever you want to do. I thought you wanted a couple of days part-time?'

'I did, I do, but what with Ron and Mum and the state of play at work – falling sales?'

Douglas reached into the brew cupboard for two mugs and the coffee jar. 'Is this about your mum and Ron, or about work?'

'You astound me, Douglas.' Paula shook her head, a smile playing on her lips.

'What have I done now?' He leant against the worktop, his arms across his chest.

'I love you, Douglas Quayle.' She moved toward him and as he opened his arms, she snuggled into his chest. 'You should have been a clairvoyant,' she muttered into his polo shirt. 'I started fretting about Ron, ordered a CD for him and then morphed into thinking noble thoughts about the state of the high street and work.'

'Kettle's boiling,' Douglas kissed the top of Paula's head and extricated himself from her embrace. 'It's no good worrying about Ron, love. You know as well as I do, he has every chance of a good prognosis, and work – well what will be, and all that, and you don't need to go back if you don't want to.' He heaped spoons of instant coffee into the mugs and poured over the water. 'The children come first; all three of them, and by the way I'm sure Izzy had a love bite on her neck.' He harrumphed and picked up his mug. 'I'll leave it with you, love – to have a word. He's a nice lad – but well, it's a bit soon for all that.'

★

Paula wrestled with the issue Douglas had casually thrown at her. Did it matter if Izzy and Joel were necking? Where did a bit of necking finish and heavy petting start? Was heavy petting still part of a teenager's vocabulary or was it "making out" these days? When had they manged a snog? They had a list a mile long of what they could and couldn't do and where they could and couldn't go together. Although his parents had agreed with the sanctions, Paula had the

CHAPTER FOURTEEN

sense that they thought she and Douglas were old fashioned, overzealous and overanxious. The dad had shrugged his shoulders and muttered something about hegemony and freedom to make choices. Joel's mother announced that she'd had an abortion when she was in the sixth form. Paula kept her mouth shut, swallowed her guilt and tried to look sympathetic.

Perhaps it was different for parents of boys unless, like Douglas, they had the shadow of Amy hovering over them. And they were laid back academics, he in far out music and she in esoteric films. Douglas had done well to keep his mouth shut when they'd come round for a drink. He'd shown unusual restraint in not ranting about the proliferation of useless degrees taught by trendy layabouts at old polytechnics, one of his many well-rehearsed soap box issues. But then again, he'd gone to town in his efforts to find vegan wine to accommodate their dietary choices. So, it was up to Paula to decide what to do, how to play it. Could she afford to ignore a single love bite?

*

The twins were settled for the night, Douglas was watching a football match and Izzy was finishing her homework in her bedroom. Paula had decided that the love bite issue needed to be sorted. Douglas was bound to ask what she'd done about it and memories of her own miserable experiences and the sad child that was now Becca conspired to return Paula to her old state of useless fretting.

She knocked on Izzy's bedroom door before walking in. Izzy was propped against the bed-head, dressed in pyjamas and wrapped in a snuggly blanket. She was mouthing a song and reading notes in a ring binder. She looked up, smiled and yanked her earphones out of her ears. The innocent, welcoming look touched Paula's heart as she craned her head to try to scrutinize Paula's neck.

'I've nearly finished – geography.' She grimaced. 'Climate change.'

'Geography never did it for me. My teacher once told me it was a miracle I could find my way home from school.' Paula sat on the edge of the bed. 'I swotted and got a good grade to spite her.' She riddled her bottom to get more comfortable, she was lost for words.

'Is something wrong, Mum? Pops?'

Paula clasped her hands together and shook her head. 'No, it's me. I've got a problem. Don't look so worried, love.' *Spit it out.* 'It's your dad, he – well – he thinks he's seen a love bite.' Paula waved a hand toward Izzy's head. 'On your neck.'

Izzy tutted, raised her eyes in exasperation before tugging the blanket away from her neck.

'Nothing there, Mum. It was makeup, I'm going to the Halloween party as a damsel in distress and Joe's going as a werewolf, I did tell you.' Izzy laughed. 'Mum, you and Dad need to let me go. I'm fourteen next week, for God's sake.' She upended herself and crawled down the bed and snuggled against Paula. 'You and Dad are obsessed with me and Joe and sex. It's illegal to have sex until I'm sixteen. Which is two years and one week away, then you can start to worry.'

Paula was caught between relief, dread and a crazy feeling of joy.

CHAPTER FOURTEEN

Jean *November 2018*

Jean let herself be lost in the deluge of the waterfall power shower. Head bent, she watched the rivulets of water run down her breasts and belly. She closed her eyes, swayed side to side, then rolled her shoulders. The thrum of the water, the heat and steam cocooned her from the melancholy that threatened to swaddle her. She told herself she had no right to wake up downhearted and moody. It would be easy to say her misery was down to Ron's prostate cancer, but that was unfair – his illness was a focus for feeing dejected but she'd always had feelings of serial despair in a morning. There were mornings when life was good and bountiful, when she had energy and verve. Then days like today when she felt as though she were walking through glue in concrete boots. *Get a grip. Get dressed. Get sorted. Get writing.*

Jean forced herself to be determined. Showered, hair dried and in comfy clothes, with a weak glass of Vimto at her side, she settled at her laptop. The scene she'd abandoned before the weekend, she decided, was a load of waffle. Her main character had become a caricature of the woman Jean was trying to portray. She stared at the screen. *Write something.* She touched the keyboard, and a previous piece of work replaced her manuscript. *Bloody hell fire.* She fiddled with the file trying to retrieve the work – it didn't seem like waffle now it had done a disappearing act. She checked her memory stick. She'd not saved her work when she was interrupted on Friday. *Bugger.* She was ready to slam the lid of the laptop shut when the phone rang.

'Jean. Is that you?' said her mother, in a voice rife with suspicion.

She slammed the lid of the laptop down. 'Yes, Mum.' She inhaled.

'What's up? You sound out of sorts. Is summat up with Ron?'

Jean's shoulders slumped, the misery that had plagued her earlier gathered momentum. *Give up, you're a crap writer anyway.* 'I can't get for going, that's all – one of those mornings.'

'You allus did get yourself into a state about something and nothing. Anyway, I've had enough of em here. I want you to get me out.'

Bloody hell.

'Are you there, Jean? I said…'

'I'm here, Mum. I'll get changed and be with you in half an hour or so.'

'I'm not changing my mind. I'll tell you that for nothing. Come now. I need the commode and there's nobody about and I can't reach my bell. Please come, Jean.'

Slumped back in her chair, Jean watched the tops of the branches of the trees waft. The faded green and the gold of the leaves vivid against the blue sky. Pushing herself out of her office chair, she chastised herself. She had avoided acknowledging the thoughts about her mother that had nibbled at her consciousness over the last few weeks; Ron and supporting Paula with the twins had been a priority. Her mother was safe, looked after and cared for. Or was she? The atmosphere at Fairhaven had changed, especially since Roza's long term absence in Poland. The new owners and senior staff had changed the emphasis of the home from that of a pleasant, supportive community to a more profitable focus on residents with dementia. The daily activities had been reduced and all the friends her mother had made had

CHAPTER FOURTEEN

died. She was the only one left from the group who had met in the sunroom and organised the residents' meetings. When had her mother's choice to spend time in her own room become a state of isolation?

Jean checked her appearance in the hall mirror – she looked a mess with no makeup and her hair flat instead of teased into spikes. It wouldn't take long to sort out things at Fairhaven and she'd be home again before Ron was back from his art group.

★

The homely smell of fresh baking was underpinned by the eyewatering tang of a cocktail of urine and disinfectant. Jean glanced around; other than the cook busy unloading an oven there was no one about. Jean trudged upstairs. Her mother's door was closed. *That's strange.*

She paused and cocked her head.

'Help, help.'

Galvanised, Jean lunged for the door. It was blocked.

'Mum!'

'Jean, help. My leg. Please, help.'

'Mum, try and budge up, then I can get to you.'

A series of strangled whimpers and groans and a muted clutter followed by a soft sob accompanied Jean's simmering fear for her mother and anger at the non-existent staff.

'Mum!' The door shifted to make a gap. Jean breathed in and turned sideways to attempt to edge her way through the tight space.

'Jean. Are you there?' Her mother's voice was a tortured whisper. 'Terry.'

'Nearly.' Jean wriggled and squirmed her body against the wall, all too aware of her mother's ragged breathing. With a final heave she was through the gap. *Dear God. No. Not like this.*

Acknowledgments

Thank you to -

Our family, James, Heather, Olivia, Charlie and Lilli for all you do and who you are.

Friends, including Kearsley Girls to whom this work is dedicated – it seems a long time since September 1959. Special thanks, as always, to Judith Thorpe for her love and first reader critique and to Judith Hilton for her encouragement and knowledge of all things literary. To my fellow writers, and members of the best ever critique group, Rhona Whiteford, Jackie Farrell, Carol Fenlon and Dennis Conlon (RIP) warmest thanks.

UK Book Publishing for their help and professionalism.

The Richards family for permission to use family photographs.

And thank you, Ron Cole, for everything.

Printed in Great Britain
by Amazon